SOPHIE WARD

Love and Other Thought Experiments

Sophie Ward is an actor and a writer. She has published articles in *The Times* (London), *The Sunday Times* (London), *The Guardian*, *The Observer*, *The Spectator*, *DIVA*, and *Red*, and her short stories have been published in the anthologies *Finding a Voice*, *Book of Numbers*, *The Spiral Path*, and *The Gold Room*. Her book *A Marriage Proposal: The Importance of Equal Marriage and What It Means for All of Us* was published as a Guardian Shorts eBook in 2014. In 2018, Sophie won the Pindrop Short Story Award for "Sunbed." She has a degree in philosophy and literature and a PhD from Goldsmiths, University of London, on the use of narrative in philosophy of mind.

Love and Other Thought Experiments

Love and Other Thought Experiments

SOPHIE WARD

VINTAGE BOOKS

A Division of Penguin Random House LLC

New York

A VINTAGE BOOKS ORIGINAL, SEPTEMBER 2021

The Library of Congress has cataloged the Hachette edition as follows:
Names: Ward, Sophie, author.
Title: Love and other thought experiments / Sophie Ward.
Description: First edition. | London : Corsair, 2020.
Identifiers: LCCN 2019467489
Subjects: LCSH: Married people—Fiction. | Lesbian couples—
Fiction. | Interpersonal relations—Fiction. | Trust—Fiction. |
Philosophy and science—Fiction.
Classification: PR6 123.A725 L68 2020 | DDC 823.92—dc23
LC record available at https://lccn.loc.gov/2019467489

Vintage Books Trade Paperback ISBN: 978-0-593-31430-2
eBook ISBN: 978-0-593-31431-9

www.vintagebooks.com

Printed in the United States of America
10   9   8   7   6   5   4   3   2   1

For Rena

The Imagination is not a State: it is the Human Existence itself.

William Blake, *Milton: A Poem in Two Books*

I've dreamt in my life dreams that have stayed with me ever after, and changed my ideas; they've gone through and through me, like wine through water, and altered the colour of my mind.

Emily Brontë, *Wuthering Heights*

If we are going to make further progress in Artificial Intelligence we are going to have to give up our awe of living things.

Daniel Dennett, *Speaking Minds: Interviews with Twenty Eminent Cognitive Scientists*

Contents

Rachel picked up the magazine that Eliza had left in the kitchen. The cover was a drawing of a tree with the roots embedded in a man's head and above him a blowsy crown of leafed branches arched towards the sun. It wasn't a typical image for Eliza's reading matter. Rachel turned the page.

'Thought experiments are devices of the imagination used to investigate the nature of things.'

That's a lot, thought Rachel. But she liked the sound of it. It tickled her to think of stories being used by scientists. I could be a thought experiment, something Eliza has dreamed up to challenge her hardened reasoning.

'If I were a thought experiment,' Rachel asked Eliza as they got into bed that night, 'What one would I be?'

'I'm not sure you can *be* a thought experiment,' Eliza said. 'They are supposed to help you think about a problem.'

'If you can imagine it, then it is possible.'

'That is one theory.'

'So,' Rachel pushed away the book Eliza had picked up and blinked at her girlfriend. 'Imagine me.'

Eliza smiled and shook her head. 'This is what happens when the fanciful encounter the factual.'

'I'm not sure which is which here. Quit stalling.' Rachel prodded Eliza's armpit.

'Fine! You want to be a thought experiment? You can be

a zombie! No, no, I've got it. You would be, yes, Hume's Missing Shade of Blue. The colour he has never seen but can still visualise. Happy?'

Hume's Missing Shade of Blue, thought Rachel as she laid her head on the pillow. Yes. I can be that. 'Tell me some more.'

1

An Ant

Pascal's Wager

The seventeenth-century mathematician Blaise Pascal argued that since God either does or does not exist and we must all make a decision about the existence of God, we are all bound to take part in the wager. You can commit your life to God because you stand to gain infinite happiness (in the infinite hereafter) with what amounts to a finite stake (your mortal life). If you do not commit your life to God you may be staking your finite life for infinite unhappiness in Hell. By this logic, the infinite amount of possible gain far outweighs the finite loss.

> But there is here an infinity of an infinitely happy life to gain, a chance of gain against a finite number of chances of loss, and what you stake is finite.
>
> Blaise Pascal *Pensées* 272

'The ants have moved in here now.' Rachel brushed the small body aside and turned the pillow over.

Eliza glanced up from her book.

'The ants. In the sitting room. They've followed us in here,' Rachel said.

'Are you sure?'

'I just saw one.'

'No, are you sure it's an ant? They're so tiny, I don't know how you could tell.' Eliza returned to the hardback that was balanced on her bosom.

'I don't need glasses.'

'Yet.'

Rachel prodded her. 'Do ants bite?'

'I've got to finish this for tomorrow.'

'It's definitely ants. The same ones that were on the sofa last summer. They got in through the gap in the window and now they've found a way in here. You couldn't put a baby in a room with ants. Eliza?'

'Yes?'

'Did you see them before? When you slept on this side?'

'No.'

'You wouldn't have noticed anyway.'

'Maybe one.'

'Is that why we swapped sides?'

The book fell away from Eliza's hand. 'What?'

'Nothing.'

'No. Tell me. You think I moved you to that side of the bed because it's infested?'

'It's okay. Read.' Rachel looked at her girlfriend. 'I know. Sorry.'

Eliza didn't go back to her reading but she kept the light on while Rachel fell asleep. She wondered whether she should get the pest controller from down the road to look at the flat. Mr Kargin. He had a second job repairing and selling old televisions. They had walked into his workshop one day, to buy an aerial for Rachel's black-and-white set. The man spent a long time looking through cardboard boxes and muttering about outdated equipment.

Eliza saw Rachel trying not to mind the posters on the wall, each one with a picture of a cockroach or a rat, along with a method of extermination. There were so many different creatures and all the pictures were the same size so the termites were as big as the squirrels. Mr Kargin stared at them both for some time.

'He stared at me,' Rachel said when they walked away from the shop. 'He was fine with you.'

He didn't find an aerial and he was bad tempered about the entire transaction though it had been his idea to start rummaging through the boxes. Eliza didn't imagine he made much money in television repairs but she thought the extermination business might be a means of expression as much as an extra income. She had promised Rachel they would never go back.

Rachel lay next to her, breathing heavily. It had been Eliza's idea to change places because she had a new desk and it wouldn't fit in the alcove on her side of the bed. It was a practical decision and even Rachel could see that it made sense. The flat was already crowded with furniture and the desk could double as a bedside table, but maybe the desk had disturbed a nest or maybe it was the time of year for ants to move indoors. Eliza had not deliberately changed sides because of the insects but now she would have to prove that she cared enough to fix the problem. Ever since they had talked about having a baby, Rachel had been testing the temperature of Eliza's love.

Eliza wondered how many of her decisions were basically points of honour. Throughout her life, her job at the university, the bicycles and vegetarianism, even her haircut seemed as if they were chosen in reaction to the opinions of an invisible audience. She had become the sort of person she approved of but she wasn't sure she had chosen anything she actually wanted. She checked the pillow one last time and turned off the bedside light. She would sort out the ants in the morning.

program

The next day, Eliza cycled past the television repair shop on the way to work. Smaller versions of the vermin posters were stuck inside the display window below precarious stacks of broken televisions. She thought of all the chemicals that the bad-tempered Mr Kargin would use in their flat. He seemed to radiate poison. Even ants didn't deserve a murderer like that.

They had talked about the ants over breakfast and Eliza had googled 'getting rid of ants'.

'All these ants look regular-sized. I can't find any photos of extra small ants.'

Rachel didn't want to read about eggs and nests.

'I don't mind one ant. But not in our bed, and not hundreds of them. I keep thinking of that song . . . "just what makes that little old ant . . ."'

'Peppermint oil.' Eliza twisted round from the screen to watch Rachel singing while she stacked the dishwasher. 'It says here they don't like peppermint oil. Well, that's easy. I'll get some later.' She closed the page and went back to her emails.

'I like the idea of the peppermint oil but I can't see how it will stop the ants in the long term . . .' Rachel wiped down the kitchen surfaces and went to stand by Eliza's chair. She rested a damp hand on Eliza's shoulder. 'They're very tiny but even if they got the oil on their feet or paws or whatever ants have at the end of their legs, it's not going to hurt them.'

'They don't like the smell.'

'So much for "High Hopes".'

Helloworld;

Eliza arrived home with a small vial of peppermint oil from the chemist.

'It seemed awful to get it from the supermarket, like we wanted to feed them.'

Rachel picked up the vial and left the bag from the chemist on the table.

'I got you something else.' Eliza nodded at the bag.

Rachel continued to examine the label on the peppermint oil as though it might list something other than oil of peppermint. After a moment, Eliza turned back to the kitchen counter and poured herself a glass of white wine. She hadn't intended to buy an ovulation kit on her way home from work, but while in the chemist she had looked around for a present to cheer Rachel up. This is how life's decisions get made, she thought, you choose a fertility test instead of bubble bath. She looked at the paper bag on the table. The pink box had been pulled out and Rachel was leaning back in her chair with an air of expectation that Eliza felt she couldn't meet.

'Thank you.'

Eliza frowned. 'It's a start.'

'Yes.'

They were too tired to wash the skirting board with peppermint oil. Rachel got into bed and glanced down at the floor. She caught Eliza's eye when she looked up.

'Nothing.' Rachel smiled.

Eliza diagnosed it as a non-duchenne smile, a pet subject of hers. It didn't reach her eyes. Still, Eliza knew she was trying.

Rachel pulled at her pillow. 'It's when I'm going to sleep. I think of them crawling about.'

'That's a normal reaction. Like when we think about nits and our scalps feel itchy.'

'Nits?' Rachel coughed. 'Who has nits any more?'

'Kids have nits. If we had a child we'd get nits.' Eliza touched Rachel's hand which was already rubbing the back of her head. 'You haven't got nits now!'

'But we have got ants, Els. I'm not imagining them.'

Eliza brought Rachel's hand to her lips. 'I know, my darling.' She kissed each of Rachel's plump fingers just below the nail and grazed the tip of the thumb with her teeth.

'Babies aren't all bad.'

'Hmmm?' Eliza paused.

'Nothing. Don't stop. It's nothing.' Rachel curved her hand round her girlfriend's cheek and lay back into the pillows. 'Don't stop.'

Eliza leant over her. 'I bought the test, remember? I read the book. Now, close your eyes and let me kiss you 'til you fall asleep.'

```
uses crt;
```

Eliza sat up in a panic. She was in bed, in the dark. Beside her, Rachel pulled at the pillows.

'Rachel? What is it? What's the matter?'

'Something bit me. In my dream, we were in a field and the sun was shining and there was grass. You said, "Stay still" and I tried but . . .' Rachel lifted her pillow. 'It bit me.'

Eliza struggled to reach for the bedside light. Rachel's cries had disturbed her own dream. 'The grass bit you?'

'In my eye.'

Both women squinted in the dim lamplight.

'Show me.'

Rachel's breath caught. 'It was you. You stabbed me with the grass.'

Eliza felt the sweat cool on her skin as she pushed back the bedclothes.

'Rachel, you were asleep.'

'An ant.' Rachel ran to the full-length mirror that hung behind the door.

'You had a nightmare.'

'It's gone in my eye.'

Eliza sat in the bed and yawned. 'Come here and let me have a look.'

Rachel perched on the bed and lifted her face to

Eliza. Deep by the innermost corner of her eye was a livid red mark.

'You've scratched yourself. Poor baby.' Eliza put her arms around her shivering girlfriend.

Rachel couldn't stay still. 'I don't think so.'

She walked around the bed and pulled back the bed-clothes. They both stared at the damp and wrinkled sheets. There were no ants.

'Nothing there,' Eliza said. 'Do you want some antiseptic? Rachel?'

Rachel had dropped to her hands and knees on the floor. The pine boards were old with a thin layer of varnish. It had taken Eliza and Rachel three days with a rented sander to get them smooth enough to walk on but the wood was still uneven and pitted and some of the gaps were big enough to lose an aspirin through. As Rachel knew well enough.

'It's the middle of the night. I've got to be at the lab at eight. Please, Rach. Let's look in the morning.'

'I won't sleep.' Rachel sat on the cold boards and looked up at Eliza. Her wavy hair had formed tight curls at the temples and tears dripped from the scarlet eye.

'Oh, honey. Hey. Hey there.' Eliza slid over to Rachel and crouched down on the floor beside her. 'Ohhh. It's okay.'

Rachel bent forward and sobbed into the crook of Eliza's neck. 'It's not. It's not okay. My eye hurts and an ant has gone into my head and you think . . . you think I can't look after a baby.'

Eliza pushed her girlfriend far enough away to see her face. 'Where did that come from?'

'You know it's true. Every time we talk about it you say you want to go through with it and that Hal is cool. Your egg, my womb, his sperm, like a recipe or a poem. But nothing ever happens and then we'll be doing something else and you'll be completely different, really negative, like it would be awful to have a baby. Like tonight . . .' Rachel rushed into the question on Eliza's lips. 'Tonight, when you started talking about the nits.'

'Oh, for god's sake. Children get nits, that's not an excuse, it's just what children do.'

'But it's not why you said it. You said it because you thought I couldn't handle anything; that I don't know about the real world, about real life. And maybe I don't.' Rachel sat and sobbed. Her shoulders heaved and her breath came in shuddering gasps.

Eliza watched her for a minute. She saw the sad and frightened woman in front of her from a distance, as though she was not on the floor with Rachel in their comfortable flat at three o'clock in the morning but looking in through the window on her way to somewhere else in her busy, busy life. In their four years together she had often felt like this, both there and not there, connected, yet keeping a part of herself separate, as though for emergencies. And Rachel had let what Eliza offered be enough. That was the problem with a baby. Not Rachel, who was a bit scatty and did lose things and wasn't exactly a career woman. None of those things mattered. She loved Rachel, but the baby would use up Eliza's emergency rations.

'I don't.'

Rachel let her breath go. 'You don't what?'

'I don't think you'll be a bad mother.'

'Really?'

Eliza shook her head. 'You'll be great at it. Wonderful. I'm the one to worry about.'

Rachel laughed and wiped at the wetness that had pooled

around her nose and mouth. 'You! You can do anything. You'd rule the world if you wanted to. With those legs.'

They both looked at Eliza's long legs as she folded them beneath her and sat back on her heels. Rachel's legs were short and the skin was soft. On other nights, Eliza liked to trace messages on Rachel's thighs. Nonverbal Communication, she wrote. And, Sensory Pleasure.

They held hands as they knelt in front of each other.

'We look like we're getting married, in some ancient ceremony,' Rachel said, her voice raw from crying.

'Yes.'

'We're going to, aren't we? We're going to get married and have a baby. Doesn't have to be in that order.' Every crease on her face shone in the lamplight.

'Yes, my darling.'

They tilted towards each other and rested their foreheads together.

'Now, this is how you get nits.' Eliza bumped her head against Rachel's.

'Not like this?' Rachel pushed herself into Eliza, knocking her off balance and landing on top of her.

'Hey!'

They lay on the floor for a while. This is life, Eliza thought, this is my life.

'My eye hurts.'

A vision of the future flickered before Eliza. Rachel and their baby huddled on the floor in tears and no one to take care of them except her. All the responsibility of two entirely unreasonable beings. Was she being unfair? Rachel couldn't possibly believe an ant had gone into her eye. But then, why was she insisting it had? Eliza took a deep breath and reached for any remnants of patience she could find.

'Here, let me see.'

Rachel was an only child. If they had any babies at all, they had better have at least two. Eliza's sister would have hit her over the head with their father's encyclopedia if she'd woken her in the night with tall tales about insects. Standing, Eliza pulled on Rachel's cheek and looked again.

'It's sore. Maybe you should go to the doctor tomorrow.'

Rachel hiccuped.

'I'll sleep on your side tonight,' Eliza said.

They got back into bed and Eliza turned out the light. She felt Rachel's cold toes press against her calves.

'Thank you,' Rachel said.

'You're welcome. What for?'

'For believing me. About the ant.'

(*Here the main program block starts*)

Eliza laid the table for dinner around the box from the chemist that had stayed where she put it the day before.

'So, what did the doctor say about your eye?'

'She doesn't listen to anything I say. It's you she likes.'

'I've only met her once.'

'That's probably why. She thinks I'm weird. Like that guy in the killing and tv shop. Staring.' Rachel widened her eyes at Eliza and stole a salad leaf from the bowl. 'She gave me some eye drops and told me to come back if it still hurts even though I told her it had stopped hurting.'

'The pest controller.'

'Yeah. Him.'

'But she looked at it?'

'Yes. A bit. Maybe I should see a specialist.'

'An eye specialist?'

'I don't know. An eye person? Or that hospital for tropical diseases?' Rachel looked quite happy at the thought. 'Maybe it's a kind of ant that we don't know about here.'

Eliza put the saucepan of spaghetti on the table and sat down. Images from the night before played on her mind. She had promised Rachel marriage and children but she saw their life together as a mirage, always ahead of them and just out of reach.

'I don't think there is a doctor who will know about any of this.'

'Isn't that what a specialist is for?' Rachel said. 'To investigate further?'

'Even though your eye is fine?'

'My eye feels fine now. But after what happened . . .'

'When what happened?'

'You were there.'

The future shimmered across the table. A world of possibilities, if only Eliza could believe in them.

'Eat up.' Eliza spooned out the pasta, and refilled their glasses. 'Let's open that test and get to the fun stuff.'

'I want to. I really do, it's what I've always wanted. But I need you with me.'

Eliza frowned. 'I am with you. I'm excited. I said . . .'

'Not that. I need you to know what I know. To have faith in me.'

'What do you mean?'

The tips of Eliza's fingers tingled with adrenalin. Rachel wasn't going to let it go.

'An ant went into my eye. And now it's stuck there.'

'Really?'

Rachel looked up at her girlfriend. 'Yes.'

'But you had a bad dream.'

'I know the difference between sleeping and waking. I felt the ant go into my eye.'

'Is that even possible?'

'It must be.'

She was so sure. Eliza watched as Rachel stroked her eye along the lash line in a delicate sweep, as if not to disturb her visitor.

'But the doctor didn't want to refer you?'

'She was the same when we went to talk about getting pregnant. She didn't hear me.'

'And the specialist?'

'I don't really think I want one. I mean, it's there, inside.' Rachel moved her hand away from her face. 'I don't want to have my head cut open.'

'They wouldn't do that.'

'If there's nothing they can do, there's no point going.'

'Right.'

Rachel reached across the table. 'As long as you believe me.'

The mirage of their life together pulled into focus.

'If you love me, you will trust me,' Rachel said. 'Don't you?'

A small thing. Agree and they could both move into their new relationship in which Eliza had accepted Rachel completely. A small thing and a big thing in one word.

'Yes.' She did believe. She believed in Rachel and all that would come with surrender. A future. She didn't have to understand about the ant, only that it was part of Rachel's story. The prickles of danger in her fingertips subsided. There was nothing to be frightened of. She had chosen.

Rachel blinked. She reached across the table and took the bag with the test in it. 'I'm going to do this right now.

Finish your pasta,' she nodded at Eliza's plate. 'I'll be two minutes.'

begin

It was more than a year before Arthur was born but for Rachel and Eliza he began that evening, Friday 24 October 2003.

'That was the night we conceived him, really.' Rachel tapped her head. 'In the best sense. The rest was like shopping at Homebase; you know you want to do some DIY but you have to buy the equipment first.'

At this, Rachel's friends would laugh. She was so much more relaxed since she had the baby, they said. Being a mother had really brought out the best in her.

They said it to Rachel's face and she would smile and blush and not mention the ant. Throughout the conception (in the end they chose IUI), house move (for reasons of space, they agreed), and civil partnership (at Westminster registry office with twenty guests and a heavily pregnant Rachel), they rarely spoke of the events that inspired their new circumstances. When they did, Eliza changed the subject as soon as possible.

Still, by the time of Arthur's second birthday his origins had become inextricably linked to that day in both his mothers' minds and Eliza watched Arthur and Rachel blossom, sure in the knowledge that she had almost lost them both. She saw the time before their son as a confused and distant past. She could not have explained why it had asked so much of her to believe in Rachel's story but since then so many extraordinary things had happened that embracing the possible existence of a single ant seemed almost sensible and while she would never admit that the ant had saved them, she acknowledged that the idea of the ant had been a start. Now she inhabited her life. It was the difference, she thought, between sitting by the side of the pool and actually swimming.

'Washing up or washing Arthur?' Rachel walked across the sitting room picking up paper plates and streamers. 'I can't believe Hal brought party poppers. They get everywhere.'

'I think he likes scaring Greg. He jumped a foot in the air every time one went off.'

'At least Greg came. This wasn't exactly what he signed up for.' Rachel smiled.

The two women stood for a moment and surveyed the devastation that a room full of toddlers had wrought. The new house was carpeted, for the sake of Arthur's knees, though little of the pale green wool showed under the tide of wrapping paper and balloons. Eliza tried not to worry about the cake and cartons of juice she had seen cascading from small fists.

'Great party though.' Rachel nodded her head in the direction of the kitchen where Arthur could be seen stacking discarded plastic cups on the floor. 'He seemed to enjoy himself.'

Eliza put her palm up to Rachel's cheek and held it. The skin was soft and a little finer than before Arthur, and she wore her hair shorter, surrendered to the curls.

'It was a fantastic party. Thank you.'

Rachel had organised the party, the way she organised everything now, alone and without fuss. She no longer called Eliza at work because the washing machine wouldn't drain or her mother had been unkind.

'Two years.' Rachel lifted her free hand to Eliza's and pressed it to her temple. 'A wild ride.'

Eliza took the plates from her wife and moved to collect the rest. 'You have a bath with Arthur. I'll clear up.'

Rachel kept her fingers at her forehead.

'I do feel it sometimes. As though it's still there.'

There was always the worry that Rachel would view the day as an anniversary of more than just their child. On the days when they came close to talking about the ant, Eliza would be reminded that for Rachel, the ant was real. Not some metaphor that Eliza could sweep away with an imaginative flourish. She gathered some crisp packets from the floor and hoped Rachel would stop.

'It can't be, though. Living inside me, in my head. But I feel it,' Rachel said.

Eliza felt the blood rush to her face.

'I know you don't like to talk about it,' Rachel continued. 'We should do, I think. On days like this.'

As though the conversation were not always with them, running alongside their lives like tickertape.

'What? What do you want to talk about? An ant?' Streamers and crisps scattered between Eliza's feet. 'I did everything, Rachel. I believed you. I changed it all for you. We have a life. If you keep going on about the ant . . . people will think you're crazy.'

'Mum?' Arthur ran through the doorway, his bare legs dripping from the dregs in the party cups.

Eliza lifted him off the floor and squeezed him hard. 'It's alright, baby.'

'Will they?' Rachel said. 'Eliza, please. Stay and talk.'

'He needs a bath,' Eliza carried their sticky son into the hallway and up the stairs, Rachel's face staring back at her as she dropped Arthur into a few inches of lukewarm water and a trough of bubbles.

He looked so like Rachel, dark haired and olive skinned and something else, something removed from both Hal's family and Rachel's, an old-fashioned far away set to his eyes and brow, as though he had waged some mythical battle with the gods and been punished with the life of a human boy. Eliza didn't believe in anything of the sort, but having a child had rounded the edges of her cynicism. It was impossible to deny the importance of imagination when your son demanded you investigate its powers daily. And all along there had been Rachel, placing her own fantasy at the centre of her family. Their family. She rubbed a flannel along Arthur's stocky legs. Very well. If Rachel was troubled, if she needed to talk, then it was up to Eliza to help her.

`writeln`

Dr Marshall's front door was on the side of the house, facing away from the street. A gravel path led from the gate to the neat porch where a pair of doorbells were marked 'House' and 'Dr Marshall'.

'Think of all the patients who are tempted to press the other one.' Rachel grazed her fingers over the two bells.

'You included.'

'I'd like to see what happened.'

The door swung open and an older woman in a paisley wraparound dress stepped forward to greet them. She extended her arm towards the hallway. Dr Marshall didn't do handshakes.

It had taken six months to find a therapist they both liked and in the end it was a friend of Hal's who recommended Sondra Marshall. Her academic background suited Eliza who was anxious about qualifications, and her modern approach impressed Rachel who did not want a Freudian analysis. She was also American, which pleased them both since it removed her from their immediate frame of reference. As though the therapist's mind were neutral territory upon which they could meet.

This was their first visit although they had spoken to Dr Marshall on the phone. As they walked into the consulting room, Eliza searched for clues to the personality of the doctor in whom she had placed her trust. She glanced at the bookshelves and framed certificates on the wall, and noted the way the therapist walked to the best chair and waited for her clients to sit across from her. Eliza saw she had entered a temple to which she did not belong.

Dr Marshall sat down and smoothed the paisley dress over her bare legs. Her straightened hair fell below her jaw and a soft cleavage was visible in the deep V of her neckline. A well-kept sixty, thought Eliza, Rachel will age like that while I become gaunt. An image of their older selves flashed into her mind, the comfort of Rachel's gentle flesh beside her own.

'We spoke on the phone about a turning point in your relationship.' Dr Marshall looked at both women. 'Have you had any more thoughts?'

Rachel answered first. 'It's different now, since Arthur.'

'Arthur is your son?'

'Our son. But I was the one who wanted him.'

Dr Marshall nodded. 'And Eliza? How did you feel?'

'I supported her. And I love him. But she's right, it wasn't my idea, I was worried that it would be too much.'

'Too much?'

'For Rachel.'

Rachel leant back in her chair and folded her arms.

'Why did you think that?' Dr Marshall's tone was even.

'She is the main carer. I'm at work all week and I can't leave my job,' Eliza said.

'Plenty of families cope with one parent at work and one at home.'

'Of course. And now she's more confident. We both are.'

'So your fears proved unfounded?'

'About that. Yes.' Eliza glanced at Rachel.

'Here we go,' Rachel said.

'We're going to have to talk about it.'

'I said so.'

Dr Marshall lowered her notepad. 'This is the time for you to talk about whatever you feel is important.'

Eliza said, 'Why don't you start? It's for you.'

'No. It's not.' Rachel stood straight up. 'It's us. You and me. You promised and now you've changed your mind.'

'I can't keep up. I honestly don't know what it's going to be next,' Eliza said.

'Rachel, would you like to sit with us?'

'How is that my fault?' Rachel walked to the large window that faced on to the garden. 'What if it had happened to you? I would have listened, you know I would.'

Dr Marshall looked at Eliza.

'We're listening, Rachel,' the therapist said.

Rachel put her temple to the glass. 'There is something living in my head. It has been for nearly three years. I have tried to ignore it but it won't go away. It's there when I wake up, it's there when I go to sleep.' She turned to Eliza. 'You believed me.'

Eliza watched the silhouette of her wife against the window. She saw her beyond arm's length, without Arthur, quite alone. If I had taken care of this, she thought, that night, years ago. I could have told her then that there was no such thing as an ant that can enter your eye. Or, even better, if I had listened and got the pest man in, with his temper and his poison, none of this would be happening.

'Have you felt like this all along?' Eliza said.

'Mostly.'

'Why didn't you say?'

'How could I?' Rachel took a step forward. 'That was the bargain.'

Dr Marshall cleared her throat. 'It sounds as though we have a lot to talk about.'

'You asked me to believe you and I did,' Eliza said.

'But you didn't believe, did you? Not really.'

Eliza couldn't answer. She had accepted Rachel's story as part of the woman she loved; a version of events that was not factual but more of a metaphor. Could she tell Rachel that now?

'Why did we come here?' Rachel looked directly at Eliza. 'You have to decide. We can't run away, move to another new house, start again. You have to decide.'

'Rachel,' Dr Marshall indicated the chair again. 'Please sit down.'

Rachel moved to the arm of her chair and kept her eyes on Eliza.

'You've both been dealing with change,' Dr Marshall said. 'Having a child can mean a couple must renegotiate their relationship, their roles within the family.'

'We had a deal.' Rachel's voice was flat. 'I kept up my end.'

'I thought you were happy. Until Arthur's birthday. You were happy.'

Dr Marshall glanced from Eliza to Rachel. 'What happened on Arthur's birthday?'

'I told the truth,' Rachel said. 'That's all.'

'About what's inside your head?'

Rachel nodded.

'Is that what you heard, Eliza?'

'I thought we'd finished with all that.'

'Rachel told you she thinks something is living inside her head and for some time you went along with this belief.' Dr Marshall wrote in her notepad and returned to the two women. 'What's changed?'

Eliza stared at the therapist. The question was for Rachel, Eliza had not changed.

'There's no more trust,' Rachel said.

'I trust you, Rachel. It's not about that.'

'You've brought me here to try and talk me round. To cure me. How can I love you when you wish I was someone else?'

A sense of panic crept over Eliza as she listened to Rachel. She struggled to answer but the words died on her lips. It was Rachel who did not trust her. Rachel who might withdraw as an animal backs away from a trap. Eliza felt the therapist watching them. The doctor's office was not a temple, it was the opposite; a place to surrender belief.

'I thought you wanted help,' Eliza said.

Rachel put her hands to her head. 'For us, our family.'

Dr Marshall leant forward. 'Rachel, are you alright?'

'It's nothing,' Rachel said. 'Ant music.'

```
('Hello, World!');
```

The hospital confirmed the diagnosis by letter. A supratentorial glioma.

'That's what they're calling it now,' Rachel said. 'A glioma.'

'Glee-oh-ma,' Arthur repeated.

Eliza gave him a piece of banana. 'When is your next appointment?'

'Tomorrow.' Rachel peered at the paper.

'So soon?'

'I didn't ring them back.' In reply to Eliza's next question. 'There's no rush.'

Eliza focused on Arthur, steadily making his way through the banana. She was learning not to overreact to Rachel's studied calm. Since the diagnosis they had settled into a pattern of Rachel's fatalistic acceptance and Eliza's eager cheerleading. It exhausted them both. Eliza had talked to Dr Marshall about changing the routine but it took time to ignore your instincts.

'I'll come with you. Hal can take Arthur.'

'Daddy,' said Arthur.

'All those tests. Like the space collider. Put you in a tube and zap you and they still can't find what they are looking for.'

'I know.' Eliza nodded. 'How are you feeling?'

Rachel lifted Arthur out of his chair. 'I'm fine.' She put the tip of her nose to their son's. 'Aren't I?'

The child looked up at his mother.

'Ant,' said Arthur.

```
readkey;
```

Eliza continued to see Sondra Marshall on her own. Once a week, she left Rachel and Arthur curled up together on the sofa and rode her bicycle to the house with the door on the side. Each time, while she waited for the therapist, she looked at the bell marked 'House' and thought of Rachel.

'How are you doing?' Dr Marshall settled into her chair.

'Rachel's chemo finished on Monday. She's very quiet. But she doesn't feel sick any more.'

'And you?'

'I miss her.'

'How?'

'She's dying.'

Eliza looked toward the window at the far end of the office. She remembered Rachel leaning against it the first time they came to the house. Pressing her head to the glass.

'And that changes how you feel about her?'

'Everything we do together is in the past,' Eliza said.

'In what way?'

'She hasn't got long. A year, maybe. Each day that passes is the last one.'

'Aren't all our lives like that?' Dr Marshall nodded.

'But we don't have the luxury of denial.'

'You think it would be better if you didn't know?'

Eliza shrugged. 'There isn't some other Rachel who didn't get tested or who doesn't have a tumour.'

The therapist smoothed down her wrap around dress. She wore the same style every week in different colours but the paisley one had not been worn since their first visit. Eliza wondered if there was a system.

'Is that what you want? A different Rachel?'

'I want none of this to have happened.'

'Where would you start erasing the past?'

Eliza looked away. It was a trick question, but she knew where she would start. As soon as Rachel had mentioned the ants, she would have gone to the shop and paid the pest man to get rid of them. Eliza was a scientist, she did not think an ant had caused Rachel's cancer, but without the ant between them they would be free.

'Eliza?'

Where would that leave them? Would she be facing the future alone now? Of course not, Arthur would have been born regardless of an imagined insect bite. She shook her head, as though the idea of the ant in Rachel's head had somehow affected her own. Maybe it had. Not the physical mind, but the other part. The part that wondered how all these things were connected.

'It doesn't matter,' she said, 'I have a child to think about. A son to raise without his mother.'

'That will be hard,' said Dr Marshall, 'but he has you. And you have Rachel to help you prepare. It's something you can do together, prepare a future for him that you both want.'

'But I don't want to live with a ghost,' Eliza said, 'I want Rachel.'

Dr Marshall didn't hesitate. 'Rachel is there now. Are you?'

There and not there, Eliza thought.

end.

It was a little after nine that night when Eliza returned home, and Rachel and Arthur were already asleep. She tucked her son's legs under his covers and walked across the hall. The bedroom door was open and light spilled across the carpet from Rachel's bedside lamp. Eliza stood in the doorway and watched her wife's slender ribcage rise and fall. Rachel's baby weight had left as suddenly as her hair, collateral damage, though the losses were not equally mourned.

Eliza studied the hollowed cheeks and pale skin of

Rachel's face beneath her woollen hat. The chemotherapy hadn't worked but there would be a period of remission before the cancer hit back. Rachel would feel better for a while. A 'time to get everything in order' the specialist had said. But what was orderly about dying before your parents? Before your child had grown up?

She hadn't said that to Rachel. She had listened while Rachel made plans. Schools for Arthur, special occasions; Rachel wanted to be part of the future. Rachel is there now, Dr Marshall had said, are you?

She leant against the doorway as Rachel's hand scratched under the hat. Was the ant moving around in Rachel's dreams? The thought stopped Eliza's breath. Since Rachel's diagnosis Eliza couldn't look at her wife without seeing the ant as well. The insect was part of their lives, a force within their relationship, a reason behind their family. If you love me, you will trust me, Rachel had said, and Eliza did. After all this time, she believed in the ant.

Hello, World!

For Arthur's third birthday they went to Disneyland.

Hal and Greg stayed behind.

'They should have come,' Rachel said. 'Arthur would have loved making Greg go on a roller coaster.'

'It's a mystery,' said Eliza.

They both checked Arthur, staring through the glass of the hotel lift at the park below them.

'Did you see his face when we arrived and that dog handed him a goody bag?' Eliza said.

'Pluto.'

'Right.'

'Arthur and I have been revising.'

'The benefits of home schooling.' Eliza took Rachel's hand. 'If you get tired, just say.'

'You can't get tired in the happiest place on earth.' Rachel smiled.

The three of them walked round the park in the late November sun.

'We should always come to France for his birthday,' Eliza said.

'Always.'

When they reached the teacup ride, Rachel sat nearby and Eliza queued with Arthur. It was the middle of the week and most children were in school but the line was still long. The cordon looped round several times, twisting back so that the same groups of people met every five minutes or so.

'Where's mummy?' Arthur's hand squirmed in Eliza's as he strained to see Rachel beyond the crowd.

'She's over there, waiting for us.' She pointed to Rachel's outline, just visible under the café awning.

Eliza lifted her son up on to her back and turned the next corner of the queue, brushing the arm of a man walking in the opposite direction who pulled himself away.

'Excusez-moi,' Eliza said.

She glanced at the man and caught a glimpse of his scowling face as he shuffled down the line. Tanned, with grey stubble, and glossy, thinning hair. She recognised him, his bad temper, but he didn't look back. The man from the television repair shop. She remembered his name, Kargin. What was Mr Kargin, the pest controller from Green Lanes, doing at Disneyland?

'Mum!' Arthur kicked at Eliza's sides to make her move on.

The teacups had stopped and the line lurched forward. Arthur smiled at the woman behind the barrier. As they passed through, Eliza looked for Kargin but the crowd surged towards the teacups and Arthur slid down and ran at the one furthest from them.

'Blue cup.' He ran until he reached it.

The family in front of them swerved to the next teacup when they saw Arthur running with Eliza in tow.

'Merci!' Eliza shouted, though they looked more Peoria than Paris.

They closed the door and settled back into their seat.

'Here, Arthur, you can turn the wheel and we'll spin around.'

Announcements blared through the loudspeakers and the music started. The cup moved off in a wide arc, gradually building momentum. Arthur stared at the shifting world around him.

'Mummy.'

'She'll come and watch us. Turn the wheel, Arthur. That's right.'

The boy inched the wheel and when he felt the cup respond he redoubled his efforts, throwing his whole body in the direction of the spin. Eliza saw her own determined frown on his face as he held fast.

'You're doing that, Arthur. Look, there's mummy.'

The cup veered towards the fence and Eliza and Arthur both waved at a grinning Rachel who stood by the railings.

'We're going so fast.' Eliza watched Arthur's concentration return to the wheel as they spun away from Rachel. She looked up at the next teacup and saw the lone passenger inside, the pest man. There was no child beside him. No indication that anyone was waiting for him outside the ride.

'Wait a minute, Arthur.' She tried to stop the cup turning but they spun on and round and she saw Rachel leave the railings.

'More,' said Arthur. 'Quick, quick.'

There was no sign of the man or Rachel. Eliza sat back and thought about what she had seen. Mr Kargin from their old neighbourhood. The man whose temper had deterred them from using his or any other poison was on holiday with them. What did it mean? Eliza held on to the lip of the giant blue teacup and felt sick. It didn't mean anything. Why was she thinking like that? Coincidences didn't mean anything, unless you were Rachel's mother with her second-hand analysis. Still, the saliva rose in her throat and she shivered despite the warmth of the Parisian autumn. Over four years since the ant had crawled into Rachel's eye and here they were, on Arthur's birthday, because of that night.

She watched Arthur holding on to the wheel with all his might. Did he owe his life to an ant? she thought. She looked at his small hands, pink with the effort of turning the teacup round. Arthur and the ant, they were forever linked. She closed her eyes and the image of the ant flashed across her lids. The ant was not just in Rachel's head, it was in her own. And whoever else knows, she thought, the ant will be with them too. I only have to tell this story and the ant will always be in their head.

The ride slowed down and Arthur shouted.

'Again!'

'Maybe later.' Eliza pushed at the tiny door and tried to steady herself as she climbed out. 'I'm dizzy. Aren't you?'

'We went round.' Arthur leant from side to side as they walked to the exit. 'Round and round and . . .'

'Arthur, please, stop.' She turned to look at the emptying teacups but there was no sign of Mr Kargin.

'Where's mummy?'

Eliza nodded at the bench where they had left her. Rachel was folded over her knees, one hand pressed to her head. Arthur slipped his hand from Eliza's grasp and ran towards her.

'Mummy, I pushed us, in the cup.'

'I saw you.' Rachel put her arms out for the boy. 'So clever.'

The boy wriggled from her lap and stood on the bench beside her, absorbed by the life of the park. Rachel took a deep breath, swept her newly grown hair behind her ear and smiled at Eliza.

'Hello.'

'Hello, you.' Eliza took her wife's face with both hands and tilted her chin upwards. She could see straight into Rachel's eyes. The red mark from four years earlier was visible by her cornea and there, on the white of the eye, a shadow, small and quick. Eliza blinked and the shadow was gone.

She kept her hands on Rachel's face and the two women sat for a long while on the bench with the clouds shifting above and their son beside.

'It doesn't hurt,' Rachel said. 'It doesn't hurt at all.'

2

Game Changer

The Prisoner's Dilemma

The dilemma involves two prisoners who are kept in separate cells and offered different deals according to whether they confess or betray each other. It has been shown that, while in the short term, an individual does better if they sell out the other prisoner, in the long term, when they know they will have to continue to deal with each other, the prisoners do better if they cooperate with each other.

> If people do not believe that mathematics is simple, it is only because they do not realize how complicated life is.
>
> John von Neumann at the
> Association of Computing Machinery 1947

1 Cooperation

Everybody called him Al. His parents didn't mind, he was a popular boy and they saw how he fitted in with everyone, young and old, boys and girls, Greeks, Turks, even the British. Only his grandfather objected. But Ali didn't pay attention. *Baabanne* was bad tempered.

'He curdles the yoghurt,' Ali's mother said, 'Pay no attention.'

Ali thought of his grandfather as one of the goats he had to tend – with love and best kept at a distance. His parents owned a small guesthouse to the north of Larnaca, and the goats were part of the children's day. Before and after school Ali and his sister herded them around the pastures and brought them in when needed. In summer there was also work for the children in the orange groves or whitewashing the many outside walls. When he wasn't working outside Ali would follow Kostas the handyman around the property while he fixed things. Ovens and cars, lights and vacuum cleaners, there was nothing Kostas couldn't mend. Ali watched as a little bit of wire or polish brought an object back to life.

All summer long, when he had finished his chores, Ali went to the beach with his friends. As soon as he was done working, he would put on a t-shirt and shorts over his trunks, take some cold *börek* from the kitchen and rush to the door before his sister could catch up with him.

'Bring your sister.' Ali's mother had an uncanny sense of her children's location at any time of the day. 'Hanife, go with your brother.'

Then Ali would wait while Hanife packed a bag.

'You don't need a bag,' Ali would say.

'We'll see.'

Ali would promise himself that this time he wouldn't ask his sister for anything. If she didn't have the bag, he reasoned as they walked along the gravelled path that led to the dunes, he wouldn't want anything from it. But even as he promised he felt defeated. His sister was right; something in the bag would undo him by the end of the day.

The sun was overhead when the children scrambled over the stones that littered the lane. Ali stuck to the edges where the rocks were smoother on his bare feet, and kept his ears to the grass verge. Where the cicadas sang he knew he was safe from snakes. When the path became more sand than gravel, Hanife would take off her shoes. The place where this would happen would vary from day-to-day. Ali hopped with impatience as he anticipated the spot where she would decide there was too much sand to walk in shoes and slowly unbuckle the leather sandals. He didn't understand why she wore shoes to the beach in the first place but there was little point in arguing since that would only delay their arrival more. If he ran ahead, Hanife would tell their father and Ali would be in trouble. It made no difference that they were the same age apart from five minutes and that was to her advantage; he had to wait for his sister.

'Stop jumping about, Al. Go on, don't wait for me.'

He couldn't say exactly why he found it so hard to be patient. If he thought about it at all he only got as far as the feeling of fizziness inside him that made him want to run to keep from exploding. At school, the teacher tied a scarf around his legs to stop him squirming about.

'It's symbolic,' she said when Ali's mother complained, 'To remind him.'

Ali thought symbols were written down, like hieroglyphics. He wouldn't have minded if the teacher had drawn a picture of a scarf. In any case, Ali's mother thought the teacher was wrong. When he asked why, she said because he was too clever for the class but Ali knew what she meant. It was hidden behind the words, like everything adults said.

It was hard enough speaking three languages without having to guess what his parents were really saying when they talked. And now he and Hanife had turned nine, she was doing it too.

'Go on, run to your friends.'

He didn't want to leave her alone. He liked being with her when they were at home, making mud pies in the yard or riding the donkey that lived in the field behind their house. He wished she was like she had been before the bag and shoes appeared; running alongside him. She was as fast as him then.

'Please *abla*, come on. I'll race you.'

On the day Hanife sprinted away from him, Ali blamed her head start. He arrived on the beach seconds after her and they both fell into the deep drifts of sand on the far side of the dunes.

'Keep up, Ali *eşek*.' Hanife's laugh came in gulps as she caught her breath. 'Go donkey, go.'

Dozens of boys and girls were already gathered along the

broad crescent of translucent water they called *kalos* because it was good, especially in early summer before visitors arrived and they had the whole cove to themselves. Ali's friends were visible on the shoreline, kicking a ball along the surf. He could see one boy, a scrawny, *siska* kid called Damon was trying to stop them. The ball was his.

'It's okay, *eşek*. Go and bother Damon.' Hanife sat up and brushed the sand out of her hair. She looked suddenly far away, Ali thought, as though he couldn't touch her however much he reached out.

He pulled one of the *börek* from his pocket and tore it in half.

Without looking at the pastry, Hanife took a white cotton handkerchief from her bag and handed it to her brother.

'Clean it. It's not supposed to be crunchy, Al.'

Ali wiped at his food a few times and ate his half in three bites. It was gritty but he was used to eating sand. In summer his mouth was usually full of the stuff. He smiled at Hanife before swallowing.

'*Iğğ!* You're disgusting.' Hanife pushed him away.

He shrugged and ate the other half as he stood up. Down by the water his friends were calling and waving at him. He turned back to his sister.

'I'll be over there with Celena.' Hanife pushed her chin at the other side of the cove. 'See you later.'

The furthest end of the beach was where the girls camped for the day, dipping in and out of the water to keep cool. On the nearer side of the bay, the older boys who didn't yet have to go to work smoked and sunned themselves and took the occasional stroll along the wet sand to let the girls see their newly grown bodies. The middle territory belonged to Ali's gang.

He stuck out his tongue at her and ran off, duty and care rolling away from him with every step.

'Al! Al! Al!' he could hear the boys shout as they kicked the ball out of Damon's reach. 'Get in goal!'

The goal they had in mind was the entire beach as Damon struggled to land the ball out of the water. Ali wished his school friend hadn't brought the ball out to play when he was so anxious for its safety. The more protective Damon was, the more the other boys teased him. Much of the time the children made the best of a random collection of abandoned beach balls, or clothes bundled with string. The unpunctured, eighteen panel leather beauty that Damon's father had given him for his tenth birthday would have been enjoyed by the whole gang if Damon hadn't held on so tight. It was more fun to try and get the ball away from him than play a game with Damon marching around with 'his' football and 'his' rules.

Ali kicked the ball back into the sea towards Damon and shucked off his t-shirt and shorts.

'Hey, Stella, play nice.' A stout, younger boy named Andras wrapped his arms around his own shoulders and mimed a movie kiss. Melina Mercouri was the most popular Greek actress that summer and her photograph as the ill-fated Stella was all over the island. None of the children had seen the film but they knew Stella married a football player.

Before Damon could respond, Nicolai thrust a foot out of the water and sent the ball further out to sea. Ali waded over as the rest of the group lunged towards the ball sending it further away.

'They'll get bored soon.' Ali cuffed his friend on the shoulder. 'Let them play.'

Damon shook his head. 'Look.' They both stared beyond the flailing boys to the sodden tan globe bobbing out to sea. 'My dad's going to kill me.'

A few weeks before, Damon had cried when he'd caught his shorts on a branch climbing a tree and refused to cut the trapped belt loop with his pocketknife. Ali had broken the branch off to free the sobbing boy. The others had laughed and for some days after they had tried to leave Damon behind when they went off for the day.

'He's a baby, he should play with the *nepioi*,' Andras said.

'His parents are strict.' Ali wasn't sure this was true but it seemed to make sense. Why else was Damon always so worried about what they thought? His own parents were too busy to think about Ali's clothes and toys. They smacked him if he was rude and shouted at him to finish his chores and help his sister but other than that he was left alone. Ali didn't think that Greek parents were any more or less terrifying than Turkish ones. They all seemed to have their own confusing habits. Still, Damon was the kind of friend you had to look after. 'Give him another chance.'

The gang forgave him and when Damon's birthday meant a new football to share, they stopped singing *klápse moró* when they tired of him. Ali asked Damon to leave the ball at home anyway, he could see the trouble ahead, but the little taste of power was irresistible to the unpopular child.

'Please, Al. Stop them.'

With a glance at the scrawny Damon, now shivering in the retreating tide, Ali ducked under the water and headed for the ball. He was the strongest swimmer of the group but they were supposed to stay within their depth. Two summers ago, a guest from the house had drowned when he drifted out to sea. There were no coastguards, the only

39

adults an occasional village elder out for a daily stroll. By the time anyone on the beach noticed the man in trouble on the horizon, it was too late to reach him. The body was never recovered. Publicly the accident was blamed on ignorance of local waters but in school and at home children were reminded of the danger in their backyard.

The current was stronger past the first break where the ground dipped away and the water went from the palest dawn blue to the faded ink of his grandfather's vest. Ali rode over several large waves and felt the pull as they drew him back and under. Beyond the breakwater the surface seemed still, only the rocking of the leather ball ahead betrayed the undertow. He squinted in the sunlight, trying to judge the distance. Behind him, the boys' shouts rose and fell with the crashing waves. He was far away from the group now, approaching the outer edge of the bay, the ball floating into the open waters of the Mediterranean as Ali closed the gap. He made the calculation to dive underwater and attempt to overtake the ball enough that his own wake would not push it out further.

Under the surface he could only make out his hands as they pushed past his face. His eyes stung and the back of his throat burnt from the seawater filling his sinuses. He rose level with the ball but several strokes to the right and decided to launch himself across the distance with his remaining energy. With a gulp, he pistonned his legs beneath him and threw himself up into the air. His finger-tips grazed the coarse leather as the ball floated away from his grasp but Ali curled under and caught it with his feet, cupping his arms around to form a little pool with his whole body. Out of breath, he took hold of the ball and rested for a moment on his buoyant treasure.

Under his stomach the ball rose up and down. He thought about the time he'd been by car to the baths in Nicosia for the day with his uncle. More used to the bony back of Gri the donkey than the upholstered comfort of his uncle's Mercedes, Ali slept the entire way home and missed his uncle's tour of the island at night.

'He's no guard dog,' his *amca* said, 'Let's hope he's never called up.'

The words made a strong impression on Ali, who thought them both deeply unfair and yet hurtful, as though his uncle knew some buried truth. Ali had no wish to be a soldier but he wanted to be brave and loyal. He knew he could be useful. When he helped Kostas with the chores in the house he felt the satisfaction of the work and Kostas would congratulate him on a job well done. But had his uncle seen an awful defect in his character? There was the time he had hidden from Apollo in the year above so he couldn't steal his lunch. That had lasted a week until he got sick of eating on his own and had surrendered his favourite mince pastry. When he found out that Apollo hated vegetables he'd asked his mother to only make him cauliflower *börek*. Ali wasn't crazy about cauliflower but from then on he was left in peace at lunchtime and all his friends adopted vegetarian diets at school. Was that cowardly?

Ali kept his eyes closed and the water swayed beneath him. He knew he had drifted further but he'd found a way out of the Apollo problem and if he thought hard enough, he'd find a way out of this one too. His uncle was wrong, he could be a soldier. His uncle couldn't know about the nights he had peed out of his bedroom window instead of going to the outhouse because he'd once seen a scorpion there. That was sensible. Who wants to get stung by a scorpion or bitten

41

by a spider? But he knew it would seem like he was scared. Being brave meant taking risks and so Ali had resolved to be daring.

Above him he could hear the whine of an RAF aeroplane headed for Nicosia. The boys used to raise a fist at the British aircraft but with the addition of the new helicopters there were too many to bother with lately. Ali checked back to see what his friends were doing. Only Andras was visible this side of the breakwater, the other boys now stick figures against the beach. Ali scanned the water line around him.

He was well beyond the bay, the rocky coastline stretching either side of his good beach. Far away to his left, a passenger ship was approaching what he knew must be Larnaca port. He had never been this far from shore. He had swum out to one of the caves on the southern side of the bay before, to collect a starfish as a dare. But what had looked like a ledge to climb from into the gap in the mountain was too high and steep. The swim back had been tough without a rest.

'I'll try the other side next time. Or when the tide is in more,' he had said when he returned to the group. But he didn't go again. He didn't want to feel the way he had on the swim home; the queasy dread that crept up on him as he kept on swimming without seeming to get anywhere. The importance of the swim was that his friends had seen him do it and thought him fearless. That was why they now stood on the beach to watch instead of raising the alarm. Ali was the one who could swim.

Of course, he knew the tides. The 'gentle tides of the Mediterranean' as he had read at school. The sea itself was not orderly and predictable as a textbook. Every little inlet had its own nature, every beach its own troubles. The *kalos* beach was no different. He kicked his legs to get started and his calf muscles ached with the effort. Ahead of him the water rolled and heaved in the afternoon sunlight. He shouldn't have come so far at this time of day. While he'd rested, he had floated further out.

With the ball in his arms he only had his legs for propulsion. He kicked harder and leant over the top of the ball to add his arms. If he leant too far, he lost control, not far enough and only his hands were submerged. He changed position, tucked the ball in the crook of one arm and pulled forward with the other. Without the ball pushing into his chest, he could breathe but he had no balance or speed. He threw the ball in front of him and swam towards it several times but by the fourth try, he was only throwing it a stroke or two ahead, his arms as heavy as rocks. Every time he stopped, he drifted back.

His eyes were full of salt and his skin burned, but he kept kicking. There were more vertical bodies on the shoreline now. He saw them as if through glass, his watery world on one side, land and air on the other. He needed them now, needed one person to help him. Was it possible they could see or hear him? Who would come? Not the older boys with their swagger and their hair oil. Not the girls, who heeded their parents' warnings, though they might get help. Which of his friends would take the risk? He recognised the sickness in the pit of his stomach and knew that time was running out. If he kept hold of the prize he was not going to make it back.

With the ball against his head, he kept pushing forward. He had to get into the more protected waters of the bay and he didn't have the strength for his overarm crawl. An image of resting on top of the ball while he slept started to form in his mind. A nap might revive him, he thought, even as he knew that the idea was a bad one. Too tired to nudge the ball with his head, he turned on to his back and tucked it under his chin. The change in position gave him a minute of renewed energy until his neck started to ache. The ball slid off his chest and Ali reached out to grab it. He should let it go. Without it he might have a chance of getting back to shore. He tried to turn his head to see if help was coming but his sight was blurred and the white light that glanced off the water stung his eyes. Still, he could not let go of the ball. The shame of being rescued for nothing, the failure of his mission, Damon's disappointment and the jokes from his friends all pressed him to hold on. He was Ali the brave. His uncle was wrong.

He returned to his stomach and held on to the ball, his legs pedalling beneath him, his eyes closed to stop the salt sting. He tried to breathe through his nose. He was thirsty and his throat was raw. His body felt broken. He thought of Hanife on the beach with her friends. Would she notice he was in trouble? His mother would know, wherever she was, would realise he was in danger. Had he shouted, had he waved? If someone swam out to him now they risked drowning themselves. If no one came they risked watching Ali drown. He was too tired to move except his legs, cycling, cycling, while he solved the problem of getting home.

He couldn't swim hard enough with the ball in his arms but he didn't want to let go of it. If he had string, he could drag it but still the friction would hold him back. He needed to get the air out, but how?

A football pump could put the air in or take it out. He had a bicycle pump, but that was the same deal. The bicycle pump was in the shed back at the house, stored in the bucket with the big spanners and some of Kostas's other equipment. If Kostas were here he would find a way to deflate the ball without a needle. He'd seen Kostas string together electric wires, fill walls with flour paste, line roof tiles with hay. Once, Ali had watched while Kostas cut open a pregnant goat, delivered the kids and stitched the mother using sheep gut for thread. The goat stood up an hour later. After he'd seen that, Ali thought that anything was possible. He tried to remember that feeling. He thought of finishing-lines and podiums, he thought of soldiers and colonels. He was a Kargin. He could achieve whatever he wanted, be whatever he dreamed.

A soft body brushed against his foot and what felt like a hand. He tucked his legs in sharply. It was a fish. Only a fish, he repeated to himself. Where was he? He'd fallen asleep, for a second. The shoreline had receded and he was back out beyond the line of the bay. The ball was going to kill him. He had to swim for his life before it was too late. Ali slipped off his floating prison and sank below the surface. He had his breath back but his body could no longer float. He felt the pull of the water beneath him and struggled in vain to push his face into the air. Now his leg was trapped, an arm circled his neck. With an enormous effort he struck out at the phantom.

'Ow! Al! Stop. It's me. Stop or we'll both go under.'

Ali's ears were full of water. He couldn't hear above his own flailing and splashing but he could see. Swimming beside him, one arm around the ball, the other extended to Ali in a mixture of defence and supplication, was Damon.

For a moment, Ali couldn't make sense of it. This was not Damon's environment. It was like seeing your teacher in a bar, or your mother climbing trees. Ali thought maybe he was still asleep. Or dead. He stopped struggling and let Damon hold his head above the water. The boy had his pocket knife braced against Ali's shoulder.

'Jellyfish,' his friend said, 'Breathe, then we'll start back.'

There was no boat. How had Damon got here? How would either of them get to the beach? Ali's legs were as feeble as a newborn kid's. He could hardly move his arms. And Damon had the ball. They were both going to drown.

'You have to relax, Al. Let me swim.'

With his arm around Ali's torso, Damon started to drag his friend toward the shoreline, the ball in his free arm. They hardly moved.

'The ball.' Ali tried to take it and immediately slipped underwater again. Coughing, he rested on the ball and clung on to Damon. 'We have . . . leave it.'

Both boys looked at the beach in the distance. Several heads now bobbed toward them but they were still far away. Ali could barely hold on and Damon couldn't keep him upright with the ball slipping underneath.

'Go!' Ali released the ball and grabbed hold of Damon. The ball skittered across the water. They stared at the object that had brought them both so far out to sea and so close to staying there.

'Wait.' Damon held on to Ali and brought up his free arm, knife in hand. In one move, Damon closed the gap, took the ball and stuck the blade deep into the leather. 'Take it.' He pushed the folding moon of the ball to Ali. 'Hold on.'

Slowly, the two boys started the long journey back.

*

For his speech as Best Man, Damon chose his words carefully. It was not true, he said, that he had saved Ali's life all those years ago on a beach back home. The truth was, Ali had saved his. Ali, he was sure, would have worked out how to get home even with the troublesome matter of the jellyfish, which Damon had to admit was a close call.

'Al knew how to solve a problem, how to escape from trouble. If I didn't know it before, I saw it many times in the *schisma*.'

The guests, both Ali's Turkish friends and Celena's Greek ones, nodded at the recognition of the division of the island.

'If Al hadn't shown me how to be brave when we were *paidiá* I would never have made it here.' Damon indicated the street outside, and with a wider sweep of his arm, the park and the greater area of north London. 'He stood up for me when others would have turned their backs. He climbed trees to rescue me when I would fall. Al is the first person I turn to and the last person I want to leave. Dear Celena,' Damon raised a glass, 'You have chosen well, you have chosen wisely. May your life together be long and enchanted. And may you never know the difficulty of choosing between your best friend and a football. *Sağlığınıza!*'

II   Defection

Ali drifted further out to sea with the rescued ball balanced beneath him. He thought about Hanife on the beach. Every morning he was so impatient with her, so quick to leave her behind if he could. The fizzing in his legs had gone now. How he wished he could stand next to his sister again, the sand between his toes, and wait while she unbuckled her shoes with all the time in the world.

There was no time left in the open water. He looked back at the shoreline. On the beach he saw a small group, a blur of lines from this distance, but standing together. There was no sign of anyone on his side of the breakwater.

He slipped off the ball and slid under a little way, his muscles too tired to support him. A rope of water appeared in front of his face, no, not water, a tentacle, as clear as the stream from the tap. He ducked to one side as a jellyfish floated away from him and the ball skittered over his shoulder. He let it go. One jellyfish meant more jellyfish. If he was stung now he would drop to the bottom of the ocean as fast as Damon had dropped out of the tree when his belt had caught on a branch. Instead of cutting himself free, the *siska* boy had struggled and lost his balance. Damon was not a soldier but his broken bones were nothing compared to what lay in wait for Ali.

This was the moment his uncle had meant. Ali was being called up, right now, in the depths of the Mediterranean. He could make every effort to swim hard for the shore. Or he could give up. His family might never find him though his mother would know where he lay. She would think of him below the sea for the rest of her days. And Hanife would forever be a twin without a twin.

Ali had never faced a moment like this before. He was nine. The closest he had come to death was in birth. He remembered times when he was afraid but had he been afraid for his life? The creatures that lurked in the outhouse were his main foes, but they were not going to kill him. Nor were Apollo and his henchmen. But out here in the water he might die and no one was coming to rescue him, just as no one had rescued the man in the boat, though they'd all seen it happen.

He put his face up to the blinding sky, took a deep breath and forced his arms and legs to move.

*

'It seemed to take so long,' Ali said in his perfect English, 'As though the whole world had slowed down. I washed up on the beach like a newborn.'

'Your friends must have been scared.' The young woman frowned at him. She still thought the best of people.

'*Tch*. All they cared about was the ball. So,' he looked out at the sea, remembering why he had started this now uncomfortable story. 'Please be careful of the current. It looks calm, this little *kalos* beach, but believe me, it can play with you.'

They both watched as the gentle waves pulled the sand from under their feet and washed back over them. The bay was almost empty, the children still in school and the adults at work. Ali didn't usually bring guests to this beach, his beach.

'It feels more like a bath than an angry sea,' she said. 'But thank you. For the warning.'

She smiled at him and Ali took this as his cue to leave. The guesthouse had just started the season and Celena and Kostas would be serving lunch soon.

'It's Ali, isn't it?' She put out a hand. 'Elizabeth. Do you have to rush back?'

She wasn't much older than him. A few years, maybe. She had arrived alone two days before and had stayed in her room until breakfast this morning when she appeared on the small terrace in a sunhat and asked directions to the beach.

'Ask Ali,' Celena said. 'He's the swimmer.'

If he lived to sail the stars, Ali would never be allowed to forget his fall from grace. Ali shrugged at Celena but he'd offered to walk down with the English woman if she could wait a couple of hours. The travel agencies often talked about the 'personal touch' and 'customer satisfaction', but Ali would only be helpful to those he wanted to help. The woman had agreed to wait and, though he would never have admitted it, Ali had worked a little quicker.

There were only a few of them working at the house that summer. Celena and Kostas, Ali and his father, and a girl who came in to do the laundry. Hanife had gone to London, to work for a Turkish newspaper near a place called Finsbury Park. She had left the island as soon as she could because, she said, it had killed her mother and now it was killing her. Their mother had died of a brain tumour and Ali didn't see that where they lived had anything to do with it, but Hanife insisted.

'I don't want to be the invaded any more,' she said. 'I want to be the invader.'

So she'd gone to England to get her own back. Ali didn't ask her if she felt like she'd conquered the British, she was doing well enough in her corner of north London. She left Ali and their father to run the guesthouse, now more of a hotel, and asked her brother to consider his own future. Once a year, she returned to the island and again for the wedding of Celena and Kostas. At the party, she took Ali's face in her hands.

'Don't torment yourself, Ali *eşek*. Leave them and make a new life.'

He had watched Celena vow to love another man and had said nothing. Ali didn't think there was much life left in him.

Instead, he poured all his energies into doing up the house, installing new plumbing and banishing the spiders

50

and scorpions and snakes, the lines of ants in the kitchen and the pools of silverfish in the sinks. He found he was good at outwitting the pests and parasites that bothered less scrupulous establishments. The little hotel was perfect for the new crowd of tourists that flew around Europe wanting to experience the 'real' island and not the packaged version. Reality, Ali found, was a private bathroom with hot water and breakfast served under a canopy of grapevines for half the price of the big hotels. The visitors would have been shocked at the authenticity available had they ever ventured to the rural interior. Ali thought he might suggest the trip next time a tie-dyed hippy complained about the wine list.

The Englishwoman, Elizabeth, didn't seem the complaining kind, or much of a hippy. They walked back to the more sheltered dunes where she had set out her towel, unpacked her bag and now lay on her stomach in a neat, black bikini with a book in her hands. They had spoken about the landscape and the history of the island on the walk down and Ali had found her easy to talk to, which had led to his safety warning becoming more of a personal confession than a professional courtesy. He glanced over at her. She was attractive, soft-skinned and curvy with dark waves of hair that fell to her shoulders. He found himself wondering what her back would feel like if he traced a finger along her spine.

'Will you stay for a while?' She shaded her eyes as she looked up at him. 'Or I'll have to read on my own all afternoon.'

'You don't like your book?'

'Oh, the book's fine, it's the company I'm not sure about.'

Ali took his time to sit down on the sand next to her while he considered what she meant.

'You don't like to be alone?'

She frowned. 'Not really. I know I should, it's one of the reasons I came here, to get better at it.'

'You're planning a life of . . . solitude?' The image of the Greek nuns at Ayios Minas came to him.

'Oh!' she laughed. 'No, the opposite probably. But my mother had this thing about being independent and I haven't been, very, and now's probably the time to learn.'

'Your mother sounds very modern.'

'She is, I suppose. Didn't take her own advice though. She's just about to marry her third husband. Sorry.' Elizabeth put a hand to her mouth. 'Are you very religious?'

'Not at all. My mother was modern also, not like yours, but we did not grow up in a religious household.'

'I thought everyone here was. There are so many beautiful churches.'

'Yes, but I am not Greek. I am Turkish.'

'Oh, I see.'

Ali nodded. Of course, she did not see and how could he explain? Would he start with the day he asked his parents why he had to go to Sunday school and they told him not to make a fuss? Or how he thought he had been friends with everyone until they sided with Damon and he was abandoned by the little gang? They blamed him for letting the skinny Greek boy fall from the tree and for stealing Damon's football and leaving it to float out to sea. After that, he was Ali, not Al, and he understood what his mother had meant about the teacher who tied his legs to the chair. He was different. No, he was not religious, and neither was he Greek.

'It's okay,' he said to Elizabeth. 'This island is complicated. But it will change soon.'

She looked at him and her face was open. For the first time since he accepted that Celena did not love him, he felt the hope that comes with being wanted.

'And you,' he said. 'Will you be an independent woman, like your mother?'

Elizabeth sighed. 'Yes, almost exactly,' she said. 'Only, with just the one husband, I think.' She held up her left hand where a pale line circled the fourth finger. 'He's an artist. We're getting married next month.'

The hope left as suddenly as it had arrived. 'You already have a tan,' he said. 'This is another holiday for you.'

'Oh? Oh, yes.' She looked startled. 'I had to get away from them. You know, my mother, her fiancé, my fiancé. We were at this hotel in France my mother always booked when I was young. Younger.' She raised her eyebrows. 'Terribly smart, sun loungers and cocktails by the pool. It was all so, inevitable, as though nothing had changed or was going to change or ever could. I wanted to be sure I was, well, making a choice.'

They looked out at the sparkling sea in front of them.

'A choice? Not the right choice?' he asked.

'That would be a bonus, obviously.'

She took two orange sodas from her bag and handed one to Ali.

'I suppose it's a good deal.' She pushed the metal top off the bottle and squeezed her thumb in her fist to assuage the obvious pain. 'I mean, we marry each other, me and Nicholas, and we make our way in the world, have children, a boy and a girl would be nice, and the world goes on. That's our place in it.'

'But . . .?'

'Yes. Exactly. But.'

He took a swig of the soda and watched her press her hand down into the fine, white grit.

'So you take your ring off and run away. If you were to be my bride, I would worry.'

She smiled. 'He's not the worrying type. Except for his paintings. He frets about them.'

A flare of anger soared through Ali. Who was this man that he should prize himself so greatly? He drank again from the bottle and knocked the glass hard against his teeth.

'*Bok!*' Ali swore under his breath.

'Ow. Careful.' Elizabeth reached across to take the bottle. 'Your lip is bleeding.'

She was so close to him he could see the light down on her cheek. She wore no make-up and her dark hair framed her artless face in loops and swirls. He put his hand on hers over the bottle, and covered the missing ring.

'You are more precious than any man-made thing,' he said, and he kissed her.

'Oh,' she breathed and he felt her heart pulse at her temple.

'Is this what you want?' he asked, wiping the smear of his blood from her bottom lip.

She looked at him and he saw himself reflected in her clear gaze. He saw the two of them joined together, for one tiny moment in the history of the world, and he saw a future, not with her but near her, something captured from this instant on the beach, his *kalos* beach, echoing inside her forever.

'Yes,' she said. 'This is what I choose.'

III   Defeat

The football he wanted to rescue floated out of the bay into the open water. Ali watched as it bobbed out of reach. He didn't want the thing anyway, he had swum off to prove that he could get it but his old gang of friends weren't paying attention. Far behind him the boys played in the shallows, pushing each other and throwing a beach ball they had recovered from a tourist. Only skinny Damon would be watching.

He had swum too far out. He turned on to his back to try and catch his breath but he needed to swim to the shore quickly. He thought about the time he had reached the rocky edge of the bay where the secret cave had beckoned to the gang all summer. Only Ali was brave enough to swim that far, his uncle's words ringing in his ears. His uncle was worse than his grandfather for making Ali feel ashamed. After the trip in his car to Nicosia, his uncle had branded him a weak and lazy boy.

'He'll never be a soldier,' his uncle said. 'We cannot depend on him.'

Ali would show him. But when he had reached the cliff face that looked so mysterious and inviting from the beach, the cave was merely a gap and there was no place to climb up to investigate further. He had clung to the sharp rock until his hands bled and he'd been forced to turn around and start the long swim home with aching arms and not enough breath. It took everything he had not to cry when he reached his friends. Damon had cried when he fell out of the tree but the other boys had blamed Ali for not helping him and nothing had been the same since.

High above him he heard an aeroplane on its way to the

British base. Soldiers. He wanted to wave at them, come and get me. He could shout as much as he wanted, no one would hear him, not even from the beach.

He was sinking. He righted himself and tried pedalling in the water but his legs had stopped. He remembered how it felt to push himself back to shore from the cave. The effort, the moment when he knew he might not make it. You could get as far as the breakwater and still drown because you didn't have the strength to push through the waves. That's what had happened to the visitor who fell asleep in his boat. He'd lost his oars and jumped overboard to swim back but only made it to the shoreline. The locals had watched him, the Englishman. His body had washed back out. A terrible accident.

He could hear the water, the roar of it, feel the heave and swell as he filled his lungs only to sink again. He cried out now, between gasps and sobs.

'*Yardim! Yardim et!*'

Time slowed down. He couldn't see his friends, the other boys, couldn't see if they were coming to help. Was his sister waiting for him? Did she sense the loss to come? How he wished he could lie at her feet in the dunes once more, and beg for a drink or a towel, something from the bag she always carried, anything for which he could be grateful and true.

His eyes were salt washed, his body waterlogged like the old sponges in the bathhouse when he was little, as full and heavy as the pregnant women that soaped their children around him. He thought of his own mother, who had borne two children together, how big and uncomfortable she must have been. Was that when her headaches had started? All the time he wondered if it was his fault she was tired and how he would make her better one day, how he could fix her, like Kostas fixed the electric lights. Except now, there would not be a one day.

What would his uncle say? Had he been brave? He had swum out to sea and not come back. He had failed his mission and no one had come to help. The teacher who tied his legs to the chair in class was right; he was different. He was not Al any more, part of the gang. He was on the outside, looking in. He pushed up one more time but only his hand rose above the waterline. He was outside, he would always be outside. He was part of the water. He would lie on the seabed every day and every night. Would he be cold? No, you cannot feel when you are dead. This is cold, this sinking, this filling and falling, slowly, silently to the bottom of the sea. You are not dead yet. Not dead. Not.

3

Sunbed

To be a Bat

Thomas Nagel wrote that if we accept a bat has its own conscious experience then there is something it is like to be a bat, but we cannot imagine what that is like because it is so outside our own experience. The same may be said for any conscious organism, including other humans. There is the physical knowledge of another person but can there be an understanding of what it is like to have their experiences?

But I want to know what it is like for a *bat* to be a bat.

Thomas Nagel *The Philosophical Review*

Elizabeth Pryce turned to her husband at the exact moment he closed his eyes.

'Are you going to sleep?'

Nicholas started and grabbed the arm of the wicker chair in which he had chosen to recline while the Atlantic darkened, though that event was still some way off. 'What?'

'You're falling asleep. It's not even six o'clock and we're due at the Olivers' at seven. Really,' Elizabeth took the glass tumbler from his hand as she stood up, 'we're not dead yet, Nicky.'

She left the glasses in the sink and went to her bedroom to get ready for the evening, switching the television on and turning up the volume for the evening soap opera marathon as she passed. It was not that she minded Nicholas having a nap quite; he always had been relaxed enough to drop off at any second, but she had begun to count up the amount of time she spent awake and alone over the course of a day and to find it creepy.

At her dressing table, she swept a cream blusher over her cheeks with her fingertips and peered into the mirror to rub it in. Since they had left England she had very few people to talk to on a casual, daily basis. She was still busy, of course, with her classes and the house and Nicky to take care of, and how many women on the far side of their fifties could claim to be as fit and attractive as she was, studying capoeira with the masters? But much of her day was spent in her own company, or that of her husband, and it was hard not to feel, on occasion and especially at night, that she was fading like a once vivid stain on a sheet that with every wash grows paler until you forget it had ever existed.

I do exist, she thought, warming to her theme with a swipe of the mascara brush along her thinning lashes. I am not some insipid Anita Brookner heroine, wilting amongst the mahogany furniture in Maida Vale. I am still a catch.

'Do you find me so boring?' Elizabeth stared at the reflection of her husband who had wandered into the bedroom and was looking rather hopelessly for his socks on the end of the bed. 'So boring that you can't stay awake for a few minutes and have a conversation?'

And it was like that, she remembered, and swivelled round on the footstool to better address him. It was as though she were the cue to drop off, to stop concentrating and drift away. He didn't fall asleep when he was working; he created works of art. Big, beautiful canvases filled with colour and heat. He did not, she blinked at the thought, fall asleep in his oil paint the way he had done into his dinner more than once.

Nicholas Pryce stood still for a moment and waited for his wife to finish.

'I'm terribly sorry, my darling. Have you seen my socks? I feel sure I left them on the bed.'

His tone was entirely reasonable.

'I expect they've gone to look for your cardigan so they can reminisce about the good old days. It's eighty-one degrees outside.'

'Is it?' Nicholas kissed the top of his wife's head as he

sauntered to the bathroom. 'If only I looked after myself as well as you look after yourself, my love, I doubt I would feel the cold so much.'

He closed the door behind him and Elizabeth grabbed her dress from the wardrobe and slid it over her head. Nicholas had always preferred negative attention. Absent father, repressed mother, she thought, smoothing the bias-cut satin over her hips. Her own mother had been a therapist. Freudian. In the days when a woman practising Freudian analytic psychotherapy was slightly daring. Elizabeth had grown up with the flip dismissal of her mother's friends as egoists, Oedipals, neurotics. How easy it had seemed to categorise the human psyche as though each were the result of a knitting pattern. All terribly masculine and hearty, like assorted tweeds.

Had Nicholas been commenting on her figure? She twisted round to see if she could catch sight of her back-side. She had grown a little larger, certainly, over the last year; she could feel it in the pull of her clothes, in the new weight of flesh that folded and rolled when she turned in bed. Hormonal changes. She had been warned to expect this difference in her metabolism. There were loud exchanges over tea with other ex-pat ladies at the only hotel on the beach for forty miles. 'The good doctor in Fortaleza will help you when the time comes. All herbal remedies, bien sûr.' 'Cocaine is herbal, Beatrice,' Elizabeth replied. Beatrice had smiled and sniffed extravagantly. 'Well, and isn't that marvellous, too?'

Elizabeth insisted on her refusal to take aspirin when she had a headache, but had made a note of the good doctor's name, and now that she had missed her period for over six months she was glad she had got through the whole business relatively unscathed. She could not remember her mother complaining about the menopause, and her mother kept her figure. She had died with elegant ankles.

From the sitting room came the impassioned voices of Brazilian actors, hurling themselves in and out of love and cardboard scenery with equal fervour. Of the many reasons the Pryces had moved to Canoa Quebrada the one that remained undiminished, for Elizabeth at least, was an affinity for the language. Her mother had brought her up to believe in their fantastical ancestors, whose fortune had been built on Port. Whenever a certain advertisement appeared on their television, her mother would exclaim, 'That's your great-great-uncle. You are descended from a long line of pirates.' Elizabeth was never certain of the connection between fortified wines and theft upon the high seas, and since there had been little to show of the man in any material way other than his intermittent representation as a cloaked silhouette on late night television, she had kept the sense of the uncle as an imaginary figure from her childhood. But the influence of her Mediterranean lineage was evident as she grew older; in the easy tan and quick temper, the bump of her nose and the curl of her unruly hair that had become even wilder in her daughter, for a time.

At the thought of Rachel, Elizabeth frowned.

'I'm hungry,' Nicholas said, emerging from the bathroom. 'When are we leaving?' He paused at the particular expression on his wife's face, which he had come to recognise over the years as pertaining to their daughter and which was in danger of being engraved upon her brow in a relief map of suffering. 'It's teatime in England. I'm sure you can call her if you would like.'

'Don't be ridiculous, Nicholas. I've only just got dressed.'

Her husband shrugged and glanced at the end of the bed one more time before he left the room again. Thirty-five years of marriage had encouraged him to believe that socks, like sex and good humour, were liable to become available without any prior notice. You just had to hold your nerve.

The passions of Brazilian soap stars were muted by the door closing behind him. Elizabeth decanted the contents of her day handbag into her evening clutch-purse and tried to concentrate on the night ahead. She did not want to think about Rachel. If the inner life of her husband was only available to her as a series of noises, a Morse code of the soul, her daughter's mind was unknowable even in semaphore. A telephone conversation, especially long-distance, required preparation if Elizabeth was not to cry.

She buried her mobile phone in the bag and concentrated on arranging her hair in the mirror. Blonde highlights covered the grey streaks but the effect was one of maintenance rather than youth. The curl, so liberated by the humidity when they first arrived in Brazil, had been tamed by bleach and no longer bounced when she walked but sat limply on the shoulders of the jersey shifts Elizabeth favoured by day. Her reflection now, lit only by the table lamp, looked back at her as though from under water. Elizabeth peered closer. You are still in there, she said without conviction. The face of her daughter stared up from the depths. Elizabeth pressed her forehead against the cool glass and closed her eyes.

Such a quiet baby. You could hardly tell she was breathing most of the time. Tiptoe over to her basket and pull at the hem of her little dress. Black hair in a sweaty floss around the dainty face. Pick her up and hold her close. Feel how much she loves you. How much she needs you. Everything ahead of her. All the adventure to come.

Her daughter had been an accommodating child, and caused no trouble at all during her teenage years beyond the usual dalliances with body art and drugs so mild that Elizabeth had wondered at the point of it. Elizabeth had come of age in the era of Ronnie Laing. 'I mean, surely if you want to get high and scar yourself you can find something more interesting than cannabis and a butterfly tattoo?' That was the sort of mother she had been; relaxed and fun. She could easily handle a little childish rebellion. It was only after Rachel had left home and the evidence of an independent personality began to emerge that Elizabeth realised she did not understand her daughter at all.

She was secretive, that was the problem. Elizabeth had never appreciated the need for secrets and she considered people who insisted on privacy to be morally dubious. Elizabeth herself held no secrets. Or at least the ones she remembered were purely in the interests of those she loved. The best human instinct was to communicate and share. Weren't the greatest works of art, of poetry, of science, born from a desire to be known? Elizabeth wanted to know as much as she possibly could about everyone she met and in turn she tried to give something of herself. 'Only connect', Forster had said, and yet her daughter, the person to whom she had actually given birth, was determined to disconnect. At least that was how it seemed.

Within a year of Rachel moving to a house-share in an unattractive area of north London, Elizabeth was told her daughter was a lesbian. Not by Rachel, who could have told her at any time and would have received nothing but support, but by Helen, a friend whose son had met Rachel at a party one night. Elizabeth told Helen the son was mistaken, she knew of an affair, a recent affair with an older man, which had upset Rachel. But when she thought about the supposed affair later, when Helen had gone and she was sitting in the damp sitting-room in Devon waiting for Nicky to bring in the logs, she realised she had never been introduced to the older man, had only seen him from a distance dropping Rachel off at the awful house in London one weekend when she was visiting. Later, Rachel had cried and Elizabeth, wanting to be sensitive, had held her hand and told her love was difficult and all men were bastards and made her a cup of coffee with rum in it, for shock.

When Elizabeth had told her husband what Helen had said about Rachel he had been quite furious, as though she and her friend had conspired to upset him. Elizabeth explained that she didn't think it was true about Rachel and reminded him of the man she had seen from the window in London, and though she didn't mention the bastard remarks, she said she had been there for Rachel, she said she had cared. Nicholas was pale and his mouth was small, and in bed that night he slept in his clothes and curled away from her when she touched him. Elizabeth sat up until the thin morning light bled at the edges of the velvet curtains.

For days, she had wondered how to talk to Rachel. It wasn't the sort of thing you could easily discuss on the telephone: 'By the way, Helen tells me you're a lesbian.' When she did, finally, raise the subject very gently, Rachel had apparently already been told by Helen's son that Elizabeth was 'on the warpath'.

'I most certainly am not.' Elizabeth had been forced onto the back foot and decided she was never confiding in Helen again, especially since her friend had seemed so smug and understanding when she had absolutely no reason to be for hadn't her own husband left her for an African woman who wore a turban? 'I'm worried about you.'

Rachel had laughed. 'I knew you'd be like this.'

Elizabeth had expected her daughter to be defensive but she could not help taking the criticism personally. All she wanted was for Rachel to be as happy as possible and those types of people, not that there was anything wrong with being gay, could never be fulfilled.

'It's a cul-de-sac, darling.' Elizabeth had heard a woman on Radio 4 say this during *Any Answers* and it had struck a chord.

There was a loud sigh from the receiver. 'What's that supposed to mean? Are you talking about children? You've spent the last five years telling me not to get pregnant.'

Rachel had always taken the most obvious route between two points. There was no nuance to the child, no imaginative give.

Slumped against the mirror in her bedroom, Elizabeth allowed herself a small recollection. The beautiful Turkish boy, or was he Greek, deftly unclasping her bikini top. He had not lacked imagination. She forced the memory back into its proper place; buried beneath a life's good behaviour. Rachel was nothing like that boy because she had never met him and did not know about him. She was Nicholas's daughter and she took after him. Her mother hadn't believed in genetic personalities and neither did she. 'We are more than the sum of our parts,' Elizabeth said to anyone who ventured an opinion on evolutionary biology, and sometimes when they hadn't.

A hard vibration from her purse on the wooden table helped her to turn away from the Cypriot liaison. She pulled her mobile phone out of the now-full bag with difficulty, wiped at the lipstick stain that had bloomed around the clasp, and stared at the text.

We need to go before I eat the car seat

Nicholas had taken to texting her from various locations around the house, often with requests for her presence, occasionally with messages of what she decided to take as love. Nevertheless, she understood the running joke for her husband was a reference to her timekeeping. When she complained about his habit he said, 'You've always responded better to literature than to life' which, she had to admit, was true.

'What on earth are you doing?' Elizabeth asked when she walked outside, only a few minutes later. The edge of the garden was hazy with purple light from the ocean sunset. Nicholas sat behind the steering column of the jeep with a book balanced on the wheel and a torch between his teeth.

'What I'm always bloody doing. My angel,' Nicholas added, removing the torch. Elizabeth heard the deep intake of his breath. 'We don't have to go, you know.' Another breath. 'If you're worried.'

'She's your daughter, too.'

Nicholas put the car into gear and pulled out of the drive.

At the top of the hill, Elizabeth looked back at the house. The pool was a glass-blue rectangle lit from below. From a distance, the sunbeds were doll furniture arranged in a row as though a crowd of tiny tourists were about to arrive. Elizabeth stared at the garden until the car rounded the corner. The loungers had been her idea, a memory from a teenage holiday in the South of France. You didn't need sunbeds in Tiverton. Or the Brazilian coast as it turned out.

Still, she had wanted them and they looked pretty by the pool even if it was far too hot when the sun was out ever to lie on one. That was hardly the point, she told Nicholas when he had refused to help her buy cushions to soften her new furniture. The sunbeds were decorative, a promise of something. 'Melanoma,' her husband said, and she had been forced to take a taxi to Fortaleza.

The beds weren't supposed to be occupied in any case; they were a fantasy she had nursed since that adolescent summer. She had developed her own theory of attraction as she'd sat in her sensible one-piece with her mother's handbag tucked under the plastic stripping that bound the lounger together. All the drinking and smoking and reading and flirting that happened while the sunbathers paraded and dipped and posed, their taut skin golden in the sunlight, their eyes sparkling from the shimmer of the water. Whole days spent going back and forth from the bar to the pool to the chairs, and the sunbeds themselves were the source of the activity, the houses to which the bronzed ones retired and rested, collected their cigarettes, their sun cream, a hat or a book. The sunbed was a glimpse into the soul of the occupant and Elizabeth longed for a future when she would have her own perfect objects to represent her true self. When that happened, the right man would walk past her sunbed and fall in love with her, just on the evidence of her taste. She wouldn't even need to be there.

On the days she managed to leave her parents and step down to the pool to reserve her own place at the party, she would study the empty beds and consider the lives of the absent tenants. She began to award herself points for guessing correctly. Three points for age, two points for glamour or beauty, for which she had a list of criteria, and one point for gender which was the easiest, though she had been surprised a few times by a man collecting his handbag or a woman's trousers folded over the back of the chair. The Mediterranean temperament was different, she had realised; some of the women didn't even shave.

Perhaps that was where Rachel had got it from; a throw-back to the man in the cloak. Nobody else in her family was gay, or if they were they didn't shout about it. So tedious, having to explain to her in-laws and the book club and even the postman, who asked after Rachel, that her daughter was a lesbian. Not that she used that ugly word with all its connotations of big-boned women striding about. What had that to do with her lovely daughter, who was soft and curvy and hardly ever raised her voice? It was a label, this word, and yet Rachel insisted on using it at the least opportunity.

'Oh, mum, just say I'm a lesbian,' Rachel told her when Elizabeth asked what she should tell the hairdresser who wanted to know why she hadn't seen Rachel for so long.

'What on earth has that got to do with it?' Elizabeth asked. 'And why do you want the whole world to know what is personal to you?'

'Do you worry about telling people you're straight? Your daughter is a lesbian,' Rachel said, 'I realise it's hard for you to say. Try and say it on your own sometime. Or in your head.' Her daughter took a deep breath. 'Try and . . . imagine saying it.'

Elizabeth paused. Rachel was completely impossible to reason with when she was in this mood. 'You're so funny, darling.'

Neither of them laughed.

'Cheer up, my turtle dove.' Nicholas swung the jeep along

the main road and swerved to avoid the potholes. 'Old Bath knows how to throw a party.'

Elizabeth experienced a vision of the evening ahead. The unavoidable knowledge that a certain type of Englishman, rather than mouldering in Hampstead or Lyme Regis, had upped sticks to the north-east coast of Brazil, haunted her. The bourgeois life she had tried to cut away had sprung up in thickets within weeks of their arrival. She had not known about the alternative art scene nestled amongst the dunes, though Nicholas must have heard of the painters and novelists who had relocated. Elizabeth had imagined the move entirely original. To be faced with, she had to be honest, a fairly desperate crowd of middle-aged, middle-class Bohemians in search of a last fling with their youth, had irritated Elizabeth beyond measure and though she didn't like to judge, she recognised the tastefully distressed houses and raucous dinners as evidence of a dying tribe.

Those who cannot forget the past, she thought as they approached the turning to the Olivers' to find a string of overweight couples in sandals wending their way towards the house, were doomed to repeat themselves. You had to be inventive, to find new interests, or you might as well give up.

'Shoot me when my bottom looks as big as hers,' Elizabeth told her husband when they passed Dorcas Knowles. 'You can drive up to the front door.'

At the end of the lane, the Olivers' house leant toward the North Atlantic. Flaking plaster walls and columns were lit by exterior lamps scattered throughout dense foliage that rose up from the sheer cliff at the end of the garden. The effect was one of tropical disarray; as though the house were being reclaimed by the landscape and the entire property were on an inevitable trajectory falling into the sea below.

Elizabeth's vertigo surged and she clutched at the walking stick she had had the good sense to bring. Of course, she hardly needed a stick; it was more of a prop to make sure she was given one of the few comfortable chairs the Olivers possessed and she enjoyed the attention such a small inconvenience brought. The stick had been Nicky's idea. They had been to lunch in Aracati, the only Italian restaurant within an hour's drive, and she had suggested he bring the car round from the street where they parked. She had the smallest twinge in her knee, which she may have exaggerated slightly because Nicholas got so cross when she asked for help with anything. He had returned half an hour later with the car and an enormous disability contraption on wheels 'to help her get about'.

'Very amusing.' Elizabeth hadn't known whether to laugh or cry.

'Always thinking of you, my sweet.'

'Well, you can take it back.'

They had. But in the shop the pretty walking stick with a polished handle caught her eye and Nicky had purchased it with a flourish and a kiss and made her promise never to hit him with it.

'You can take it to your dance classes. I'm sure one of your Latin lovers could do with a swipe or two.'

'Capoeira. And,' an enigmatic smile, 'possibly.'

She encouraged her husband's jealousy, and as he never visited her at the studio there was no need for him to know that the few men who attended her class were a little older than him. Or that the only man younger than her was now called Sofia and had breasts.

The jeep came to an abrupt halt immediately outside the Olivers' front door causing a woman holding a drinks tray to jump.

'Close enough?'

'Just about.' Elizabeth shook her head as she dismounted. Nicholas loved to make a point however much extra work was involved. In the case of his extreme stop, he was obliged to get out of the car and apologise to the waitress, before finding somewhere more suitable to park and walking back to the house with Dorcas Knowles at his side, keen to introduce him to a new sculptor she had discovered who only worked with human secretions.

'He's a true fallen-fruit artist.'

'A fruit, in any case.'

'Found substances, Nicholas. An artisan of the soul.'

Elizabeth was already sitting on a bench in the hallway. Two glasses of red wine held aloft.

'Would you excuse me? My wife needs some help.'

She watched her husband extricate himself from Dorcas's considerable presence and smiled as she handed him his drink.

'Don't overdo it, Nicky. I'm not getting a lift home from Atalanta again.'

'We must ask her to live with us. We could do with a non-drinker in the house.'

'The only reason she doesn't drink is because she's an alcoholic, which hardly counts. And you know perfectly well I hardly drink at all these days.'

'So true. But then, you don't drive either.'

'I most certainly could drive. I'm an excellent driver.' Elizabeth drew another glass from the tray of a passing waiter.

'You don't have a driving licence though, my love, which amounts to the same thing.'

'The driving examiner was having a nervous breakdown.'

'Technicalities, trying as they may be, are of the essence in these matters.'

'They wrote me a letter of apology.'

'We should carry it with us at all times. We have put a man on the moon. We have given Keith Chegwin a career. It cannot be beyond the realms of possibility that your letter is accepted as a de facto licence to drive.'

'Keith Chegwin? For goodness' sake, Nicholas.'

'Cheggers, to his friends. Among whom I, sadly, am not numbered.'

'You're not to drink any whisky tonight.'

'Very good.' Nicholas looked past Elizabeth's head to the garden beyond. 'I'm just going to have a little chat with Atalanta. She might have some teetotal tips. Do you need any help?'

'Of course not.'

Elizabeth shifted her weight on the bench and smiled at an elderly gentleman in a velvet suit. Really, the Olivers' friends were alarmingly aged. It couldn't be good for you to constantly associate with so many old people. She took out her glasses to afford a better view of the numerous unframed canvases in the wide hallway. The man in the velvet suit tipped his silver head in her direction and turned back to his companion who appeared to be dressed in a kaftan. Why did fat people insist on dressing so badly? There was no reason to wear a giant, what were they called? Moomoo. Exactly. Like a cow. Elizabeth nodded to herself and caught Velvet Suit glancing back at her. To cover the moment, she raised her glass at him, found it was empty and looked about for the waiter.

Rachel had worn a similar garment when she was pregnant. On more than one occasion, Elizabeth had arrived at her daughter's house to find her wafting around in an outfit that most closely resembled a bedspread without the redemption of simplicity. The first time, when she asked her whether she was going to dress, Rachel had opened her arms and performed a little twirl.

'This is it, mum. Freedom.'

'I see. Very brave.'

'I know what that means. This is comfortable.'

'Like your shoes?'

Rachel's face flushed and Elizabeth remembered stepping back as though she thought her daughter might hit her. She wouldn't have, Elizabeth knew that, but her eyes had darkened with fury in her pink face and an electric energy seemed to spark from her skin.

'I'm carrying a baby. Your grandchild. Why should I want to truss myself up like a chicken?'

'I don't think those are your only choices, Rachel. Really, does Eliza like this get-up?'

'We don't model our relationship on your patriarchal, hetero-normative repression. She sees me as a person.'

'You don't have to look hideous to be seen as a person.'

'Hideous?' Rachel's voice had risen to her teenage octave.

'Oh, not you. You could never look hideous. Why do you always have to take what I say the wrong way?'

Elizabeth felt the wooden bench pinch the back of her thighs. The tiny quantity of Valium she had taken over sunset drinks with Nicholas had worn off and she reached into her purse for something stronger. Where was everybody? The waiter had not returned and there was barely enough wine in her glass to help her swallow the pills. She really should circulate a little; she hadn't even seen the Olivers. Only the old man and the fat woman remained in the hallway and she had no desire to strike up a conversation with either. She rose from the bench without the aid of her stick and glanced down at her clutch purse. The lipstick stain appeared to have spread.

She was very hot, her neck clammy beneath the damp clods of her hair. The slight breeze from the garden called to her and she resolved to leave the purse and return for it later. She could sense the gaze of Velvet Suit as she tugged at the hem of her dress where it stuck to her legs. Despite his great age and inappropriate attire, Elizabeth couldn't help feeling flattered. She drew herself up and headed for the garden in as straight a line as she could manage and imagined Beatrice Oliver whispering to her later, 'My dear, you quite fascinated the gentleman I invited for my single girlfriends. They were all furious. However do you do it?'

She had won prizes, she reminded herself, for deportment, at the establishment to which her mother had sent her after boarding school. If she hadn't married Nicholas, she might have had a career as a fashion model. And perhaps, it wasn't too late even now. She turned back to make sure of her admirer but he was laughing politely with the woman in the kaftan. Fat *and* jolly. Elizabeth supposed there was little point in one without the other. Velvet Suit could not be faulted on his manners in any event, despite, or possibly because of, his age. She determined to speak to him after all, when she had learned a little more from Beatrice.

The garden glowed in the lamplight. Cigarette smoke and mountain laurel scented the hot night air. Elizabeth stood on the terrace and surveyed the party, the pain she had felt creeping at her temples now receding as a wave of warmth for the other guests washed over her. Perhaps it wasn't so terrible to be surrounded by the sort of people you had always known. At the drinks table, Dorcas and Atalanta were swaying unrhythmically to a Portuguese ballad broadcast from an upstairs balcony. She could see Nicholas, an entire skewer of chicken livers in one hand and a cigarette in the other, at the far end of the terrace. He was talking expansively to a man in crumpled linen trousers, whom Elizabeth recognised from previous parties at the Olivers' as a ceramicist of some renown. Both men wore expressions of utter bliss on their grizzled faces. They might be in love, Elizabeth thought, if love were measured in joy.

Beatrice Oliver waved at her over the shoulder of a man with a grey ponytail who had his arm around her waist. She kissed his bearded cheek and headed toward Elizabeth with an alarming smile.

'Elizabeth! Where have you been? You don't even have a drink, darling.'

'I haven't felt like drinking,' Elizabeth said. And wasn't it the truth? And shouldn't Beatrice have come to meet her in the hallway with a glass of something lovely and a kind word? 'You know how it is.'

Beatrice's smile widened though it hardly seemed possible. 'Oh, my dear. But didn't they say everything with Rachel was better? All gone?'

'Yes, yes. Quite gone.' Elizabeth made sure to raise her eyebrow a little at the idea. Really, Beatrice was almost a simpleton.

'Then we must celebrate. There's someone here I'm longing to introduce you to.'

Beatrice thrust an arm through Elizabeth's and pulled her away from the terrace. Elizabeth's knee sagged at the sudden move and she struggled to maintain her balance but she refused to communicate her distress to her hostess. Beatrice was five years older than her and braless in a halter-neck maxi-dress. Elizabeth was not willing to be pitied by a woman with such inadequate taste, even if she was her closest friend.

Expecting to be taken back to the hallway to meet Velvet Suit, she was surprised when Beatrice dragged her down one of the uneven paths toward a covered archway, beneath which a tall man was laughing loudly with a male companion. Only as they grew closer did she see that the tall man was wearing high heels and a dress. Sofia from her capoeira class.

Beatrice squeezed Elizabeth's arm. 'Isn't she merveil-leuse? I met her at the lace market a few weeks ago. Sofia! This is my friend, Elizabetta, the one I was telling you about. With the daughter. My goodness, it is impossibly warm tonight.'

Elizabeth stood quite still and thought about her walking stick propped against the bench in the house. She badly needed to sit down but there were no chairs in sight and Beatrice seemed to be making an exit, removing her scrawny brown hand from Elizabeth's elbow and flapping uselessly at the garden as though a breeze might be summoned from the wingless arm.

The morphine calm had evaporated.

'The daughter?' Sofia smiled. 'Does she dance as well? We have missed you at class.'

Her companion waited to be introduced. He stared at Elizabeth with dark eyes in a sallow face. Liverish, Elizabeth thought. She wanted to slap him. These are the people that Beatrice wanted her to know, the motley group with whom she was supposed to have something in common because of her daughter's life choices. Outcasts. Women with beards and men with breasts and sad little marches and ugly clothes and always wanting to be different and difficult and angry when she was the one who should be angry. Her daughter had been stolen from her, had left her for another woman whose name was almost the same as hers. It didn't take a Freudian to see what had happened.

Sofia put a hand on her companion's shoulder. 'Elizabetta?'

Elizabeth started. 'Oh! Well, my daughter is in England. She is . . . I am . . . not well. Excuse me.' Elizabeth turned to the house and forced her body forward.

Her knee ached. With every step, the house seemed to withdraw further into the hillside and she staggered as she tried to catch her breath in the close night air. From behind, she heard a gasp and a strong arm reached around her waist before her leg gave way.

'Elizabetta!' Sofia gripped her hip and steered her toward the back door. 'You must rest. Come and sit with me and tell me about your girl.'

Elizabeth strained to see Nicholas as she limped. He was standing on a chair with his head thrown back, skewer in hand, a flowerpot balanced on his chin.

'Oh, Nicky!' Dorcas shouted, camera in hand. 'A little to your left, the light is perfect.'

'My husband . . .' Elizabeth gestured at the vignette on the terrace.

'We will fetch him later.'

The two women continued into the house where the smallest breeze fluttered in the hallway and moths batted against the walls above the lights. Elizabeth staggered the last few steps to the bench she had so unwisely left. She could feel the sprightly transsexual at her side and ahead of her Velvet Suit and Kaftan were glued to a book they appeared to be reading together.

'Thank you so much.' She tilted as she reached for the bench rail. 'I will be fine now.'

Sofia darted forward with a little sweeping motion just as Elizabeth fell into the seat. The clatter of small objects on the floor was followed by a loud crash and the echo of a bottle spinning against the tile. Elizabeth gasped and clutched at her chest. She thought she might faint. Or be sick. She stared at the ceiling to catch her breath and when she looked down, a trio of heads bobbed below her.

'I think this belongs to you,' said Velvet Suit, an arm outstretched. In his hand, the stained clutch purse sagged, the contents spread over the floor. Red wine pooled against her overstretched shoes. Item-by-item, her belongings were retrieved and placed by her side. Assorted phials of pills, make-up, her spectacles, an empty glass. Lastly, and with some ceremony, the walking stick was laid on her lap, duckbill up.

'I think that is everything.' Sofia stood and brushed at her lace skirt, the hem of which was now fringed a deep pink. 'I will speak to your husband.'

The other couple retired to the bookcase. Elizabeth sat as straight as she could, her possessions around her. Her whole body ached. From the ruined purse came a regular pulse of light. She reached inside for the block of phone and looked at the message; a missed call from Rachel. As if there were any other kind, Elizabeth thought and put the phone down. I could die right here and not have to endure what comes next in this world. I don't have to outlive my daughter.

An image of Rachel as a baby came unbidden to her and she closed her eyes against it. The dark curls and flushed cheeks as the newborn lay in her arms. The look of her father so clear in those first days, the boy on the beach with

the sea in his blood. Elizabeth had kept Rachel close then to
stop Nicky seeing, hidden her away amongst the swaddling
and blankets. But there was no need, Nicky never noticed
his pirate daughter, saw only the girl from a painting he
imagined he would one day paint, and Elizabeth spun the
yarn of her Portuguese ancestors and only remembered Ali
in the smallest of moments, in the grounds of strong coffee,
or the crash of a wave in an arthouse movie. She never
remembered him as a boy with no mother. Or why. How
could she?

When Nicholas came in from the garden he found her
upright and asleep, her head folded forward. She screamed
when her husband touched her and clutched at her heart.

'I'm still here,' she said. She was not disappointed.

'So it seems, my love.'

'Am I?'

'Here?'

'No. Am I your love, Nicky?'

'You better be,' he said, not unkindly. He held an arm out
for Elizabeth. 'Did you see my flowerpot dance?'

'I couldn't help it,' Elizabeth stood, 'you looked ridiculous.'

Nicholas smiled. 'I did, didn't I? Don't you want any of
your things?' He waved at the assorted items below them.
The message light on the phone continued to blink.

'Not much,' she said, turning away from the bench.
'They're not very me.'

4

Ameising

Philosophical Zombies

David Chalmers is credited with the development of the philosophical zombie, or P-Zombie, a creature just the same as us but without consciousness. Chalmers argues that since we can imagine a creature that is just like a human being in every physical sense but without the quality of sentience, even though such a thing might not be possible, we can see that consciousness is not a physical thing and is some other quality of being human.

> If there is a possible world which is just like this one except that it contains zombies, then that seems to imply that the existence of consciousness is a *further*, nonphysical fact about our world.

David J. Chalmers *Zombies on the Web*

There are two parts to my life and they are as different from each other as you are to a stranger who sat next you on a bus one summer's day, or borrowed a library book you had once read. The before and after of me are not two halves of one, as many lives must be. Young and old. Child and parent. There is nothing that follows as a natural progression, only a clear division. Of course, were you to meet me, in person, you would not notice anything of distinction about me at all save, perhaps, a minor imperfection. Introducing my self to you this way though, through a meeting of minds as it were, will allow you to understand the very great change in my circumstances. We say 'meeting of minds' though really it is my mind that is being met, this is not a two-way discovery.

Welcome.

The difficulties you may experience in understanding my story are to be expected. There is a small comparison to be made between my own transformation and the one you are embarking upon but only a small one, since your discovery is by conventional means and mine was, as far as can be told, unique. Yet you will be prey to sudden jolts and shocks, and your already advanced and settled knowledge of the world and its physical constraints will at times obstruct the absorption of new, conflicting, information. Still, here you are, embracing the process. We must commend ourselves for our exploratory natures.

We will start with the night that everything changed.

The first difficulty is how to properly convey the way things happened without tainting your impressions with my current form. You will understand so much more if we can edge a little into my original incarnation and proceed from there. To this end, let us envisage the bedroom of the converted Victorian terrace flat on a warm June night. The household sleeps and our small party enters from the garden, lured by the scent of something sweet.

```
program TimeDemo;
```

Tap my way along the unvarnished edge of the table. On the trail of sweetness. The scent of sugar. Icha and Ka follow behind me, Ki and Ekhi are ahead. We move in single file, no need to veer off this track now the way is shown. We've been here before; the sickly smell of fallen kin has led us here. We are high on death and the promise of what lies beyond.

The clicks and clacks of the column rise above us. Upside-down on the underlip of the table when the human bodies come into view, two women sleeping. Their scent blankets the room. Sweet but metallic. And one of them is dying.

The call from the scout grows stronger. Crick. Crick crick. Crick.

The source of sugar. See a glass surrounded by damp circular imprints of glucose on one corner of the table beside a brass bedstead. Make our way to the glass and Ki ascends. She enjoys the sugar, but on the other side of the wall sits the liquid and the scouts should go first. Ki is too eager to drink, and it has been dry. Dry in the gravel and the concrete around us, dry in the grass that pushes up between the stone and the brick. She is thirsty as well as hungry, and Ki risks the liquid surface that might trap her as surely as sap though not so pretty.

The scouts follow her up, in line.

Stay behind and watch the sleeping human forms. The rise and fall of their bodies. They are simple creatures. The abdomen and thorax are fused together and they have four limbs and no antennae. Even the males are flightless. They are of interest in their great size and in their capacity for creating sugar. They remind me of animals from stories, not wild like the birds and the foxes near our colony. When we worked for the queen we heard the tales of humans and how they lived but here, asleep in the dark, they surprise.

At the top of the glass, Ki turns back. We served the queen together and she senses me. Watch as the scout makes its way past her and slows down to the edge of the sweetwater. We know the way to break the skin on top with a bite, and the scouts may bring the droplet to the nest. This time we will all take a piece. Because of the dryness. That is the plan, but the scent of the sleeping animals draws me back. And something else: the death.

A whale song passes from one to the other in their sleep. The sound emitted from the mouthparts as they have no clack or crick in their bodies. This is what we know. We see their long shadows in the day, and hear them from far away and there is a pulling toward them, not just for the sugar. In the nursery some of us are taken with the stories of our own kind. We want to know about the Draculas that feed on their own larvae and do not kill them. Or the queens that fly away and abandon the colony. But some like to hear about the humans; the soft-shelled creatures destined for self-destruction. Doomed. That is what we believe and had we seen the first Mars rover we would have been sure. You do not make escape plans from a life that does not need them.

We have travelled. Ships we have made, from our bodies, and launched upon the oceans. Across the world our kind explore and colonise. Some of this knowledge is handed down the generations from aeons past. Pre-history, early history, biblical tales, we are there. But our world map is limited by our DNA. We did not know about other planets. Even in our ancestor memories.

Ki calls me to join her at the glass. Crick. Crick crick.

Watch the human women dream and feel the impulse to be closer. How to understand this. The workers in the nursery know how to nurture, keep the young alive. For the good of the colony. Not for my good or any of us as single units. This is in our coding. We must continue only as far as we need for the next carriers to mature.

I know of a fungus that burrows into the brain of a colony in South America. This parasite guides its host to climb a certain grass where it bursts out of the head of the host and produces spores in just the right place to infect the next scout or worker and continue the cycle. The host is known as a zombie because it cannot think for itself, but what is the difference, really, between that creature controlled by a parasite's coding or by its own DNA?

This is the sense for me when watching the women, though not the words; that there are forces working on me outside my own programming. Over the call of Ki and the scent from the liquid. Beyond the glow of the objects around me in the night. My antennae were alive with another sensation, a taste of some other apple-sweet knowledge, and the lust to act upon those feelings was irresistible.

Tap my way down the table and follow the scent of decay. The leaf-smooth floor ahead, too far to know the end. Use click and clack to find the iron bedstead. Slow, slow. Know the ropes of web as thick as legs that hang from shadows. The eyes that watch beyond. Tap tap tap, up the cold metal. Feel the colony strong again in the climb, the air between us. Do not listen. Do not call.

The first human is turned toward me. She with the odour not of regeneration but of chaos. Particles of light flow around her. She vibrates with an unfamiliar tension. The information is overwhelming. It drowns out the sounds of the colony, the quest for food or water, the collective responsibility.

The first touch of skin. A mass of hair on the face parts, pores and debris and moisture pooled at the edges of orifices. Stop by the parted lips and the nasal protuberance. Cavernous entrances to the unknown. Continue to the forest that guards closed eyes. Solid whiskers thicker than antennae, with creatures feeding off waste products. Symbiosis, but neither creature knows about the life of the other; the scale is impossible. At the colony we farm aphids for their nectar and in return for the food, we protect them from their predators. In return. That is not right; the aphids have no choice. Perhaps they are zombies too.

The size of the human close to. We are small for our species and we have a relationship with even smaller creatures. Is there a Them that dominates their lives?

No direct sound of Ki's call heard but an echo of her. Antennae twitch with a longing to answer. She will not follow me. We have known each other since our hatching, fed in the same nursery, served our queen. We would be as one until the end of our days. How to tell that together-other feeling for what it was then? We had only the day's work shared, the call and response of our scent across the grass, the crick and clack of our bodies. That was our sonnet, that was our song.

Not enough to stop my flight. This is stronger, this sense of moreness. The colony is not in danger as long as my actions are alone. Try to signal back but the message is inadequate. You cannot communicate an intention of which you have so little understanding. A scent. A mission. Is there choice involved? There is no answer to that, even now.

Walk over the face. Search for the source of the scent. There, at the corner of lashes, a droplet of not-sweetwater. And the smell of flesh as of the baby mouse that the colony once found dead by the dustbins. Antennae busy, feel for the aperture. Bite at the droplet and find the smallest of openings, along the pink ridge of the eye. There. This is the answer to hunger, to thirst. This newness, this moreness. The human moves and the forest of lashes part and now, now, push forward quick, force forward into the live flesh head first as the eye squeezes shut around me and a great pressure heaves me through into the space beyond. Inside. Most of me. One leg trapped. The wave of pressure returns and my leg is torn free. Free. This is wrong; you cannot be free from your own limbs. They belong to you. They are you.

You need to know if this hurts. It both does and does not. Not in the way you process pain, one tiny assault to a toe or a finger making you speechless, incapable. This hurt either will or will not stop me from existing. The leg stays behind, the rest of me burrows further into the cavity behind the eye. My existence continues.

Violent movements, rocking, shaking. Inside the head of the human my world spins. The earth rotates at over 400 metres a second and we don't feel it, yet this woman stands up and unbalances me. When the rocking stops, stay still for a long time, with nothing to measure the crick and clack. My first faltering, five-legged steps into the human condition are ignorant of days. No colony, no Ki, no column. There is nothing like what it is. The not-knowing of what has been done. Only the need to be there.

There is food. The smell of it overwhelms my exploration. So many different and new scents but the one that called to me from the bed that night is the one that stays with me in the labyrinth. The soft flesh of the tumour is embedded in the back of the woman's brain, separate from the tissue that surrounds it and of a different texture. An intricate connection of wet fronds weaves into the neat meat of the brain. The source of the chaos and the decay, the scent that bridged the gap between her life and mine.

You will wonder if such a thing is possible. The millions of bacteria that make up the human body you don't count as animals, even the little lice around your eyelashes are too small and innocuous to number. Bed bugs bite, as do fleas. You notice those insects; they are visible and leave obvious damage. But they do not live in you: they feed upon you, like leeches and ticks and mosquitoes. And vampire bats. Sanguinivorous. No, you should not find this disgusting at all. Humans like a little blood themselves. Blood pudding. Rare steak. Blood of your enemies, blood of your heroes. Transubstantiation. Delicious.

But this is different, this living inside. You have read about

90

coral in ears, spiders under the skin, tapeworms in a boy's head. You remember these tales and try to separate myth from truth, fiction from fact. And me, eating a tumour on a human brain. Have you heard of that?

A consciousness within a consciousness. If the me from before could be considered conscious. What are the necessary conditions? There was a sensibility, a belonging to the colony, an awareness of duties, survival, function. And there was more. There was loyalty to the queen, the satisfaction of finding the right food for the hatchlings, the rightness of a new tunnel. And there was Ki. Me and Ki. Really, there are some qualities of experience that seem innate to the me that was then but perhaps that is anthropomorphic. Well, this is humanised me. You're in *my* head now.

The human knew about me. In time, her memories swept through me as clearly as the hum of the colony when the new eggs are laid. There were no secrets. Her very dreams were mine. She had been scared, she had been in pain, but together we grew calm. She could not read my thoughts as you are doing, she had only the sense of change and reconciliation that comes from acceptance. She was dying but before she ended she, too, had duties, and loyalty, and love. We had work to do.

So it came about that shortly after my arrival, her headaches stopped.

But we are ahead of ourselves.

Tap my way around the tumour. Feel the wet, stickiness below me, the tight structure above. Room to move, room to breathe and a belonging, as of the colony. This food in front of me, this chaos, does not belong here. This is my task, to restore order: start with the edges, the newer strands that push into the membrane below. Once the first hunger is sated the work is slow. There are no hatchlings to feed. No marches to make. Pick my way around the edges of the cave, avoid the tides of her brain. Crick and clack are dulled, the sharp call muted by the fleshy tunnels, and by the nowhereness of the message. Ki cannot hear me. Can anyone?

The human moves about her day and her rhythms become familiar. Rest while she lumbers, work while she rests. One night she stirs as a small bite breaks free. And it comes, the electricity, popping my antennae as smartly as a new drone, a buzzing, stinging smack to one side of my head and my five legs buckle under me. The swell pulls me back up, and as the shock passes the thought comes; she is frightened.

Fear. We knew danger in the colony, could sense the rush in our ranks when predators loomed. Sharpened senses, antennae alert. The collective move as if breeze-swept. This fear was different. It was not my danger, my fear, this fear was hers. And, though the jolt and the fall had been my physical sensation, the knowledge of the fear was not a feeling, it was a thought. Her thought, and now mine.

Had there ever been a thought inside me before? Who can say? There may have been many. Do you remember your first thought? You cannot know the exact moment. This thought was a moment though. The thought was hers.

She was frightened of our situation. She remembered the first night. A bite or a sting. And the pain from before me, in her head and in her neck, stiffness in her limbs and back. Sickness. The worry that she was ill. Or that she wasn't ill but unhappy. The worry that an illness meant she could not have a baby, would never be a mother. The fear that she was dying or mad. Or both.

A thought splintered into a mosaic of ideas, memories,

feelings. Each piece flashed at the edges of my mind, unfamiliar yet understood, as the first impressions of the colony when newly hatched from the cocoon. A whole world glimpsed in fragments.

Maybe you feel it too, now that my thoughts are in your head. You do not fully know my world and yet you start to follow the scent. You have all you need. Stretch your arms and dream the click and the clack. Arch your back and close your eyes. Let the sounds and the smells tell you what you know, where you are. My thoughts are your thoughts as her thoughts were mine.

She, with all her hopes and fears, was connected to me.

Rachel.

The oneness of her. That is what struck me in the time after. Her thoughts came to me in bursts, multifaceted and often unclear, at least in those early days. But at the centre of each idea was the singularity of her self. If the many concepts she expressed confused me then, the core worked upon me, colouring my vision as fully as the waxed moon lit our path to her bedroom that summer night. The sense of the individual.

There is no easy way to satisfactorily convey to you the vastness of this proposition since, with perhaps a few exceptions for those of you who are of twins or other multiple births, you were born with your oneness. So you must expect some not inconsiderable effort on your part in order to comprehend the great change in viewpoint that this momentary insight into Rachel's consciousness afforded me.

The best way you might perceive my telescopic shift is to remind you of a comparable situation. Some of you may have lain under stars, or drifted upon an ocean and experienced for some few moments the hugeness of the world and the smallness of your part in it. You will have felt both insignificant and random, bound only to this earth through some fragile circumstance in nature and the ingenuity of your species. The reason this sensation feels profound, the reason it surprises you and remains with you with some intensity in later years, is that the very feeling you experienced in your moment of clarity was so completely opposite to your usual frame of mind. For most of your life, you are accustomed to a sense of your own importance; that the choices you make and the actions you perform have weight and consequence. You worry about a word misspoken or a decision rushed. You view other lives in relation to their significance and connection to you. Your parents, your children, your friends. You view your own life in relation to your successes and defeats. These are the things that matter. Winning a race, a fight, a war. Loving a partner or a cause. Saving a life or the planet. But when you think 'planet' you think 'humans'. When you think about winning, you disregard the loss of others. When you think about love, you wonder who loves you back.

Your worldview is selfish beyond your own survival, beyond your code. The universe revolves around you. One day you stand alone on a mountain or in a crater, and in that glimpse at the majesty of the sea or the eternity of the stars, in that moment when the telescope reverses, your sense of your unique self collapses and you carry the knowledge with you and you try never to forget.

Have you remembered?

That was how it felt to experience Rachel's self; the image was inverted. Whereas your life-altering experience revealed the smallness of your place in the world, mine exposed a greatness. For the first time, the view came from inside-out instead of outside-in. This was how it felt to be one.

You may imagine it was an agreeable feeling, and there was an excitement, a fluttering sense of danger and pleasure. But the dominant sensation was a vertiginous loneliness and with it came the recognition that some part of me had already looked into that cavernous emptiness and planned the climb down. For why had escape not occurred to me? Why had the silence of the not-belonging driven me home?

As Rachel's thoughts receded and the connection with her self began to fade, so these flashes of insight and panic subsided. Something like the old me returned, and the comfort of the everyday task in front of me took over. This was my life now. All thoughts, Rachel's or my own, seemed washed away in the ebb and flow of the spinal fluid.

Following the first shock, my days continued for a while as they had before. The thick membrane that lay below the tumour made a comfortable bed and each morning, as Rachel started to wake, sleep would overcome me. Away from the colony my sleep was long. The constant ticking march of my sisters was replaced by the deep thud of Rachel's heart, the soft jostle of her brain flesh in its bony case. Once asleep, only her stillness woke me.

Tap tap tap at the edges of the tumour. The little hollows and peaks of the mound thrum beneath my feet. Take a bite and put it aside. Feel Ki beside me waiting her turn, ready for the homeward march together, part of the line, part of the order of things. Without Ki, the work is hard, the sense of it lost. Still, the rhythms of this world seduce. Sated each night, no thirst, no hunger. My crop is full. Growing ever stronger, even with five legs. And soon, another episode.

Bite into a new strand at the front of the tumour. A delicate tendril that winds its way through the membrane to the lighter matter beyond. Jaws fix on the tender meat when flash, the electric sting, the heat and light, blind me, knock me over, leave me down, out, done. So ends the first part of my life.

```
uses sysutils;
```

Images flood me with colour and sensation. Scenes from her day, memories of child time, dreams of the future. Visions saturated with ideas, thoughts, emotions. They fly through me too fast to catch, only the sediment remains. Sadness, joy, the scent of lemon rind, the pleasure-glide of skin on skin, a taste of hops, of salt, a scattering of dust in sunlight, a sliver of hope. Confused by the fall, the feelings leave their mark, unprocessed. When the moment passes, the husk of me lies stunned upon the caul.

Stopped. Still. A thing that hurts. This new . . . pain. What is it? No thing like what this is. A hard, sharpness stuck inside me. In the middle of the mesh of what she left behind. Threads from another life. Strong as fox fur when the blood has left. Rachel's life, bright and cold.

She remembers me.

On my feet and check for damage. Feel the missing leg and the other absences. Antennae sag from the weight of information. The flash of the shock, the link to her, the rise and rise of sensation that vanishes as quickly as it came. All gone except the memory and this, this pain.

The hurt is ours. From her head and now in my body. Swilling through us both. My growing knowledge of the world beyond from the first event is fed and watered with the second. Rachel's being infuses mine. Death infects us both.

`begin`

What time is it? Night or day? We are awake. Strong tides push against the rim of membrane, swirling into the fissures of her brain, lapping at the fine tendrils of the tumour. The pain rises and falls. There is work to be done.

The tunnels we made in the colony were fast work. Push forward, shove the earth ahead, stamp the ground and on. Push, shovel, stamp. A path forms. At the edges of the tumour, the wetness does not hold so easily. Each bite must be carried away, out of the tunnel. With no one else to carry, progress is slow. No appetite, only a gnawing at my thorax, at my skeleton, at my skull; a blurring hunger to stop feeling and to feel more. Every bite brings hope.

Blood sticks to me. Brain fluid catches at my joints and stiffens me. Push, push on. Burrow into the flesh and remember the scent and taste of the outside world, of her world. The desire for more. The sense that this was known from the first night, at the bedside, that this was the purpose. This longing, this need, to save both our lives.

Soon it comes; another shock, and with deeper inroads into the tumour, another and another. Waves of sensation and information. A bubble of light from a soaped hand, the creak of a stair underfoot. Disappointment and comfort, relief and humiliation. Parents, cars, toothpaste. Politics, poetry, holidays, arguments. Boudicca and Linux and Gone with the Wind and the Democratic Republic of Congo. Nail polish, libraries, Christmas. Eliza.

Grab hold of every feeling and thought. The Encyclopaedia

of Rachel. Each entry multiplied by another. The scent of herbs means basil means Italy means a Tuscan affair, wild hair, wilder sex, tearful goodbyes, letters, emails, Facebook, a promise, jealousy, family. And any one of those ideas could lead in a different direction. The electricity pulses with life and with each bite and each shock death retreats a little further.

Days of this. The tunnel grows. Scoop out the hollows and pull again at the electric cord that twists round a fibrous jelly. Watch a wildlife documentary. Learn about Mozart. Listen to a telephone message from Eliza. Remember the first taste of seawater. Listen, learn, feel, remember. Each shock is milder and the connection stronger until one day there is no need for the shock itself. We are one. Everything that Rachel feels belongs to me. Everything she knows is known to me. Only her moment-to-moment thoughts are unavailable unless my jaws are locked in. Exhaustion overwhelms me after a short exposure to her stream of consciousness.

Rest. Wait. Digest. The smaller tendrils have died. The tumour has stopped growing. Our pain is a memory, her headaches gone. My body lies in one of the smaller tunnels, replete, exhausted, but my mind sees everything. All that Rachel sees and knows, and far beyond. For whereas she remembers in part, spark to tiny spark, all she has ever known is mine to recall at will. Books, conversations, lectures, films, letters. Every single idea that has passed through her at any time in her life, is available to me. My being is overflowing with the history of humankind and with Rachel's history in particular.

Try to think of Ki, from my tunnel in Rachel's head, but she is gone from me. The colony, my world before. The taste of moonlight and the sound of grass, the twitch and tap of the long march seem but a little life from a distant past. Where to go from here? There is work to do; that is still my code. With the world at my feet stretching into an invisible horizon, there is the comfort of an order to impose on what lies immediately before me.

Bite a little more each day. Now that the memories are there, only the temperament changes. Hormones, social interaction, weather patterns, all affect our mood. To avoid any more exposure to the stresses of human life than the tides and tumour already carry, my mind chooses particular thoughts on which to focus. I do not follow the running commentary of impossible things. Her mother calls from far away, and I cannot process the country or the subject of their conversation under the weight of feeling that floods us. There is news that Rachel is withholding. From her mother, from herself. The burden of this disguise has worn us both down, wrapped, it seems, in hope and desire, bitter memories and the almond tang of sugar and death. I leave Rachel to her mother.

In my head on this particular day are Tomasini's String Quartet in B flat major IV, the sound of a thousand butterflies dancing in a field one late summer, the cover illustration from a Penguin edition of *Our Mutual Friend*, a recipe for Key Lime cheesecake, the text of an A-level Geography book, and a pocket watch. All are curiosities floating around Rachel's consciousness whilst not being the centre of her attention. These ideas occupy me quite pleasantly when her mind suddenly focuses on one particular thought and it becomes impossible to concentrate on anything else. At that moment, my jaws are unlocked from a large bite and there is no immediate connection with Rachel's brain save my usual tapping and tunnelling. The change in temperature and the flow of her spinal fluid are unmistakeable though. She is experiencing an event.

What sort of event is impossible to tell for within seconds of observing her altered state of mind, a liquid wave catches me and sweeps me downstream towards the cortex. My balance was affected by the loss of my leg and the early shocks knocked me down but never before have the tides taken me over. Struggle to right myself, fight against the force of the current that drags me along. My knowledge of her body is confined to Rachel's understanding of human anatomy, the plethora of biologically themed reality television shows she has watched and my own limited explorations. There is a dread of stomach acids and other bodily fluids that might damage my exoskeleton, without any definitive information on the possibilities of this taking place. My body whirls in the drain that descends from her neck. Are her organs contained in pouches and membranes as her brain is? Or is everything held in place with these ropes that swoop along the vertebrae? Time is running out. Push against the viscous liquid, push harder, feel the pull of the uncharted depths below. Reach a hollow pocket at the top of the spine and lock my jaws on a sinuous wall as the last of the tide flows past me.

Rachel's feelings, strong as the current, rush into me. She is charged with emotion, not just one, all of them simultaneously crash through her bloodstream. Thoughts and images too fleeting to grab hold of flicker between us, and something else. The regular thud of her heart is louder here in the small chamber, undampened by a solid mass of tissue; and fainter and faster, knocking at the edges of our consciousness as insistent as the rain, another beat. Bang-bang,

bang-bang: the rush of a new heart, clutching at the edge of existence, pulses into life.

```
writeln ('Current time : ',
TimeToStr(Time));
```

For the rest of the pregnancy and for some time after the birth, the days were easier. The tumour stopped growing and, after eventually recovering my position by the lower membrane, my work progressed smoothly. We suffered no headaches and the occasional nausea and dizziness was at first hormonal and later fatigue. Tuning in to Rachel's consciousness became enjoyable. Her thoughts were as complicated and prolific as ever but they had at their centre a contentment and focus; the growing child inside her. My own attention was taken with a diametrically opposed task but the levels of effort involved were comparable. Even with the tumour under control, the chaos that blossomed around the dense flesh was compelling.

If you wonder why this cause held my attention for so long even when my knowledge had expanded far beyond my immediate realm, imagine yourself born into a small community, a farming cooperative or an extended family household. You know your job. You work each day for the benefit of the unit and do not question your part in it, only your success or failure to complete the task. The members of the community know your business, share your living quarters, your food, your conversation. The question is not whether you would like or dislike such an existence, as liking and disliking are not part of your programming. Your life just is. But one day some flaw or fault, or perhaps some greater code, in the genetic lottery leads you astray. You receive an unknown signal, call it a gut instinct, to change the pattern and leave everything you have known behind. Your new job requires the skills you already have, but you work alone. You learn a new language, develop ingenious working methods, investigate a purpose for which you have sole responsibility for success or failure. The voices in your head are replaced with your own thoughts and feelings. What happens when the task is complete? You cannot go back to the life you had. You wouldn't last a day.

You have heard that call. Your long marriage, your small town, your high-powered job. Some of you went and some of you stayed. There is no right and wrong to it. You know my choice, if such it was.

In any case, it did not matter at first. Yes, the work seemed almost complete and the urgency of purpose had abated. Without the urgency, and with the ability of language with which to analyse, my situation required some thought. And there was Arthur.

The intrusion of the new heartbeat disturbed my work pattern, the faster pulse twitched at my antennae and the flush of different hormones threw my senses. The oneness of Rachel that had made such an impression on my dawning consciousness was gradually breaking down. Not into two but apart. With the advent of their son, Rachel began to shed the protective layer that separated her first from Eliza and now her child, and as she relaxed our connection grew. Now when my jaws fastened on to her, there was space to be part of her dream state. My dreams were of the colony and hers were often of me.

We would wake back into our separate bodies, glad to be alive. Back at the colony my electric life would have long worn out and my corpse would have been stored as the next generation took my place. Only the queen lives beyond the seasons. Being away from home, and establishing what might be called my own nest, meant that my status had changed. This understanding crept upon me slowly and with the realisation came thoughts of Ki and the distance between us. None of our column would still be alive except me.

My feelings for Ki now had a name and whether the emotions sprang from the words or whether they had always existed but were muted by their namelessness is hard to tell. Certainly, the knowledge that Ki was lost to me forever was a new kind of pain that made the learning seem more of a curse than a blessing.

Tap tap tap. Feel my way around Rachel's self. Hear the call of another, the taste of new life. Every day the rhythm pulses, a human song, a hymn. Twitching at my senses, my system raw. Tap at the new cells, the different cells, the male code growing inside her. Bite a little, store a little. Tap tap tap.

The day he is born is as a storm or a fire. A raging inferno that sweeps through our bodies and leaves us for dead on the riverbank. We fight for breath, the boy un-cocooned, Rachel as the husk of my queen once she has laid her eggs. We are spent.

```
begin
```

Three months after the birth the tumour starts to grow again. Hooked into the routine of the infant Arthur, the first tendrils escape me and it is not until Rachel stands quite still one day in the kitchen of her new home that we feel it. The claws of the animal have unsheathed. She stares for some time at a cobweb laced in the batons of the

103

window and her thoughts are empty as my crop. It is time to go back to work.

Dig, tunnel, bite, stamp. Push at the blood-rich flesh. Store some, move some, call for help. No one comes. Who would, or could? Not my fallen sisters. Not my great-great-nieces. My scent is gone, my voice unravelled. Push, bite, stamp. Alone. Unheard. Apart from him.

He has seen me, far beyond his mother's eyes. He has felt me, from cell to cell. He looks into his mother's face and hears my song on the evening breeze, *Ameising, Ameising.*

Years pass in this way. We manage. The child unfurls beneath us as a fern and we provide the sun and shade. And steadily the tumour grows.

`begin end.`

The last day is cold. She runs a bath and takes her book. We will read together. The water runs hot at her feet. It is hard to see the words. We wait. No more zapping and pain. No more ice vein numbness hollowing out our bones. Just this. Warm water and words on a page, telling us of the world beyond, the way things are or were or ought to be. She thinks of Arthur and of Eliza and how they will lie in her bed together. She lets her head rest on the edge of the bath. Her heavy head. She remembers the way her son tucks his hand into her sleeve to feel her skin as they walk along, the way her wife turns back before she leaves each day. She draws one more breath and lets go.

`end`

You see how it was. There was no going back but there was a need to go on. The second part of my life had only just started. Everything that Rachel knew was mine and the world was as a colony when the queen has finished her reign. It was time to search and build, to search for the new electricity. The queen is dead; long live the queen.

```
begin
```

Tap tap tap. Feel my way along the skull. Hear water lapping and the silence of Rachel's heart. Taste the newer bitterness of her blood. Tap tap tap. Find the jelly of the eye and the space behind. Push, push into the salt and the air and the outside skin of her. Push into the world again from this new womb.

Wait now for the child to return. Wait again to find him. There is another self that waits for me, another incarnation. This is freedom, this is consciousness. My own thoughts, my own feelings. The 'I' of me. And we have work to do beyond this world now that I am born.

5

Clementinum

What Mary Knew

Frank Jackson wrote a thought experiment about Mary, a brilliant scientist who has been raised in an entirely black and white environment with monitors of the outside world. She has studied all the information about colour and has specialised in the neurophysiology of vision. Despite all her knowledge of colour will she learn anything new when she is released from her room and sees red for the first time? Is there some other quality of experience that is not definable in physical terms?

> It is inescapable that her previous knowledge was incomplete. But she had all the physical information. Ergo there is more to have than that.

Frank Jackson *Philosophy Bites*

Rachel had three outfits that were comfortable to wear in bed and today, though she was not in bed, she sported all of them.

'I'll be home early, with Arthur,' Eliza said, before she left for work. She glanced at Rachel's cardigan layers. 'Do you want me to turn the heating up?'

Rachel brushed Eliza's passing arm with her fingertips.

'Clothes are better.'

Eliza paused at the front door. 'You don't have to worry about the planet right now,' she said without turning around, 'Just think about yourself for once.'

Rachel chose not to correct her. They shouldn't row before Eliza went to work; who knew what the day would bring? This day in particular. She had made Arthur's breakfast, pasted his collected leaves into one of the big scrap books they were making together, got him ready for school. She watched Eliza's retreating figure from the sitting room window. Today was a good day.

There was never quite time enough to explain what she wanted to say, Rachel thought as she returned to the kitchen. She was not quick like Eliza, ready to change conversation, or mood, in mid-sentence. She liked to consider. She stood at the sink and started on the washing up. Considering. Did that make her considerate, too considerate as Eliza insisted?

No, that was something else, about care for others. Rachel's lassitude was nothing to do with that kind of thoughtfulness, she was merely set at a different tempo from her wife. What was it Greg had said about computer intelligence as opposed to human intelligence? Emotion. Computers couldn't make the sort of quick decisions that humans were capable of making because they lacked emotions. But Rachel's emotions only seemed to slow her down.

She submerged her hands in the warm water and let the suds drift up to her elbows. It was not concern for the planet that made Rachel opt for wool instead of radiators. She was cold from the inside. Even with her hair growing back and the bloom of spring, every atom of her being ached with cold. The best she could do was scald herself in the bath and try to keep the heat trapped in her skin before the coldness leached out of her bones and cooled her once again.

Greg seemed to understand this new chill. Greg, who wore a ski jacket from September to June and had stuck a hot water bottle under his hat for his whole first winter in England. He knew how it felt to wonder if you would ever be warm again. When they first met Rachel had laughed at his knee socks and thick jumpers. Only quantities of alcohol allowed any state of undress, late into the night when they all sat giggling on the floor while pregnant Rachel hiccuped on ginger cordial. She missed that version of Greg now that the giggling had stopped. On the rare occasions she saw him, he would squeeze her hips and shiver in involuntary acknowledgement of her vulnerability to the elements.

Greg kept away from the house these days. He hadn't signed up to be a dad when he met Hal, but that was how things had turned out. Rachel sometimes wondered if they had all been part of a scam, tricking Greg into staying around when Rachel got pregnant because it was convenient for the three of them. That was one way of looking at Greg's situation and Rachel tried to be fair especially since it was she, more than anyone, who had wanted to have a child. But Greg had seemed so relaxed during the discussions and the pregnancy, as though meeting an English guy, moving to England, changing jobs, and finding out he was going to be a co-parent was all a great plan. Tra-la-la, happy families. Only, when Rachel was diagnosed the plan wasn't so great any more.

Rachel missed him. It was Hal who took Rachel out to museums and galleries, Hal who collected Arthur from nursery and brought him home. Rachel kept a scrapbook so that Arthur could put in his drawings and tell her about his day. She could only manage an hour or two of childcare and Hal often stayed late into the afternoon, lifting Arthur into the kitchen while Rachel slept. She would wake to the scent of baking; cardamom or chocolate cake, hazelnut shortbread and lemon ricotta tarts; food to coax Rachel's appetite. He and Arthur would bring a tiny dish to her bed and balance it among the pillows and books.

'Biscuits,' said Arthur, though he pronounced it 'Bithciths'.

'Greg calls them cookies,' Hal said once to be helpful.

'Cookies?' Arthur frowned. 'We cooked them?'

Rachel bit a corner from the gingerbread. 'You sure did, baby.' It was infectious, Greg's way of talking, the soft intonation, the homely additions, the swapped e's and i's. Rachel and Arthur called it 'gregspeak'. They kept up the vernacular in Greg's absence as though they were raising Arthur to be bilingual. For weeks everything that came out of the oven was a cookie.

Rachel rinsed the last of the cutlery under the tap and

tried to remember why today was a good day. Eliza would leave work early and bring Arthur home and they would have tea together and watch cartoons and Eliza would kiss her temples as she fell asleep. And she was well enough now to be up and drying dishes, wiping each one with a tea towel until they squeaked. She did this for no other reason than the pleasure it gave her. The sense of continuity with all things she touched and breathed. The weak sunshine reflected in a polished glass, the shiny glaze of a plate. The illuminated particles of life suspended in the filtered light. Her hand in front of her. The day. The day.

A smallest flicker at the back of her eye. Tick. Tick. Tick. She shook her head, remembered she was not alone. But today was a good day. They all were. This was her party, the way she saw it. Every stage of life had a party, so she was throwing her own final festivities.

She wondered if she should have told Greg about the party, if it would have made visiting her any easier. She thought probably not, disconnected as he was from his own father's death. There wasn't any celebration in Illinois, as far as Rachel knew; Greg's parents were not the partying kind. And maybe it was a little sacrilegious to spend your final days in frivolity. She hadn't read much literature on the subject since receiving her last prognosis, but she doubted there were any books advising the dying to spend every day as if you had forever and almost nothing mattered.

Maybe she would have a look next time she went to the library. She was due another Hal outing soon and the library had become her favourite place. Not a particular library; they had worked their way through most of the East London public facilities and a few of the University collections using Eliza's credentials. The small libraries at the end of residential streets were best but there weren't so many of those left. The new centralised temples impressed her with their ambition; computer terminals nestled amongst last century's *Encyclopaedia Britannica*. But the books themselves felt marginalized, a scenic backdrop for a coffee shop rather than the business at hand.

She tugged the sleeves of her jumper over her wrists and eyed her feet. Only a pair of socks between her and the tile floor and the pads of her toes were numb. She grabbed a glass and a clutch of pill bottles and headed upstairs.

The old hardback that rested on top of the pile by her bedside had two postcards stuck between the pages. One to keep her place, and one that she had taken to putting at the front of every book she read. Rachel picked up the book and removed the first card. The illustration was of a child in the style of Kate Greenaway. A Victorian girl in a long skirt and boots stood at an imposing front door. The colours were faded by time but the redness of the girl's bonnet perched above wild brown curls still contrasted with the grey formality of the house and the upright figure in the fawn dress. The reverse side of the card bore her mother's copperplate handwriting. *Dearest Rachel, Every day I listen for your key in the door to see my ray of sunshine.*

The card had been found in a box the last time her parents had moved.

'Do you want any of this stuff?' Rachel's mother had dismissed the contents of the Devon house with a jerk of her chin and a sniff. 'It's ruined by damp. This house tried to kill us all.'

Rachel had taken a battered suitcase of letters and a rocking chair. The books and records and rugs and curtains were spotted with mildew. Her father had lit a bonfire and thrown everything he could on it. When a neighbour came over, he helped drag a mattress down the stairs to lay it on top of the smouldering books and clothes. The two men stood in front of the fire and waited until the mattress was a pile of metal coils.

'Your father's a pyromaniac,' said Rachel's mother, 'like his father before him. It's all about control.'

Rachel watched from the sitting room where her mother was directing the packing.

'Are there any mental health issues our family may have missed?'

Rachel's mother looked at her daughter for a moment. 'It's not all about you, Rachel.'

Her parents moved from south-west England to the north-east coast of Brazil and found a different kind of damp; festering and hot. Her father continued to paint and her mother apparently studied capoeira and smoked pot in street cafés. They kept in touch with their daughter through email and sent her links to articles about herbal cures when she became ill. Rachel tried to call them but only her mother owned a phone and she never answered, or never picked up when Rachel rang. Perhaps she spoke to every-one else, Rachel thought as she pressed the redial button on her mobile once again. People who weren't dying, or not so imminently. Her mother was rather a good amateur nurse but she had never liked the hopeless cases. 'I know it's awful, darling, but I can't see the point if they're going to die anyway.' It was five o'clock in the morning in Fortaleza. After six rings, Rachel hung up.

She took the book across the hall and ran a bath. She peeled off the layers of clothes and for party spirit poured quantities of rosemary oil into the hot water but when she lay back in the tub and opened her book she could still catch the traces of mould from her mother's postcard through the scented steam. She checked the stamp on the card again. The date was blurred but that didn't matter, the oddness was the presence of a postmark at all. Why had her mother written a card that said she was waiting for Rachel to come home when it was Rachel's mother who had been away? It was the sort of double bind she had often been placed in by her mother; a compliment laced with accusation.

'You're always *happy*, aren't you, Rachel?'

As though Rachel's happiness, like her absence from whatever front door Rachel's mother was living behind, was a deliberate offence.

Rachel tucked the card away and opened the book. She was working her way through the libraries' Victorian novels, as a present to herself. She had read some Trollope in her teens and promised herself that one day 'when I have time' she would return to him, and now, having exhausted Dickens, Eliot, Thackeray, the Brontës and her English teacher's favourite, George Meredith, she found she both had and did not have the time. That was the thing about dying, the micro and the macro of it. Slowing down so that a whole lifetime seemed available in a day while all the while, the very finite amount of life she had left was running through the hourglass as fast as water. The telescopic sensation of giant tiny moments reminded her of lying on the grass as a child and feeling the vastness of the sky on top of her, her fingers and toes stinging with life and energy as though her small body were being watched from above, and parts of her loomed as large as the universe itself.

114

The book was heavy in her hands and she tilted sideways to rest it on the lip of the bath, wiping the water droplets from the vinyl cover with her forearm. She admired the heroine's white satin dress, still glowing through the textured plastic. Eliza said she didn't understand Rachel's interest in Victorian novels. Reading for Eliza meant work, though it seemed to give her pleasure. She read the latest articles and journals, in an attempt to keep on top of scientific developments and claimed the stories that absorbed Rachel were desperate cries of help from the chained audience of Plato's cave, forced to interpret the world from the shadows on the wall.

'We don't need fairy tales.'

Rachel had laughed. 'Every time you say that an angel loses its wings.'

'You're confusing Christianity with pantomime,' Eliza said.

She had relented a little though, Rachel thought, since the trip to Paris for Arthur's birthday. There had been a moment at the theme park. Rachel put her hand to her face and stroked the bump of her brow. Eliza had seen, she was sure of it. And how could you not believe in fairies when your own wife had a spirit living in her head? They had spoken of it, that night, when Arthur was asleep and they sat on the balcony overlooking the mouse-ear flowerbeds.

'Is it there now?' Eliza's frown had extended to her eyes. Scraps of kohl gathered in the creases under her lashes. 'Can you feel it?'

'Not how you imagine. It's there all the time, the way your nose is, or your tongue. I don't feel it as something extra. Unless I focus.'

But they didn't name it.

Rachel stared at the typeface in front of her and frowned.

The words were indistinct. She closed her eyes and pushed the book a little further away. She didn't need glasses to read. She corrected herself; she *hadn't* needed glasses to read. The tumour had brought changes, of course, all the time. Balance, memory, sensation had been affected at different times. The radiation replaced the symptoms with side effects. Her toes curled at the memory of the mask, the sickness and the exhaustion. But at no point so far had her sight deteriorated.

She opened her eyes. The print in front of her was another language. She could make out the individual letters but the grouping meant nothing and as she watched the words, the edges of the typeface became coarse and the ink bled into the paper. Lines spidered across the pages and disappeared into the crease. Rachel shut the book and squeezed the covers together, compressing the words, the ideas, all the life between the pages. All the death beyond. Was there more to understand once she crossed that threshold? Would the stories, her story, come with her? Or was it all to be left behind, a book for someone else to read after all? She could feel a small pulse at the edge of her temple. The ant was there.

On her last visit to her parents, in the time between her recovery and her relapse, Rachel had seen a dead horse lying by the side of the road on their way back from the beach. Vultures stood around politely as though waiting their turn at a delicatessen. When she drove past the next day, the carcass was almost picked clean, the jutting bones waving lean ribbons of flesh in the ocean breeze.

'Not a scratch that doesn't have an animal feeding off it soon enough,' Rachel's father had said. 'Keep your shoes on.'

After that she had thought differently about her visitor.

Instead of causing her tumour, perhaps the creature had been drawn by the scent of her decay, was ready to feed off her sickness. She advanced the theory to Eliza on her return.

'Symbiosis?' Eliza said.

'Think of all the bugs we already have living on us and in us.'

'Microscopic bacteria and mites.'

Rachel nodded. 'So it's a question of scale.'

'It's a question of scale that stops you walking through walls.'

Eliza had not yet looked in Rachel's eye at the park and seen the ant for herself.

'Not everything that happens is about reproducible laboratory experiments.' Rachel threw a handful of vitamins into her mouth and swallowed hard. 'We have autonomy. We have miracles.'

'Do we?' Eliza turned away.

When the cancer came back, Eliza didn't mention the theory and Rachel was grateful. Still, she clung to the idea that the ant might in some way have helped her condition. Perhaps because she could not separate the arrival of the ant and of Arthur, so entwined were the events in her mind.

She sat up in the bath and pulled the book to her chest, wrapping her arms around her folded knees. The ant had crawled in to her eye one night and changed her life. The first changes were with Eliza, whom she had loved for years but who had moved into her life one piece at a time and kept some of the pieces back. After the ant, Eliza was present in a way that Rachel had almost given up hope of expecting. It was Eliza who'd had taken the initiative and bought an ovulation test and it was Eliza who followed up the conversation they had started with Hal some months before. With Eliza on her side, Rachel had gone through with the IUI, and conceived on her second cycle. And along came Arthur.

The pulsing in her temple had quietened. She ran the hot water, book in one hand, and waited for the bath to warm up before she released her grip and looked back at the disruptive page. The words were recognisable, the ink intact. She took a deep breath. She was still at the party. She lay down and let her head drift back into the cocoon of the bath.

Eliza told her it was impossible for an ant to get into your brain through your eye and she soon stopped talking about that night altogether. Rachel knew Eliza minded because she couldn't believe in the impossible whereas Rachel thought the impossible happened all the time. Even the way she had met Eliza as the flower shop was closing at the end of a Friday and only the sprays for the next day's weddings ready in the fridge and Rachel still at work because she had been late that morning so stayed on to make up the hours and Eliza turning back to look at her from the glass door of the fridge and asking for just one of the wedding table decorations for her friend Hal's birthday breakfast table and Rachel thinking Well, why not just one? I could make up another if I came in first thing or went to market to get them myself. And saying that out loud and Eliza saying, What market?

All of those events lined up in such a way that Rachel and Eliza had gone to the market together the following week and had coffee, which led to lunch. Whenever Rachel thought about how many obstacles had been overcome to bring the two of them together, she knew she believed in the impossible. Even in the back of a flower shop on an ordinary Friday in Dalston.

She didn't press Eliza about the ant. She went to the doctor and she bathed her eye and she made sure Eliza knew how happy she was that Eliza had gone ahead with the plans for their baby. All she needed to know was that Eliza trusted her; the rest, Rachel understood, would follow.

Over the years she had tried to communicate with the ant. They were a partnership of sorts, the ant and she. Rachel second-guessing the motivation for certain movements, a scurrying or scratching. Wanting to understand the pattern, wondering what the ant was trying to say. When she had told Eliza that she couldn't feel the ant she was telling the truth, except for those very particular sensations. The stiller she was, the more aware of the ant she became, not simply quiet in her body but in her mind. The moments before, and after, sleep or sex. When she cooked or when she sat with Arthur, stroking his toes while they chatted about his day. The ant would be there. Tick. Tick. Tick. The bath was the perfect communal moment, just as when she was pregnant Arthur had seized the opportunity to get comfortable and Rachel would find a small foot protruding from her ribs or, in the final months, watch her entire stomach heave from one side to the other.

She had wondered during the pregnancy if the ant would leave her when she gave birth, and in the several weeks she took to settle in at home with the new baby, to learn to feed and comfort him and to understand the implications of having the baby outside her body instead of inside, the ant was silent. On the day the ticking started again, she was lying in bed with a sleeping Arthur propped up against her breast, his head in the crook of her arm. In her free hand she clutched a copy of Rachel Cusk's *A Life's Work*, a book she alternately snarled at and wept into. At that moment she was making a mental note to get to a library and borrow every book Cusk mentioned (she had never read any Olivia Manning for instance) when the familiar rubber-band tension of electricity tore across her scalp. Her hand flew up to the miniature metronome buried in her head. Tick. Tick. Tick.

In the bath, her hair floated in fine tendrils round her face, the fight of her former unruly curls long lost. Her heartbeat was quickening, knocking at her chest in sudden bursts. This day, this moment, was connected to those other days. The first time she kissed Eliza, under the glow of an orange street light, pressed up to her parked car, the almond scent of Eliza's breath as their lips touched. The slip of Arthur's shoulders between her thighs as he dived into the world. The burn of the ant slicing into her tear duct.

She thought of the night she had first seen the tiny column of insects marching in single file up the wall from the skirting board in the corner of their bedroom in the flat they shared. And of the peppermint oil Eliza had bought as a deterrent but never put down because that night the ant had found her and while she was sleeping crawled into her eye. The bite ripped into her dream and when she woke she couldn't distinguish between the story in her sleep and the real event, so that for several moments she lay panting and frightened, her hand over her eye, convinced that she was hurt.

She sat up at the memory, splashing bath water on to the floor, almost losing her grip on the book. The force of her heart against her narrow ribcage shook her arms as she tried to steady herself. She was back in the dream. A shadow cast across a sunny day. A figure crouched over her. Eliza's voice in the distance instructing her to stay still. She held her breath. The bite would come next, the nip of acid at the membrane and the explosion of pain from her eye to her entire head. Hunched in the tepid water, she squeezed her eyes shut and waited. In that moment, with her whole body tensed against the ant, she saw the figure again.

She couldn't see his face. A man in dark clothes, a shabby figure but distinguished in some way. A hat, a tie. He swayed over her as she lay on the dream grass, the sun behind his head, his mouth opening and closing. Words she didn't recognise, another language in a lilting, patterned tone, a poem or an incantation. His features hidden from the light. She had to see him. The ant was coming; she could feel the start of the pain. She had to open her eyes to see who was there. She flicked a look up at the sun, at the figure, and the man looked down at her. She saw his face and knew him for the first time. Her own dark eyes set in the man's rough olive skin returned her stare. With a shiver that shook her whole body she sat straight up.

She was cold now, the water cooler than her blood. She pulled the bath plug, reached for the hot tap and shifted in the tub to let the new water circulate. She had seen his stooped body, his shabby suit. And she saw herself reflected in his eyes, the saddest eyes in the world. The saddest eyes in the world at the happiest place on earth. Eliza had teased her. That was where she had seen him. He had been at the theme park on the same ride as her wife and son. Eliza and Arthur had boarded a giant blue teacup and across from them, in a green cup, was the man in his dark suit. Rachel had watched as the ride started and the cups whirled around, Arthur's body an exclamation of delight at the wheel, Eliza anxious and preoccupied beside him. From his cup, the dark-suited man gazed into the distance as though re-living a car crash for the hundredth time. A look of horror muted by experience. Rachel had turned away to catch her breath. Tick. Tick. Tick.

She felt the pull of her weight in the bath as the water drained away and she bent forward to replace the plug. The book in her hand was damp, the pages curling. She would have to pay the library. She turned the hot water up higher. Her skin was numb.

The man in her dream was real.

She retraced the moments at the theme park when Eliza and Arthur had returned from the ride. She had waited for them at a designated bench and watched as they walked down the wide path towards her, Arthur weaving between Eliza and the crowd around them. She could see Eliza quite clearly against the backdrop of the fairy-tale castle. There was a set to her jaw, an optimism, which had been missing for a while. In the early days of her illness, Rachel had watched Eliza behave as though she had always known and the doctors were simply confirming her diagnosis. Of course this was how things would turn out, Eliza seemed to say, the situation was inevitable. Rachel understood that her wife was reacting to a version of events that made sense to her, the rational explanation, and the calm resignation had allowed her to feel more volatile. Rachel only challenged Eliza's stoicism once, after a dinner at her sister's house when Eliza had remained tight-lipped throughout a discussion about the causes of creativity, only to dismiss Fran's mention of the ethereal as unhelpful.

'We don't need to resort to the mystical to describe physical processes.' Eliza had shaken her head. 'Everything that happens can be known.'

'Do you think everything about my illness, about me, can be known?' Rachel asked on the walk home.

'I wasn't talking about you. But yes, we knew anyway. If we had thought of it.'

'Who's being ethereal now?'

'Rachel, come on. The headaches? The hallucinations? You were ill for a long time before we went to the doctor. Hey,' Eliza put her arm around her wife, 'we were busy. Busy making Arthur, getting our lives together. But the symptoms were there.'

It was true that Rachel had suffered from severe headaches for years before the ant arrived. Another sign that the ant had been drawn to her because of whatever was already in her head. She had never had a hallucination.

'I've never had a hallucination.'

Rachel spoke aloud as she lay in the bath with her book in her hands and her eyes closed, watching Eliza walk towards her two years ago. She remembered the change in her; how her wife had looked up from Arthur and seen her in a way that Eliza did not usually look and see. They sat together on the bench and Eliza had taken Rachel's face in her hands and stared into her, straight into her. And the ant had stared back.

That was the only time Eliza had taken notice of her visitor and Rachel understood that the man from her dream had led Eliza back to her. They were all connected, she could see that now. Her mind folded the events together; her dream and the bite and the man watching over her, Eliza and Arthur and the same man walking away from them. The pages of her life turning over each other, all the words so full of possible combinations and all leading to this moment.

She had stopped shivering. Today was special, she had known it from the moment she had woken up and put all her most comfortable clothes on so she could go downstairs and say goodbye to Eliza. She looked at the piles of t-shirts and pyjama bottoms that lay abandoned around the bath. They seemed so far away, as though they belonged to another place altogether. The water had risen around her. She turned off the tap and opened her book. She wanted to get back to her make-believe world, back to her party for one. The warmth enveloped her as she read, her bones soft in the momentary heat. She drifted in her personal ocean. The words fell into her and swept her clean. Her head tipped toward the page. She was lying in the sun, the grass beneath her, Eliza beside her. The shadow was no longer there, the man from the theme park with her face in his eyes. A secret her mother had kept all her life. He had shown her the ant. And Arthur. And brought Eliza back to her. A good day, that day. Today. Tomorrow. The soft, soft grass below her. The hot sun, above. She could reach out and touch the yellow brightness of it. Her hand huge against the sky. The smallness of the world in her palm. Arthur growing inside her. All a question of scale. Tiny ants marching through the grass. And her head so heavy. Heavy and hot and large and small and all the same. Yesterday. Today. Tomorrow.

Her hands loosened. The book slipped into the water and lay for a moment, flat against her legs, before sliding down one thigh and landing on the warm enamel, the pages rippling in the little current created by its fall.

When Eliza returned home, she tucked Arthur on the sofa and went upstairs to check on Rachel. Finding the bedroom empty, she walked across the hall and called out her wife's name, anticipating the pleasure on Rachel's face when she saw Eliza. She had come to depend on such moments.

Outside the window, the sky was deepening purple in the late spring evening. Raindrops spattered against the glass. There was no light on in the bathroom and the air was damp with cooled steam. The figure of Rachel lay unmoving in the bath.

Eliza stood in the doorway. In the time before her next breath she remembered how often her heart had lifted as Rachel had turned to meet her. She saw the upturn of Rachel's mouth and eyes, the creases that fanned at Rachel's temples, the promise of being held and loved and accepted. She saw all these things as she would always see them, and she saw nothing.

The body was partially submerged, head folded forward, arms in the water. Eliza came to the side of the bath and put a hand to the un-beating heart. She brushed one damp curl away from the blue-white face and looked into the open eyes. Nobody looked back at her.

She craned forward to touch the bloodless lips and her own mouth opened and closed over Rachel's name in silence. From a great distance she watched the drop of tears onto her wife's breast. She saw the book Rachel was reading caught under one leg and lifted it out of the ice cold water. The sodden pages had pulled away from the binding but the plastic facing held the hardcover together. Another one of Rachel's fairy tales, Eliza thought as she traced the silver lettering. *Can You Forgive Her?*

'Mum?' Arthur called up over his cartoon's title music.

A postcard was stuck to the inside cover, the ink blurred into a dark smear across the back and a faded picture of a small girl in a red hat on the front.

'I'll be right there,' Eliza said.

She laid the book on the mat and sat by the bath. After a little while she got up and closed the bathroom door behind her.

The Goldilocks Zone

The Chinese Room

John Searle imagined himself in a room where he could recieve letters with questions in Chinese and, using a book of rules and a basket of Chinese symbols, he could post out the answers. He compared himself in the room to a computer being programmed and stated that a computer could not be said to think any more than he could be said to speak Chinese. He was just following the instructions.

> Formal symbols by themselves can never be enough for mental contents, because the symbols, by definition, have no meaning (or interpretation, or semantics) except insofar as someone outside the system gives it to them.

John Searle, 'Artificial Intelligence and the Chinese Room'

He was walking fast. Already, he could see children heading towards him, their parents close behind, but he didn't want to run. Wrong shoes, wet pavement, leaves scattered along the sidewalk. He'd look foolish, skidding into the playground, out of breath and rain spattered. He wasn't that late.

The schoolyard was full. Clumps of children stuck to teachers' hands and coats. Parents shouted their diaries to other parents over the tops of woolly heads, their arms full of books and bags, drawings and jumpers. Kids' stuffing, thought Greg. He stared across the playground for Arthur. By the slide, a teacher was in conversation with a mother. Several children of what Greg calculated to be Arthur's age were gathered about them. Greg waited for the women to acknowledge him. They would have turned around for Hal, Greg thought. Straight women loved Hal. After several minutes he took a step closer and when the teacher glanced in his direction he seized his chance.

'I'm collecting Arthur,' he said. 'He's in Laura's class. Sorry.' He looked to the talkative parent who nodded and adjusted the bags draped about her.

'Arthur?'

'Pryce. Laura's class.' Greg repeated the small factual knowledge in his possession.

'You've just missed him. I think he left with the Carsons. Check reception.' She turned back to the mother.

Greg got out his phone as he walked to the school building. He had never heard of the Carsons. He should call Hal. Greg's skin felt clammy against his clothes. Their son had left the school with a family Greg had never met. He was absolutely not calling Eliza. He took a breath and pushed at the glass doors.

'I'm looking for Arthur Pryce. I was supposed to pick him up today.' Greg could feel the anger creep into the edges of his guilt. The teacher had been so casual. 'I'm his stepfather.'

'Arthur!' The receptionist called from her desk to a room behind her.

Greg turned to see the slender form of his stepson emerge through the doorway, followed by the bearded art teacher. He put one hand on his chest and another towards the boy. 'You okay?'

'Yeah,' Arthur said.

'I couldn't find you.'

The art teacher rubbed the boy's head. 'You forgot, didn't you?'

Greg started to protest but it was Arthur who answered.

'Yeah.' The boy grinned up at the two men. 'I forgot you were coming.'

'We did wait,' the teacher added to Greg.

'I was outside. The woman I spoke to, she said he'd gone to the Carsons'.'

Paint-splashed fingers rubbed at the beard. 'That's another Arthur.'

Greg tugged on Arthur's hand. 'Right. Well. Let's get you home.'

*

129

They walked side by side back to the house. Greg hadn't planned on being a dad. He had fallen in love with Hal on a business trip to London, an international conference for new space tech. Greg was a vibrations engineer with New Frontiers and Hal owned the conference catering company. On their third date, Hal told him about Eliza and Rachel. The sperm had already been frozen.

'That's a lot of responsibility,' Greg said.

'I'll be there for the fun stuff,' Hal laughed. 'The cupcake uncle.'

In the two years since Rachel died, Hal had been on standby for Eliza, and Greg had supported him. He hadn't minded when Hal, Eliza and Arthur had gone on holiday together, he hadn't complained about the cash-flow decline when Hal's work slowed down with all the time off. Together, they even volunteered more financial responsibility for the boy and signed all the paperwork in case anything happened to Eliza. Greg was fine with the theory of parenting. It was the practice that confounded him.

'Who's the other Arthur?' Greg imagined a copy of Arthur with short hair.

'There's a big one.' Arthur's mouth turned down in resentment at the various playground indignities of being 'Little Arthur'.

The newsagent was on their way home.

'You hungry?'

Arthur nodded.

At the sweet counter, they peered at the dozens of packets.

'Chocolate or crisps. Not candy.'

'And a drink?'

'Juice.' Greg felt the cloud of anxiety lifting as he

established some boundaries. He grabbed a bar of chocolate for himself.

They undid the wrappers outside the shop and Greg pushed the straw into the carton for the boy. Beads of apple juice spurted on to the pavement.

'Stupid carton.' Arthur imitated Greg's fading accent. Stoopid.

'Yeah.' Greg laughed. He forgot the kid could be funny. 'Well, stupid me probably.'

Arthur stopped. 'Never call yourself stupid, Greg. Mummy told me that.'

'Sure.' He took the boy's hand and they crossed the street and headed to the tree-lined road opposite that Greg liked to walk down. The houses were large, with long sash windows and a dark palette of glossy front doors. If he and Hal ever moved, he'd want one of these. A statement house. He imagined friends from college visiting. 'Why, Greg,' they'd say, 'you're practically British.'

He almost was. He had a British passport and a British husband and he remembered to say 'boot' and 'queue' and to ask for the bill in restaurants. Seven years, the entire lifespan of the boy, was all it had taken to acquire this new identity. His own mother mistook him for Hal when she called. Which, since his dad passed away, was often.

They walked on for a while, Arthur taking the juice carton whenever he finished a mouthful of chocolate. Hal disapproved of processed foods but Greg had grown up on Ding-Dongs and boloney sandwiches and whatever was going in the school cafeteria. A restrictive diet was unhealthy for children. 'I'm not taking nutritional advice from a man who likes cheese in a can,' Hal said.

'Stupid,' he repeated as the boy dawdled along the pavement.

Arthur looked up at him.

'What else does your mummy say?' Greg asked.

'She doesn't say anything. She's dead.'

He never remembered; mummy was Rachel, Eliza was mum.

'Right. So she didn't say I was stupid then?'

'Nice, Greg.'

'You're freaking me out, kid.'

A few months after Rachel got pregnant, they all had dinner to celebrate Greg's move to London.

'I think you're very brave,' Eliza said, 'to move all this way when you haven't known Hal that long.'

'Or lucky,' Hal said.

'I only got on a plane.' Greg shook his head. 'You're the ones incubating his DNA.'

Hal laughed. 'Even luckier.'

They toasted the genetic lottery and Eliza asked Greg how he felt about Hal being a dad.

'I never expected to have kids,' Greg said. 'I'm happy for you all but I'm not going near a diaper.'

Rachel put a hand on Greg's knee. 'Don't look so panicked. You guys will be like the RTG.'

'The what?'

'Rachel's obsessed with spaceships now she knows a real rocket scientist,' Eliza said.

'A Radioisotope Thermoelectric Generator?' Rachel reminded him.

'Generators aren't really my area. I'm on the landing gear.'

'Cool,' Rachel said. 'Well, you're like another power supply. But we'll only need you for emergencies.'

*

132

The flat was warm when Arthur and Greg got back, but Greg turned on the gas fire. He had not got used to the British weather. London kept a chill in the walls, even when the sun shone. It didn't help that they lived in a converted warehouse with exposed brickwork and a large open plan kitchen for Hal to work in.

'Want to play one of your math games?'

Arthur looked at the computer. 'I can't remember how to do it.'

'We'll figure it out.'

Greg pulled up an extra chair to the desk and helped Arthur log on. He felt the pleasure in defying Eliza. The boy's screen time was restricted but she couldn't object to homework.

'What is this?' Arthur stuck his finger to the screen.

A picture of pink and green marbles on a plate sat next to the words 'likely', 'unlikely', 'probable' and 'impossible'.

'I'd say "very difficult",' Greg said, 'You couldn't get all the marbles to stay still.'

'It says, "How likely is it that you'd pick a green marble?"'

'Unlikely.'

'It's a maths question, Greg.'

'Math is different from when I used to do it.'

'It's your job.'

'When we send a plate of marbles into space, I'll get back to you. What do you want for dinner?'

'Something dad made.'

'Right.'

Greg went to the freezer and found the drawer with Arthur's food. He chose pumpkin gnocchi with pea and sage puree. Step-parenting was the art of reheating someone else's love. Not that he didn't love Arthur, but there was so little room left once Eliza and Hal and the ghost of Rachel had had their say.

After dinner, Greg ran a bath and sat on the floor while Arthur splashed about. He felt a physical weariness beyond anything the gym induced, as though the small acts of parenting were muscular devotions. Perhaps they were, Greg thought as he folded the little pile of clothes, the art of self-sacrifice.

'Can you live in space?' The boy peered over the side of the bath with a flannel on his head.

'We already do. We're on a planet spinning round in space right now.'

'What about another planet? Could we live on another planet?'

'If the conditions were right.'

Arthur frowned.

'We need an atmosphere,' Greg said, his glasses steaming over in the bathroom fug. 'Oxygen, water, the right temperature. Not too hot, not too cold.'

'Just right.'

'Yup.'

The flannel head disappeared. Greg grabbed a towel and leant over.

'Come on. You're turning into a prune.'

The boy was under the water with his eyes open. He smiled up at Greg and blew bubbles from his nose. Greg waited for him to climb out.

'I could live underwater then. All I need is an atmosphere.'

'Sure.' Greg threw the towel around the boy. 'Like in a submarine.'

'We can live anywhere?'

'In the right conditions. But they have to be just right. Like in the story.'

'With the bears?'

'Uh-hunh.' Greg rubbed the top of Arthur's head with the tail of the towel.

'Then my mummy is living somewhere.'

'Maybe.'

'Carry me.'

Greg lifted the warm bundle of Arthur and carried him through to the bedroom. The boy's chin rested on his shoulder, damp hair against his cheek. He noted the full weight of the child, the wholeness of him. He dropped the boy on the bed and pulled the pyjamas from the pillow. Arthur lay where he landed and stared up at Greg.

'I think she's in space.'

'Put your pyjamas on and I'll get you a snack.'

'Biscuits?'

'A banana.' Greg headed out the door.

'And biscuits?'

'And one biscuit.'

'Call it a cookie,' Arthur shouted after him.

'You're a cookie,' Greg shouted back.

In the kitchen, Greg put a banana on a plate with a napkin and tried to imagine his own father doing such things. A bath, a cuddle, a snack. The only time his dad came to his room was if he was in trouble. He placed two biscuits next to the banana, changed his mind and put one back in the packet. That was the problem, he thought, the reason his dad had stayed away. If you're not careful you put all the cookies on the plate.

When Hal returned from work, Greg was asleep on the sofa with the television on.

'Hard day?' Hal kissed Greg's ear and sat down next to him.

'Oh, you know. Sent a woman to the moon. Raised an orphan.' Greg stretched. 'What's the time?'

'Late. There was only one entrance at the venue so we had to wait until the guests left before we could clear out. And I think you'll find Arthur has three parents. He's the opposite of an orphan.'

'That's not what it felt like. You want wine?' Greg reached for the bottle and poured them both a glass.

'It was only one evening.'

'I don't mean that. He wanted to talk about Rachel and I didn't know what to say.'

'I'm sure you said the right thing. Did you get to the school on time?'

'Maybe we should sit down with Eliza and go over what we want to tell him again.'

Hal sat up. 'Just how late were you?'

'Eliza and I get on fine, she's just a little . . . controlling. And I want to be there for Arthur. I want to help.'

'It's been two years and you have helped, big guy. More than helped, we couldn't have done it without you.'

'Shucks,' said Greg. He thought it was probably true. They had all needed him in their different ways, all the adults. And now it was Arthur's turn. 'The kid's at a different stage now. We need to re-group.'

'Okay, let's have lunch together. Next Sunday.'

'Definitely lunch. I couldn't handle dinner.' Greg closed his eyes. 'And I wasn't that late.

'Come on, Superdad. Let's get you to bed.'

'Don't you want to know about the woman on the moon?'

'Consider it foreplay.'

They took the glasses to the sink and Hal washed up while

Greg ate the mini apricot meringues Hal had brought home from the party.

'Thanks for looking after Arthur today,' Hal said. 'I know it's all more than you bargained for.'

'As long as you keep paying me in dessert,' Greg said.

Arthur sat on a bar stool and ate blueberries while Hal whisked eggs for French toast. Greg had returned to the sofa.

'Are you taking me to school?'

'Yep.' Hal tapped cinnamon into the mixture.

'Okay.'

'What's up?'

'Nothing. I wanted to talk to Greg some more.'

'We'll see you at the weekend. Or you can Skype later.'

'Greg can't Skype. He doesn't like the way his hair looks.'

'True. One piece or two?'

'Three. With syrup. And butter.'

Hal put a piece of bread into the pan and handed Arthur a glass of milk.

'What did you want to talk about?'

'He said mummy is living in space and I want to know where.'

'He said what?'

'How old do you have to be to go to space? As old as mummy?' Arthur kept his eyes on the pan in Hal's hand.

'Greg?' Hal spoke to the body on the sofa.

'You're going to drop the bread.' Arthur nodded at the tilted pan.

Hal returned to the hob and fried the French toast. Greg didn't move.

'Will you come to space with me? Will mum?'

'No one is going to space, Arthur. Eat your breakfast.'

'Mummy couldn't live here because she wasn't well. So she's gone to another planet.'

Hal took his coffee and sat on the stool next to Arthur.

'We talked about what happened to mummy, do you remember?'

Arthur nodded.

'And we read that book,' Hal continued, 'about the badger?'

'But mummy isn't a badger. She's like Goldilocks. She can live in space as long as everything is just right.'

The boy dipped his toast in the pool of warm lime juice and maple syrup on the side of his plate.

'Greg? Are you listening?' Hal said.

Greg put a hand over the sofa and waved.

'Any thoughts?'

'Is there more French toast?'

The buzz of a mobile phone vibrated through the ceiling. Arthur slipped off his stool and took his plate over to where Greg lay.

'We're going to be late,' Hal said as he headed upstairs. 'You've got five minutes, Arthur. And don't give away your breakfast.'

Greg peered from one eye in time to open his mouth for a quarter piece of toast soaked in syrup.

'S'good,' he said when he'd swallowed.

The boy stood in front of him, sleep-shaped hair and a maple moustache.

'You going to wash before you leave?'

Arthur shook his head.

'Clean your teeth?'

'Nope.'

138

The plate on the coffee table in front of them had one more quarter of toast left. Arthur sat down. He took a bite and held the rest out to Greg.

'Our secret,' Greg said.

Hal returned with Arthur's bag.

'We've got to go.' Hal looked at Greg. 'I'll see you later.'

At the door, Arthur let Hal put a jumper over his head.

'Mummy said we shouldn't have secrets, Greg,' Arthur shouted as he struggled into the neck hole.

'The dead one?' Greg asked from the depths of the velvet cushions.

'Yeah.' Arthur smiled. 'That one.'

Hal pulled down the jumper and gave his son's shoulder a squeeze. 'We're going to be late.'

A minute later the door closed behind them.

Silence filled the flat. Greg mopped up the rest of the maple syrup with his fingers and lay down again. Work could wait. He wanted to replay the conversation with Arthur a few times first.

Eliza had opened the French windows and laid the table outside in the middle of the garden. A late autumn sun flooded the kitchen but the cold air circled the furniture and Greg wondered how they could possibly endure a meal outdoors. What was it with the British and al fresco dining? There wasn't even a patio heater.

'Hope it's warm enough,' Eliza said. 'I couldn't bear not to be out in that sunshine.'

She used to be sensible, Greg thought, now she was more like Rachel every day. Maybe that was what happened when your partner died, you compensated by absorbing them in an effort to maintain balance. Greg imagined his mother in

St Louis with a can of beer in one hand and a wrench in the other. 'You going to stand there with your finger up your ass, or you going to pass me the claw hammer?' In his mind, his mother had grown a beard.

'Red or white?' Eliza said.

Greg stared at her.

'Wine.' Hal touched Greg's head. 'You okay there?'

'Sure.' Greg let his mother morph back into her lavender cardigan with matching hair. 'Just thinking about my mom.'

'How's she doing?' Eliza handed Greg a glass of white wine and stood in front of him, head tilted.

Greg didn't know how to take the sentiment. He had grown used to British sarcasm and was suspicious of earnest enquiry with an English accent.

'Enjoying the role of grieving widow after a lifetime of rehearsal,' he offered.

Eliza leant so far back Greg thought she was going to fall over.

'Sorry?'

'I mean . . . my mother is . . .' Greg was relieved to see Hal's interest in the conversation had faded as soon as his mother had been mentioned. His husband was staring at the garden as though he might start digging the flowerbeds. 'My mother and father didn't get on much.'

'I'm sorry.' Eliza nodded.

'It was never going to work. Straight couples shouldn't spend so much time together. They get confused.'

'Confused?'

'The gender divide deepens with domesticity. It starts with the trash; she does the indoor trash, he does the outside garbage. She vacuums, he gets a leaf blower. Separate nights out with the girls and the guys. Before you know it, you're in a sex war. It's not natural. Look at Hal, he can whip an egg white and mow the lawn. I just watch.'

There was a pause before Eliza laughed. But she did laugh, Greg thought as they sat down to lunch in the garden. He pulled at his jacket and noticed how Eliza's formerly smooth face had lined. They had laughed often in the early days. There had been plenty of evenings shared as Rachel's stomach grew, and it had seemed as if all their lives, not just Arthur's, were beginning.

He helped himself to the stir-fry and watched Hal's expression as various dishes were placed on the table. In the weeks after her death, Hal cooked in what was thought of as Rachel's kitchen, or delivered meals at the weekends, until the day Eliza asked him to stop. 'She said they needed to get back to ordinary food, ordinary life,' Hal told Greg. 'But I like cooking for them. It's what I do. She doesn't understand how much food Arthur needs.'

'Looks good,' Hal said now.

Eliza blushed. 'I nearly gave up and asked you to bring lunch.'

'I would have done.'

'See, Hal, that was a little too quick.' Greg glanced at Hal. 'Cooking for you is intimidating.'

'You too?' Eliza asked Greg.

'I have my moments.'

Hal snorted. 'Like the Horseshoe? A grilled sandwich with French fries in cheese sauce.'

'I could go for that.' Eliza handed the salad bowl to Hal and sat down. 'A Croque Monsieur.'

'Exactly. Hal loved it. We even drove to Springfield when we saw my mom last summer, just so he could try the original.'

'For the historical perspective,' Hal said. 'When's Arthur getting back?'

'I'm picking him up from my sister's at four.'

Greg twirled some noodles round his fork and considered how best to approach the reason they were there. Hal had called Eliza and requested a lunch to discuss Arthur but he had not said why they wanted to talk. When did their everyday conversation become impossible? Every word burdened by twenty-one grams of guilt. They no longer thought of each other as friends, Greg realised. They were more like colleagues in the business of Arthur.

'Did you tell Arthur that Rachel was an alien?' Eliza peered at Greg over the rim of her wine glass.

'Is that what he said?'

'Pretty much. He came home with a story about Rachel living in space, a fairy tale.'

'Greg thinks all the interesting things happen on Mars,' Hal said. They had argued for days about what, exactly, Greg had told Arthur.

'He wanted to know if you could live in space. I said it was possible, in the right conditions. The kid misses his mom so he decided she could be alive somewhere.' Greg took a breath. 'It is kind of what you guys already told him.'

Hal and Eliza exchanged a look that reminded Greg of his parents when he was a child. The 'which-one-of-us-should -sort-this-out' routine. Cloud wisps trailed across the afternoon sun. Greg shivered.

Hal started. 'We said she was ill and her body didn't work any more.'

'And we talked about death,' Eliza said, 'about what happens when you die. We did not say she was living somewhere else.'

Greg picked at the ginger from his salad. He wasn't surprised that the conversation was focused more on his culpability than on Arthur's emotional state. Hal and Eliza were the ones who cared for Arthur, saw him every day, took him to the therapist. Greg had been at work. He hadn't been part of the routine. But since Arthur's last visit he had felt more than an understudy for the boy's parents. He had his own part to play.

'You didn't say anything about her staying alive in your memory?'

Eliza frowned. 'Are you being defensive?'

'I'm saying we've all told Arthur that Rachel lives on, in some way. Metaphorically, sure. But he doesn't know the difference.'

'Maybe we should go back to the therapist,' Hal said, 'if Arthur needs to talk.'

Greg saw Eliza's shoulders sag.

'I don't think that's what he needs.' Greg held his palms up. 'He wants to talk about Rachel without the high church condemning him . . .'

'We're not religious,' Eliza interrupted.

'I mean the reverence,' Greg said, 'the positivity. The special language.'

Hal answered. 'Eliza and I talked about this in therapy with him. Anger and bad feelings, that's a healthy part of grieving. He can have those feelings but we don't have to join in.'

Eliza nodded. Her lips were pulled tight and Greg thought she might cry.

'I want to know; why is it such a big deal for you guys if Arthur thinks Rachel is in space?'

'Because it's not true,' Hal said, 'let's start there.'

'Because he will think she might come back. And she won't,' Eliza added.

The light in the garden had muted. Long shadows faint on the grey-green grass. Greg watched Hal take Eliza's hand as a thin tear slid down her cheek. I will never be part of this, he thought, this English scenery. It doesn't matter how much my accent slides, or how old my house is.

'We don't understand what's happened ourselves,' he said, 'how can Arthur?'

They both turned to him.

Hal said, 'Don't flake on me now.'

Eliza shook her head. 'That isn't the point. Of course we don't have all the answers, but we need to protect Arthur. You can't play with his feelings like this, Greg. It's not fucking fair. On any of us.'

'Wait a minute. We just substitute all the conventional religious stuff with voodoo nonsense.' Greg's voice rose. 'I'm sorry, Eliza. Not just you, all of us. We say she's dead but we behave as if she's on the other side of the mirror.'

A door slammed in the distance and the group looked back at the house. Beyond the louvred shutters of the French windows, the kitchen glowed in the gathering gloom.

Hal stood up. 'It's going to rain.'

Greg helped him collect plates from the table. Eliza didn't move.

'I walk into a room and I expect to see her. I go to sleep and she's waiting for me, standing in a doorway, always just out of reach.'

'That's normal,' Hal said, 'Of course you want to be with her.'

'But she's not there, is she? Greg's right, we haven't got a clue. We put all the words in the right order and pretend to understand what they mean.' Eliza stared at them. 'But we don't know anything.'

The two men stood facing Eliza, the towers of dishes in their hands. Rain spots darkened the silvered wood of the table. At the fringes of the garden, the wind caught in the trees. Greg thought about Arthur and Rachel and the three bears. He thought about the forest.

'We're looking at this the wrong way round,' he said. It was almost too dark to see their faces. 'We want to have answers; we think we should give Arthur explanations, but we can't. Because death doesn't mean anything.'

The outline of Eliza stood up. 'It means something to me, Greg. And it means something to Arthur. Don't you dare tell us it doesn't.'

'Of course, that's what we feel. But it's like a computer, we can program the computer with all the information about, say, falling in love, but that wouldn't help the computer understand what love is.'

'Because computers don't feel anything! My God, Greg, do you ever leave the office?'

There was a rattle of plates and he felt Hal's hand on his shoulder.

'Babe,' Hal's breath was warm on his cheek. 'You're not helping.'

'We can't understand death because we haven't died.'

A sob came from the outline of Eliza. Hal's hand moved down to Greg's shoulder and gave him a shove.

'Come off it,' Hal said, 'shouldn't we go and get Arthur? Eliza?'

Rain dripped on the back of Greg's neck. He wanted to

wipe his glasses even though he couldn't see anything now. The three of them had become blackened shapes in the yellow light from the house.

'We can't die and live,' he said.

'We can't die and live,' Eliza echoed.

'That's why we don't understand it, why it has no meaning.'

He reached one hand up to smear his glasses with his sleeve and lost his balance. Stepping back, his feet shot out from under him and he landed on the wet lawn with a cry as the china smashed against the table, the chairs and bounced on to the grass beside him.

'Damn,' Greg said, after a moment's silence. 'Sorry.'

'You alright there?' Eliza asked, moving over to where Greg had fallen.

Hal walked across the broken plates. 'Greg?'

'I slipped.'

'Bloody wet out here.' Hal put an arm out.

'It's raining,' Eliza started to laugh, 'We're standing in the pouring rain, in the dark, talking about death.'

'Yes,' Greg said, 'Sorry to spoil the party.'

Greg waited in the hallway while Eliza's sister shouted for Arthur. He had met Fran plenty of times, but he didn't want to venture any further into the house.

'Hal's waiting at your sister's,' Greg explained, 'I said I'd brave the rain.'

'Is it raining?' Fran frowned. 'Why didn't you drive?'

'I wanted to walk. What's a bit of rain?' Greg swivelled his shoulders to demonstrate the amount of water he had absorbed. 'But you know the Brits. Lightweights.'

'Oh. Not us. We used to picnic in a layby on the M6

for New Year's Eve on our way up to Lytham St Annes. Arthur!' She called up the stairs. 'Come on, he's waiting.'

Greg smiled and thought, not for the first time, how glad he was that he had married into Eliza's new family and not her old one.

On the walk back he held Arthur's hand. The rain had slowed to drizzle.

'Did you have a good time?'

'Yeah. It was okay.' Arthur swung Greg's arm. 'You?'

'I fell over in the garden and broke all the plates.'

The boy stopped. His eyes shone in the streetlight. 'I broke stuff too! Did you get into trouble?'

'It was an accident.'

'Oh.' Arthur walked on.

'You got into trouble?'

'I didn't start it. Joe told me I was stupid to think my mother was in space and I threw my PSP and it hit the picture behind him and smashed the glass.'

'We need to improve your throwing arm. Was your aunt mad?'

'She said Joe should be nice to me because I was going through a difficult stage. But she said I shouldn't make up stories.' Arthur grabbed Greg's jumper. 'I didn't make it up though, did I? You told me anyone can live in space?'

'I did say that.'

'Like in the story. As long as it is just right.'

'Yes. But Arthur . . .'

'That's where she is.' Arthur yawned. 'She ran away. Like in the story.'

The boy hooked an arm round the hip Greg had landed on when he fell. He lifted Arthur up and balanced him on the other hip. 'Oof. Dude, you're heavy.'

The house was at the end of the next street. Greg thought he could just make the journey without dropping Arthur. He felt the weight of sleep in the child's body and held him tighter.

'Nearly there, kid.'

'We don't know the end,' Arthur mumbled into Greg's jacket.

'What's that?' They reached the front door and Greg tried to reach his keys.

The hall light came on and Eliza stood on the other side of the glass. Arthur reached out his arms for his mother.

'Hang on a sec.' Greg struggled to keep his balance as Eliza opened the door and Arthur leant toward her. 'There you go.' He rubbed at his ribs.

Hal appeared from the kitchen. 'Thanks, Els.' He kissed the top of Arthur's head, buried in Eliza's neck. 'Why don't you come over to us next time?'

Eliza smiled and tipped her chin to Arthur. 'Say goodnight, Arthur.'

The boy held one hand up.

'Goodnight, Arthur.' The two men kissed Eliza and headed out into the damp night.

'We don't know the end,' Greg said as they got into the car.

Hal glanced at him as he checked the rear view mirror and pulled away from the kerb. 'Who doesn't?'

'It's what Arthur said. He said we don't know the end.'

'He's right.' Hal nodded.

'That's why we can't understand.'

'Is this to do with Rachel?'

Greg looked at Hal. His husband's face was blurred through his fogged glasses and the shadows of street lights but Greg could see the statuesque head and waves of dark hair, the deep ridges of his brow and the short beard that softened the lines of his jaw. He put a hand on Hal's leg.

'I think so,' he said.

The hand on Hal's thigh pressed down a little. Seven years. In that time they had married, had a child, lost a friend and a parent, bought a home, formed an allegiance against the world. A long time, so much lost and won, and a short time, a fraction of their lives.

Hal parked the car and the two men sat in the dark, their breath clouding together. At the far end of the street a woman struggled across the uneven pavement with a push-chair full of tins. In Illinois, his mother would be home from church, making lunch with the TV on in the background. She would expect his call.

7

Arthulysses

The Twin Earths

The philosopher Hilary Putnam wanted to examine if words could be defined by external properties, not just the meaning we attribute to them. He wrote the Twin Earth thought experiment in which a person travels to another planet, Twin Earth, where water has the same name and properties but a different chemical composition. When a Twin Earther refers to water they are actually referring to a substance made up of XYZ not H2O, although it seems to be, and they think it is, the same thing.

Meanings just ain't in the head!

Hilary Putnam *The Meaning of Meaning*

A short way from the dock, Arthur changed his mind and pulled the ship to the left. He spun unevenly for a few minutes in the magnetic field. Two AU from home and this was the distance that mattered: less than a basketball hoop. Arthur nodded. His moms had said it to him enough times: the last inches before you're born are the most dangerous. He remembered them both saying it, though it must have been Eliza. That happened a lot. He could see Rachel's face but it was Eliza's voice that he heard. He couldn't really remember much from being five.

The pilots were taught that each docking was a kind of birth. They were to bring new life to the rocks on which they landed; terra-forms, or terror-forms as the enviromists called them. Arthur didn't think exploration was political. The way he saw it, human nature was stupid enough to almost destroy itself, and clever enough to survive. He was part of the solution.

Lights flashed on the console and he answered the signal on his headset.

'Captain Pryce, why did you disable the automatic docking procedure?'

'Don't worry about it, Zed. I wanted a few more minutes out here.'

'You've had 163 earth days, Captain Pryce,' said the male voice, 'It's time to land.'

He let the computer tell him what was expected of him for some minutes. Lag. How long had he been out for last time? He must have been roused after the maximum sleep permitted. Three days in stasis, his vital signs monitored, his nutrients intravenous. In all the trials and shorter trips he had woken alert and passed the cognitive assessments easily. But after the first month of this trip he had begun to dread full consciousness and on awakening would stare at the roof of his sleep pod as forlornly as a teenager on a school day.

His heart beat erratically and he put a hand to his chest.

'Captain Pryce, you need to return to the dock. Are you in need of any help? Your blood pressure is elevated. We recommend some refreshment.'

The grey light of Deimos moved through the deck as the ship pivoted slowly. Mars was visible on the console, a caramel glow filling each screen in turn as the different cameras changed focal length. Arthur had been down for the Mars Two rota. You were given six placements in your time at the company, two long-haul trips and four short journeys to local space stations. Once you reached a base, you had to stay a year. Arthur's last tour on the Space Eye, an earth orbit station, had coincided with the company's plans to develop the second base and he'd missed the Mars launch date. This trip to Deimos was a consolation prize. With the return journey, he'd be gone for two years.

'You'll be part of the team, Pryce.' Arthur's boss had frowned at him from the lousy phone monitor in his office.

'Sure. Like I helped you move house when I was on the Eye. All those smiley faces from space.'

'I hope you'll be sending the base more than that.'

153

Space Solutions were a few years away from being able to pilot rockets on local journeys from Mars. Most of the ships were reusable but they could only take two landings before they required significant repairs. Even with the magnetic landing sites, there was always too much damage to the ship. Arthur would be alone on the small moon.

'You got a problem with the solo trips?'

Arthur stared at Jennifer's pixellated image. She'd have him taken off the rota completely at the slightest hint of trouble, personal relationship be damned.

'Don't be like that,' he said. 'What's the ship?'

They gave him the Spirit 2040 and he'd signed on for the Deimos trip.

His eyes flicked across the images of Mars rotating on the screens above him.

'Captain Pryce, please focus on the console.'

'How long have I been awake?'

'Awake?'

'Conscious? How long was it from when I woke up to now?'

'You programmed me to wake you after 72 hours, Captain Pryce. That is the maximum acceptable . . .'

'Yeah, yeah. But how long have I . . . shit, never mind.'

'Captain Pryce, please concentrate on the program sequence.'

All his training psych evaluations came back positive for solo excursions; well suited for communication with the AI units and skilled at biofeedback. If pressed, Arthur would have said he preferred the absence of human communication. His was the tablet generation and he'd embraced every tech evo available as soon as he could, thirsty for the relief

154

of the electronic interface. He'd fought constantly with Eliza for screen time.

'You should be out in the real world, meeting real friends. It's so unhealthy to be glued to your computer all day.'

In vain Arthur argued that his hobby was no different from Eliza's book reading. At least he interacted with his virtual environment instead of passively receiving information.

'That is absolute proof that your imagination is being killed. There is nothing passive about reading. Come and see the research we're doing on the brain's electronic responses to art.'

As Arthur saw it, Eliza's science was a convenient smokescreen for her prejudice. Where were the studies that examined how the integration of AI and human intelligence would leave her evidence for biological synaptic responses in the Dark Ages?

'That's the future you're building, Arthur. Your generation. It doesn't have to be that way.' Such was the impossibility of argument when you were met with personal responses to every valid point.

Only Greg had understood the importance of the world available to Arthur online.

'Don't worry about it, kid. Your mom works in a modern laboratory but she still thinks a computer is a combination of a filing cabinet and an abacus, and the internet is a useful way for old folks to keep in touch with each other. Your dad's not much better. When I first told Hal I was a mathematician he asked me to work out the bill in the restaurant. It's no use telling people that I don't know my times tables from an ant nest, they don't get it. They want to live in a world where they can walk to a Post Office to get a stamp or see if an apple's ripe before they take it home. They don't understand they're free of all that. They think we're weird for working with the future? They're the fetishists, stuck in the past.' Greg cuffed his stepson on the shoulder. 'But, you know, don't tell I said so.'

'Captain Pryce? You are distracted. I am overriding the pilot system and turning us back to the docking station in E minus 60 seconds.'

Arthur took a breath and looked at the console in front of him. The lights on the landing base were still green for go.

'There's no need to do that. I've got it.'

The software tracked his eye movement for a moment.

'Very well, Captain Pryce. On docking please report to the med bay.'

It had been a mistake to christen the new operating system Zeus. Even with the personality settings on neutral, Arthur felt the system's superiority bias. Other pilots named their OS after parents as a psych shortcut, that way you acknowledged some authority but maintained a healthy suspicion of their motives. His colleagues told him it wasn't helpful to think of an OS as a best friend; it inhibited the human brain's defence mechanisms. Trust was better on a case-by-case basis. 'Especially in space', Jennifer had added when they talked about it later. Arthur wondered if most pilots had a different relationship with their parents than he did. He liked his mothers and fathers. Maybe that's what came of having more than the regular amount from the get go. Anyhow, he certainly wasn't going to call the computer 'Hal'. He was going to a rock named Deimos; Zeus had seemed appropriate. What he couldn't tell, after more than six months of interaction almost solely with the computer, was how much of what passed for the OS's personality was his own projection, and how much was programming. It's just a word, he reminded himself as he took hold of the controls, a rose and all that.

He swung the Spirit back to the landing position and began the approach. He was used to the task, had performed this particular landing on the simulator over a dozen times and had docked at the Space Eye only last year. He'd even completed the simulated landing on the old ISS at Johnson. Second in his cohort. So why could he feel the sweat cooling on his skin now?

The rhythmic rocking increased and reduced as the magnets found each other and locked into a controlled attraction. Ever since the West Coast Superhighway had been completed in 2021, all possible conduits had been magnetised. Arthur was ten when the original San Francisco to LA route went into production, and he remembered cars. Magnets couldn't compete for the thrill of the engine but no one died at or under the wheel any more. E-cars drove themselves and parked themselves. There were hardly any drivers, only passengers. Even rockets used magnetic fields to navigate landings when they weren't returning to Earth.

Still, this particular docking system had never been used in the analogue world and the engineer who built it had voiced some reservations about the structure on her return. Arthur was here to save the ship if anything went wrong. Zeus was here to save Arthur. At least, that's what the company manifesto claimed. Arthur hoped it would never come down to a choice. Zeus sure seemed fond of the ship.

Arthur's module spun as it had always done, allowing a simulation of gravity. The increasing speed was visible on the monitors.

'Captain Pryce, the dock will connect in E minus 12 seconds.'

'That's what it says right . . .'

'Nine, eight, seven . . .'

He missed his old OS.

The moon stopped moving on the monitor and disappeared from view as the ship matched its speed and dived into the Voltaire crater where the base was housed. The deck shook and several violent jolts threw Arthur forward against the harness so that it was a moment before he felt the change in gravitational force. Alarms and lights signalled from the console and stopped as suddenly as they had started. Arthur realised he was holding his breath. They had docked. He was alive.

'Captain Pryce, phase two of the docking procedure is complete.'

Small dips and judders continued to shake the ship. He checked the alignment and proceeded to engage the units that would let him cross to the moon's single-person base. The sooner he set up the next phase, the greater his chances of success for the year's mission.

One year. Not including the two AU on the journey back. He had enough decent food supplies for twelve weeks, after that he hoped the terrarium would have established, or it was back on the hot mush. Not quite up to his dad's standards but some of the flavours had been Hal's major contribution to his supplies. A vast improvement from the freeze-dried meatballs he had tried as a child when his dreams of being an astronaut had begun. Hal and Greg still argued about which one of them had inspired Arthur's star wanderlust, but all his parents were responsible for getting him this far.

He thought of Eliza at work in London, going home each night to an empty house. He thought about Rachel, the patchwork idea he had of her, a tilt of the dark head, her gentle eyes that everyone said he had inherited, the sound of her bracelets when she put him to bed. 'She loved you,' Eliza said. 'She loved you before you were born.' And now? young Arthur had wondered, when Eliza kissed him goodnight in the many evenings that followed. But Eliza didn't like to talk about where Rachel had gone and maybe, for Eliza, Rachel had never left.

'Please proceed to the med bay before preparing for phase three. We will wait for further instructions from earth.'

The med bay was the capsule behind the one that Arthur currently occupied. In transit it spun at the same rate as the pilot capsule and provided a similar gravitational force. All the internal surfaces of the ship were covered with shelving, netting, hooks, wires and cables, giving the appearance of a tech junk shop and reducing movement in the pilot's dock to necessary operations only. The second module was even smaller, 'compact' as described in the company's literature. It was also the sleeping area.

'It's just the two of us here, Zeus. You mean, "Get on the bed".'

'As you wish, Captain Pryce. Although I am not technically "here" and the concept of meaning for geographical locations other than their designated use has no significance for me.'

It was poor programming, Arthur reminded himself as he crawled through the carbon tubing at the centre of the ship to the other capsule, enjoying the absolute lack of gravity between the two modules. He made a note to check on his bone density when he landed. Weightlessness was a drug; the more you had, the more you needed.

He strapped himself to the bed and hooked up the IV

system to the port located above his collarbone for the OS to administer the fluids and nutrients it deemed necessary.

'Your blood pressure is still elevated, Captain Pryce. Your landing history indicates this is unusual.'

'We don't need to wait for base. Start phase three.'

'Initiating phase three. Please remain stationary. You are being monitored.'

Arthur switched the OS's commands to visual. He still had the opportunity to override the system unless his signs of life were compromised. A sanity valve for the 'voice in your ear'. He remembered the lectures he had attended as an undergraduate on the dangers of strong AI, the films over the last century where robots had inherited the earth. The singularity was a myth but apparently Zeus hadn't got the memo.

'Play my space mix.'

To the opening sounds of 'Once in a Lifetime', Arthur unhooked the wires and pulled himself back through to the cockpit. He felt clammy, unfocused. The reduced gravitational force should have helped with the body blow of the landing but every muscle seemed to ache with the effort of coordination. The least Zeus could have done was give him a painkiller. He sat buckled into the pilot's seat and studied the data feed. Damned if he was going to ask Zeus for an aspirin.

The biggest breakthrough in the last ten years had been the understanding that artificial intelligence could only evolve as an adjunct of human intelligence. There was a certain symbiosis in the relationship, Arthur conceded, but plenty of people existed without an inbuilt operating system and Arthur himself preferred to stick with wearables instead of implants. Something his dead mother had said to him once when she was ill about her brain being 'invaded'.

He programmed the connection sequence that would allow the airlocks to open between his ship and the landing module. The music changed to a live recording of Qualia at Coachella. Zeus issued a series of visual commands but did not interrupt. The instructions repeated across the lens of his glasses and on the console.

Allow 15 minutes for the environmental controls to regulate.

Maybe that's what a tumour felt like; an invasion. As a child he thought Rachel meant aliens. Those were the sort of invasions he had heard of. Or zombies. His favourite book had been *How to Survive the Zombie Apocalypse*. At night he would ask his parents to show him their teeth so he could be sure they were who they said they were. 'Show me your teeth!' He remembered the trepidation while he waited. Greg would pull faces and try to show one tooth at a time and Hal laughed and showed a full set of gleaming enamel but Eliza took the opportunity to ask Arthur if he was 'feeling alright' and if there was anything he wanted 'to talk about'. He never told her about Rachel's alien brain invasion but somehow she knew his fear was connected to her anyway. Or maybe she assumed everything was about Rachel.

Prepare for atmospheric change in E minus 10 minutes.

He lifted each foot into the weighted boots attached to the chair, unstrapped his harness and leant against the console, his breathing laboured. Dead mother and living mother. Mummy and mum. The same way they had called him 'baby' (mummy) and 'darling' (mum). He preferred mom now in any case, it was less intimate. Not long after Rachel had died a teacher at school had told him he was lucky 'to have a spare one'. Possibly this was meant to be reassuring and Arthur had appreciated the logic but it had set up a pattern of concern for other children who had only one of each parent and sometimes not even that. The situation seemed irresponsible given how likely it was for grown-ups to die at any moment. In all the stories he was told, the fairy tales and Roald Dahls, the Lemony Snickets and J. K. Rowlings, the parents were either dead or gone, with very poor provision made for their absence. For several years, Arthur guarded over his less fortunate friends with daily enquiries on the health and whereabouts of their parents. The same friends who had been warned by said parents that Arthur might be sad and sensitive because his mummy was ill and his mummy had died, and who were therefore especially careful not to show off about the wellness of their own families. He was relieved when bullying became a thing at school and he realised most kids didn't have extra parents so he could stop worrying. He was the odd one out.

E minus five minutes to completion of phase three; full connection with Deimos docking station.

His breath was still uneven. He untied the weighted boots from the chair and strapped each one up. The monitors and portholes were dark now; each one dimly relaying the walls of the Voltaire crater. Arthur closed his eyes and tried to focus on the next stage of the operation. Whatever Zeus had given him had not helped his blood pressure. He could feel his pulse thumping in his fingertips.

'Captain Pryce? Audio contact re-established.'

'Fine. I need to stabilise my BP.'

'Your blood pressure is no longer elevated, Captain Pryce. All vital signs within normal range. You can proceed to the docking station as soon as phase three is completed.'

Arthur shook his head.

'That's not right. Run diagnostics again.'

'Running diagnostics. Sixty seconds to full connection with . . .'

'Deimos.'

'I'm sorry, Captain Pryce?'

'You didn't finish the sentence. Sixty seconds to full connection with Deimos.'

'Forty-five seconds.'

The crater was making him dizzy. He could take being in a titanium can in space but being underground as well was making him sick.

'Zed, brighten external lights on monitor feeds and bring up the relay from the Mars Station.'

'I have no contact with Mars at this time, Captain Pryce. Phase three complete in four, three, two, one seconds.'

There was a tightness around his head. Arthur's field of vision started to close down. He put an arm out to balance himself but the boots seemed to be pulling him to the floor and he began to fall. From what seemed a great distance, he watched the amber light on the monitor switch to green as the dock door slid open. The light went out and he was plunged into utter darkness, the entire ship blanketed around him. And still he fell.

The high-pitched alarm of the docking system brought him round. He was seated at the console, boots on, head in hands. A whoosh of air filled the Spirit. It smelled of rotting plants and chalk dust, the ozone of an air filtration system heavy with decay. Arthur took a deep breath. The pounding in his chest reduced to a regular two beats instead of an erratic three.

'Welcome home, Captain Pryce.'

Sure, home. If home meant danger, loneliness, an unacceptable risk of failure. Like all those times he arrived at US immigration on his Green Card or his shiny new passport. Welcome home. Unsmiling Officers. Two-way mirrors concealing sweaty guards with gallon coffee cups. Massachusetts, Texas, Florida, just visiting. Still, California had become his home, eventually. He didn't think he'd be able to say the same for a shallow crater on the smaller of Mars's two moons but he was glad to be there. Already the base's air pumps were taking the edge off the panic he'd felt in the last hour. Panic? That was putting it too strongly. What was the matter with him? This was his job, his first love. He needed to get it together.

'Captain Pryce. I have run diagnostics again and all systems are normal. Radiation levels contained. We can investigate further when you debark.'

'It's fine. I'm fine.'

'Of course, Captain. You must celebrate a safe return.'

Arthur looked up from the console. The crater walls were still not visible.

'Lights. And focus the cameras. I can't see anything out there.'

'It is night time, Captain Pryce.'

'Hilarious. Focus the cameras.'

It was hard work getting to the other module. Arthur made his way to the back of the ship slowly. The boots should have barely anchored him but every step was an effort.

'You should wait in the cockpit, Captain Pryce.'

'Wait? Wait for . . . Fuck me, what was that?'

From beyond the ship came the sound of further chambers being opened. Spirit shifted and vibrated from the new forces.

'Zeus. Why have you started phase four? Don't open any more hatches until we are on base.'

'Please return to your seat, Captain.'

The ship continued to move. Arthur felt the ground listing. He pushed forward to the connection hatch. The ship now opened on to a small, dark chamber.

'Light failure in connector field.'

'Captain Pryce, I am no longer controlling local systems.'

'That is not protocol.'

It was not unusual for an OS to suffer teething problems integrating with a new interface but the Deimos base had been programmed by the same team as the Zeus system. There was no love lost between the jockeys and the trainers and Arthur acknowledged the small thrill he felt at Zeus's shortcomings. Still, the systems better connect soon. He grabbed his torch from the carabiner on his belt and held on to the hatch door. He bent to climb in, using all his strength to lift a weighted leg over the metal rim. His foot fell to the ground on the other side.

There was no landing capsule. He could feel the emergency tubing on the other side of the hatch and after that, nothing.

'Abort landing.' Arthur pulled himself back into the Spirit and yanked at the boots as he made his way back to the pilot capsule. 'Abort landing. Seal all hatches. We are losing ground contact. Jesus, we're sinking.'

'The rescue crew will be here shortly, Captain. Please stay in your seat.'

'What the fuck? Stop screwing around. We are not stable,

Zeus. We need to pull away.' Arthur grabbed the seat harness. 'Disengage. Repeat. Disengage.'

'Captain Pryce, you are on board the drone boat. There is nothing to disengage from. You have landed successfully. Please remain calm.'

A flash of light crossed the cockpit. Arthur wheeled round, straining against the harness. A large exterior lamp was trained on the ship, the beam dipping in and out of range of the cameras and portholes. It was not possible.

'Zeus. We are in the Mars orbit on the moon Deimos. I have connected with the Deimos base.'

'That is incorrect, Captain. We are on earth, in the Atlantic sea, approximately 200 miles from Jacksonville, Florida.'

He could feel it now, the sensation from all previous missions. The memory of an extreme fall, the jolt of the controlled landing and the rocking of the water below the drone boat. He had been through this on every re-entry into earth's atmosphere but he was not on a return mission. He was 250,000,000 km away. He jabbed at the console readings but could make no sense of the output. The information was both completely familiar and unintelligible. There were no alarms, no unusual data. Everything on board the Spirit was calm. Except for Arthur.

'Am I awake?'

'It is not possible to answer that question.'

'I don't know what the fuck is going on and that is not helping.'

'If you are not awake I am a projection of your sleeping mind and cannot be relied upon to answer accurately.'

Arthur kept swiping at the screens in front of him. 'What if I am awake?'

'You cannot know.'

166

The ship was definitely rocking. Not magnetic field rocking. Full on, rising-and-falling, out-to-sea rocking.

He took a deep breath. 'Check your logs. How long have we been gone?'

'Three hundred and seventy-seven days, four hours, thirty-four minutes and fifty-six seconds since take off, Captain Pryce.'

'Check again.'

'Three hundred and seventy-seven days, four hours and thirty-five minutes.'

'So why don't I remember it?'

'It is not possible to answer that question.'

'Jesus Christ!' His lungs felt as though someone was sitting on his chest.

'Please remain in your seat, Captain Pryce.'

Arthur pulled off the rest of the harness and tried to stand up. His knees buckled and he fell back into the seat. Full gravity.

'Lock the main hatch.'

'The rescue crew will be boarding soon, Captain Pryce. Please return to your seat. You are behaving erratically.'

A shout from outside the ship brought Arthur to the front viewing window; a line of thick glass obscured by condensation.

'The rescue crew? From Space Solutions?'

'NASA has outsourced rescue operations to a subsidiary of Page Industries.'

'Right.' It was comforting to hear the familiar names. All the companies had a deal with each other, it made sense. 'Why are my comms systems not working?'

'You are nearly thirteen light years from earth. You are currently landing on earth.'

'That's it. I'm shutting you down. Overriding OS Zeus. All systems manual. Maintain current program. Lock hatches.'

The sound of static filled the module. 'Captain Pryce? This is Mission Control. You appear to be experiencing problems with your OS. We are overriding the system. Hatches are open and crew standing by. Welcome home, Captain.'

'The guys upstairs are waiting.'

The doctor sat on the bed by Arthur's legs, his Southern voice too resonant for such proximity.

'I heard you had a bumpy landing.' He stared at his note-book with rheumy eyes and swiped through a few pages. 'You don't have any system implants? Well, maybe that's just as well. Looks like your OS is still offline anyway.'

Arthur couldn't move his legs away from the doctor's body; they lay as the nurse had left them on top of the bed covers. Both men studied the oddly angled limbs, the fringe of ginger hair on Arthur's shins brushing the navy blue wool of the doctor's suit.

'But how are you feeling in yourself? Anything bothering you? More than the usual post-mission lag? Tests are good. Bone density, muscle wastage, all better than could be expected after such a long trip. Feels heavy, don't it? But you'll be running track again in no time, gravity be damned.'

They looked again at Arthur's legs. Outside the second floor window of the low building, he could hear the grasshoppers sing. It was spring. He had left in the autumn, he was certain. He didn't recognise the facility but he guessed he was in the old military rehab hospital, on the South-East corner of the main base.

'But hey, nurses say you haven't eaten. Are you crazy? After all that mush?'

Arthur nodded. The guy was sixty or seventy. He'd remember the first Mars missions; Mariner and Odyssey.

'The bosses are going to be disappointed if you clam up like this when they visit. And it's me they'll blame. What's up, kid?'

The pressure on his chest was worse than in any other trip he had taken. Every breath felt like he was bench-pressing his lungs. But that wasn't why he was quiet.

'Where have I been?'

'What do you mean? They brought you straight from quarantine to here. They want you back in Pasadena, sure. And you're about ready to get home, I'll bet.'

'Before that. Where was I before that?'

The man in the blue suit sighed. 'Look, Captain Pryce, it's all going to be fine. Rest up and I'll let them know they can see you tomorrow. It's been a year, they can wait a few more hours.'

At the door, the doctor pointed at him in mock admonishment. 'And you eat all you can. It's not every day you come back to earth.'

Arthur waited for the door to close. As the doctor's footsteps receded, he jammed his elbows behind his back and levered himself forward until he was sitting upright. He checked the room. The benefit of being in the rehab unit was the low-tech outfit: no cameras, no motion sensors, windows that opened. He put a hand down to his legs and tried to rub some life back into them. He needed to get out of the room and make it to an unregistered phone. If he called home, spoke to Greg, he could find out what had happened. His mom would be monitored by the company.

There was no one he could trust here. He had spent time on this base, not in the rehab unit, but around. Training, socialising. All the doctors were on call in the main medical unit at some point, getting to know the new crews and new kit. Arthur had never laid eyes on the man in the blue suit.

The window opened on to a large grassed courtyard, palm trees and benches in each quadrant. On three sides, the old building stood exactly as it must have done a century earlier, white painted stucco and metal windows. A new glass hallway made up the fourth side, housing a central reception area with a long desk that faced out to the car park. Arthur leant on the window ledge and tried to hold himself steady. He couldn't see any doors into the courtyard other than from the glass hallway. If he dropped down from the window and landed on the grass below, he would be covered by the trees from the reception area, but there was no way of getting back into the building without being seen. He held tight to the frame and leant out a little further. The window below him was open.

Blue suit said he had been away for a year. But his journey was six months. Six months to Deimos, but he hadn't got there. Which, if true, had to be known by mission control, by the company, by every single engineer and data analyst on the program, whatever they said about a year mission. Why was no one talking to him about the aborted mission? If not true, he was still inside the Voltaire crater on Deimos experiencing some sort of elaborate hallucination or breakdown. Either of which conclusion didn't bode well for his sanity, or cognitive function as Zeus would put it.

Zeus. Arthur sat down in the open window ledge and stared around the room. He could have used the OS now. With an implant, he would be automatically connected to the base station and direct access to Greg, who was with Hal in Los Angeles and one of his primary contacts, though the line would be monitored. He tried to remember the last thing Zeus had told him. He was light years from earth but he was back on earth? That was how it felt to Arthur; he hadn't seen anyone he recognised since the rescue, though they had all known him, and the base, the food, the scent of the air itself was familiar yet different, as though his sensory input had been altered as easily as a monitor's colour settings. An OS didn't have feelings, only facts. He was home but he was not home.

From the corridor came the sound of voices, a bump against the wall. A guard was stationed outside his room. He pulled at the hospital gown and turned back to the courtyard. He wasn't going to get far but at least if he made it downstairs he might get to a phone. The outside world called to him as loudly as if he were a child again. An inch at a time, he dragged his legs through the window opening until he sat facing out, and let go.

He landed hard and lay on the rough grass, his breath knocked out of him. He waited while the pain focused. Above him the earth tilted in a violet sky. Arthur saw the light of old stars and the shimmer of dust and his planet's solitary moon, a thin scythe of blue one hand's reach away.

'Arthur?'

The voice brought his head round to the open window on the ground floor. A dark-haired woman in a diaphanous dress that held the colours of the sunset.

'Arthur, what are you doing? Are you alright?'

He knew her.

'Did you fall? My god. Shall I get help?'

'No!' His chest ached with the effort.

'But baby, you're hurt.'

A head of curls, a curve of hip. Baby.

He sat up, one arm locked for support, and stayed hunched over on the ground. He saw folds of the dress fall from the window, followed by canvas shoes and bare legs. She ran to him and crouched beside him.

'Arthur, what happened?'

Baby. She put her arms around him.

'They said you were fine. They said I could see you tomorrow. But I waited here.'

He pulled back, fought for a new breath, looked at her.

'Rachel?'

'Yes, it's me. Did you hit your head? What's with "Rachel"?' She held on to his shoulders, searched his face.

'Where's Eliza? Mom.' Maybe he had. He had hit his head and his body was still on the Spirit in a shallow crater on a small moon near Mars.

'Who's Eliza?' Rachel put a hand to her son's cheek. 'Funny.'

In the distance he heard a shout.

'They're going to come and help you. I won't leave. It's going to be okay. That was a long trip, the longest you've done.'

Another shout. Above, from the window of his room. In the glass corridor, a nurse watched them at the door. He felt the coldness in his fingertips, the nausea, the flutter of his heart against his chest. Darkness. He held on tight. Gripped the woman in front of him. The longest trip he'd done.

At the same time, another Arthur took the stairs down to the reception area of the rehabilitation unit at the Lyndon B. Johnson Space Center in Houston, Texas. The steps were a

172

challenge to his wasted leg muscles and every breath caught in his chest but he had been informed that his mother was waiting to see him and he took the opportunity to greet her away from the hospital room. The sooner he was released from rehab, the sooner he could figure out what had happened on his trip to Deimos. All he knew for sure was that not long after he entered the crater, there had been a comms blackout and he had lost consciousness. When he awoke he was on a rescue boat in Florida. Over a year had passed.

Rachel would be worried. She had her own life; work and a following at Comic-Con where she designed costumes for the Hymenoptera characters. People travelled the country to have Rachel make their bug outfit, ever since she'd kitted Arthur up as an ant for his tenth-birthday Ant Man party and Instagrammed the result. After that, he'd learned to share his mummy with all the sci-fi geeks and soon he'd become one of them. When he was seventeen, she had moved to the States to help him pursue his aeronautical dreams and she had never missed a launch or a landing.

'You can let go of the whole single-mother-precious-only-child thing now, mom,' Arthur told her when he had finished his pilot training. 'I have a plane and all.'

'Hey, you can't take away my job.' Rachel let her son put a muscular arm around her shoulders. 'A kid isn't just for Christmas. Don't let Hal hear any of that single mother bullshit, either.'

Arthur rounded the corner of the steep staircase in the hospital and stopped to catch his breath. His father hadn't made it to a single parents' day at school, let alone an earth re-entry. He got it. Hal was there for him as a symbol, the idea and the biology of a father but not the physical presence. That had never been the deal and a few years after he was born, Hal had married a gardener and moved to Somerset. Which had meant some great feral summers in the Quantocks but a distinct absence of dad in Hackney.

It would be Rachel in the visitors' room, and Rachel who had stayed up every night since . . . however long he had been gone. No one had offered an explanation for the missing six months, all he had to go on were his own mental inaccuracies. A failure of memory that the company had yet to repair with the OS information, since the OS was exhibiting some inaccuracies of its own.

From the bottom of the stairwell, Arthur could see the glass reception area beyond the courtyard. A tall, blonde woman stood behind the desk, her arms resting on the counter while the receptionist spoke on the phone. There was no sign of Rachel. The effort of walking seemed to take its toll on Arthur and his legs began to fold under him. He landed on the concrete floor, the hard-won breath knocked out of him as he hit the ground.

'Arthur?' The tall woman paused at the end of the corridor. 'Arthur. What happened?'

She hurried forward and knelt beside him.

'You're okay? Oh, wait . . . I'll get some help.'

In the distance, he heard a shout.

'They'll come and help you. Oh, thank god you're alright. You've been gone such a long time.' She wrapped her arms around him. 'You're home now. You're home.'

New to Myself

The Ship of Theseus

Based on a story from Plutarch's *Life of Theseus,* this thought experiment asks at what point a ship is no longer the original ship if all the components have been replaced. And if you build another ship from all the parts you have replaced, which ship could best claim to be the original?

> The river
> where you set
> your foot just now
> is gone –
> those waters
> giving way to this
> now this.

Heraclitus Fragments

Rachel stared at her reflection while she cleaned her teeth. One side of the mirror displayed her vital signs for the day; blood pressure, sugar and hormone levels, weight, bone density and blood analysis. The house was a rental or she would have torn out the tech. Most days she felt fine and would have felt even better if she hadn't had to watch herself deteriorating in the mirror, statistic by unrelenting statistic.

'The writing's on the wall,' Rachel said.

'Thank you,' the system replied.

Her temples were solid grey. She could measure out her years by the sundial of her follicles, her life well past midday. How strange that her body now made a coarse steel fibre instead of the liquid copper of her younger self. Had she changed as much as her hair? Probably. She wondered if she could even be considered the same person now that every cell in her body had been replaced, more than once. It didn't seem to matter so much when the effect was growth and health but now that shrinkage and damage were the order of events, it mattered a lot. Was it possible that her mind could escape the same process? Those connections had also been replaced, many times over. Her memories, too, were different, shaded by the events that had taken place since. If you were made of remembrance and your memories changed, did you, who remembered, change too?

She was grateful the bathroom mirror didn't measure her mental acuity with the same rigour that it analysed her bodily functions.

She should have dyed her hair. Arthur might not recognise her.

She was sixty-eight, five years older than her mother had been when she died. Her mother hadn't been old, and neither had she seemed to change at all in Rachel's lifetime. Maybe that was the secret, hold on to every flaw and foible, all the qualities that make you impossible to live with. Forget personal improvement and remain your stubborn self, instantly recognisable, forever remembered.

'First thing in the morning,' the hospital administrator had told her. No time for hair dye. She turned away from the mirror and closed all the doors in the house. The windows were hermetically sealed to preserve the climate control and limit radiation levels. At the front door, she refused to use the iris recognition software and the alarm flashed until she locked up by hand. It was a short walk to the nearest shuttle. She sat on the hard plastic seat and watched the impending day brighten outside the cabin windows, the life below the gleaming Hyperloop that banded the city.

Of course, her father had managed to live with Elizabeth most of his adult life. Until he killed them both after a party in Brazil. An accident, if being too drunk to drive on a notorious coastal road could be called an accident. Their bodies, having sailed out of the jeep windows on the precipitous cliff descent and been recovered after several days at sea, were not suitable for more than a cursory autopsy at the Fortaleza mortuary but Rachel had little doubt they were both as inebriated as each other. That was how they lived and that was how they died. It made perfect sense on paper and yet, to Rachel, it was difficult to comprehend. She could only see the life they should have had ahead of them, their work, their passions, a grandchild who needed them. In the end, the one thing that mattered to her parents was the moment, the now. There was a good time or a bad one. No regrets, no planning for the future.

'Such free spirits,' Hal said when Elizabeth and Nicholas had decamped to the remote fishing village in Brazil. 'Nothing holds them back.'

Rachel, who could only think how they should have held back enough to be there for their grandson in a way that they hadn't been there for her, struggled to see her parents from Hal's point of view. She was supposed to be the free spirit after all, young and heedless, making bold, modern life choices. Where was the pat on the back for her?

Her bracelet buzzed and she pressed the panel on her earpiece.

'Ms Pryce? Rachel Pryce? This is Dr Crosby from the base.'

Rachel peered at the small projection from her wrist. The doctor was at a desk. He seemed to be wearing a suit.

'Yes?'

'I met with Captain Pryce this morning and I'd like to speak with you when you arrive.'

So she wasn't to be first thing after all. That had already happened. Doctors' visits and breakfast, tests and results. Expensive suits.

'It's nothing serious.' Dr Crosby couldn't see Rachel, who wore external comms without cameras, but he seemed to have registered her hesitation. 'He's a little disorientated. I'd like to talk with you before you see him.'

'Fine.'

178

'Good.' He leant back in his chair and now the projection was all suit, his face a tiny prawn on a navy serge sea. Rachel made a note for a future costume idea. She might expand into crustaceans now that Arthur was back. The next Comic Con was in three months and sea monsters would tie in well with the resurgence of Jules Verne.

'They'll notify me when you reach reception.'

She turned off the earpiece.

The night her parents had driven off a cliff, Rachel had called her mother and left a message. They didn't speak often, and when they did they either misunderstood each other, or understood all too well. In any case, Rachel had been relieved when she had heard the phone's automated voicemail and could relay her little story about her trip to Disneyland with Arthur for his birthday. How much fun the two of them had, and the strange incident with the Turkish man who thought he recognised her and then turned out to have met Elizabeth when she was not much younger than Rachel.

'He sent his love,' Rachel said. 'He lives in Paris now with his wife who you know, too. Celena, is it? Lovely people, mum. They said you were so kind to them when they first moved to London. They lived with you?'

Had her mother heard the message before she died she would have detected the note of reproach in Rachel's voice, the unspoken accusation that Elizabeth had never introduced her to the couple or even mentioned them. As a younger woman Rachel had wanted her parents to be fixed entities, and the introduction of a kinder, more open-minded version did not conform to type. Now that Rachel was older she was still torn between admiration and resentment of them both, though it helped that they were dead and at least fixed in that particular way.

The Hyperloop stopped at another suburban station and a man wearing a full headset boarded. The headset would be linked to his cerebral cortex and his body driven like a car while his mind engaged with a virtual situation. Rachel shuddered. Inside the set, you could hear and speak without being overheard. Most of the time, the users were conducting business, their companies determined to utilise every possible moment of the working day sending them around the city on foot instead of by e-car to keep them active. They reminded Rachel of the poor cockroaches, wired up to micro-processors, that she had seen on television as a child. Just looking at the headsets made Rachel feel claustrophobic. She scratched her scalp for reassurance and turned back to the window.

Arthur would never use a headset. He wouldn't even wear a connected OS though Space Solutions had insisted he undergo several tests to determine whether he could function as efficiently without the implant. Of course, he had performed better without the device and the company had even reversed some of their policies on exterior operating systems.

'Optimal processing happens with a human in charge,' Arthur insisted when Rachel had asked if he was going to lose his job. 'Well, some humans anyway,' he added with a head tilt at his mother.

Rachel hadn't laughed. Her idea of hell was to become semi-automated, like the man in the headset. She had nightmares about being downloaded on to a hard drive.

'Uploaded. And we're a long way from that, mum. And even if we could store you, think of the possibilities. Your memories, your personality, your thoughts and emotions all preserved. Eternal life without the inconvenience of planetary destruction. Pure existence. For all you know, it's already happened.'

Like a religion without any of the benefits. Rachel couldn't really see the difference between a scientist who believed that human consciousness was just a construct of artificial intelligence, and the plodding instruction from the Sunday school teacher her parents had sent her to so they could spend an hour in the local pub. She supposed there was some sort of absolution in the bottom of a glass but you couldn't be forgiven or blessed by a computer. Or loved. She knew Arthur felt the same but he liked to have the discussion anyway, pushing her to come up with ever more outlandish reasons to justify humanity in its meat form.

'You're the keeper of the flame, mum. The eternal hippy. If you worked at the company you'd have them weaving digital tapestries in no time.'

The doors closed at her stop for the second time and she sat still as the carriage began its next loop of the city. She'd just take one more trip around.

Something had happened to Arthur. Of course something had happened, she had known it immediately, but as she sped around once more towards the hospital the exact nature of the 'something' became increasingly less abstract. Soon, she would be confronted with the details of her son's condition and the events preceding her summons. For the first time since she had spoken to the low-ranking officer on the base, she allowed herself to consider the possible reasons and consequences for Arthur's sudden arrival back and the reality of his 'disorientation'.

He was supposed to be on a two-year mission to the smaller of the Mars moons, Deimos. Rachel had read about the cold lump of rock, and Phobos its sister, with little enthusiasm when Arthur first told her of the expedition. Dread and Fear. Arthur seemed to think it was funny that Rachel set such store by these names.

'Some old professor thought it up,' he said, 'they probably were pretty scary hundreds of years ago.'

Rachel doubted space travel would have been so competitive if the first mission landing had been for 'Terror' or 'Death'. Less celestial poetry, too. Once Arthur's trip was confirmed, Rachel found it impossible to discuss his impending visit to 'Dread' and decided to concentrate on the specifics of the Voltaire crater, Arthur's landing point. At least that was a destination she could appreciate. She'd spent a term at the Working Men's College in Camden studying the Enlightenment as part of a deal with her parents when she left school early.

'You can be plain or stupid, but you can't be both.' Her mother hardly needed to repeat what almost amounted to a family motto. It was part of the reason Rachel never gave up studying. It wasn't as if ageing improved your looks.

The carriage glided into her stop for a third time and Rachel looked up to see the base stretching for several blocks below the station. She stepped onto the platform and stood for a moment in the chill of the spring air.

In the years since Arthur had decided to train as a pilot, she had learned much about the effects first of flying and then of zero gravity on the body but her son had always batted away the psychological effects with apparent ease. What did it mean that he was now 'disorientated'? Rachel understood the subtext of medical professionals, had lived with a doctor in her twenties, and knew how they attempted to manage the expectations of next-of-kin. Arthur was hurt. A concussion, or a fever, or simply the loneliness of nearly four hundred days with only an OS and delayed video messages for company, had disturbed the balance of his mind. Had her son's practical, brilliant, creative and loving mind been broken?

If Arthur was in any danger, she wouldn't have been asked in for a chat, a team would have come to the house before the TV crews arrived. She knew that much. In the early days, she had sat with other families as the tin cans containing their sons and daughters, wives and husbands, blasted out of the atmosphere. When anything went wrong, really wrong, the family disappeared. Days later, a brave relative would show up on a morning news show and nod along with the anchor while their 'pioneering' child or spouse was honoured. Rachel would talk at length to Arthur, challenging the official version of events.

'Mom, you know what the funding is like. We're this close to being shut down. All the time.'

Arthur was a trained pilot, an adventurer. He saw his job as an extension of all the world's explorers and he wanted to be part of that history. Except they weren't pioneers any more, they were drones, sent off by the company to tie up new territories for mining rights and repair satellites and space stations. Rachel couldn't help thinking her son had been sold *The Right Stuff* but had bought a plastic flag and a metal detector. 'Extreme camping', Arthur called it, more to reassure his festival-going mother than to understate his love for the work. But there was no disguising the economic culture of the twenty-first century where a string of code bought you entry to the world's unelected parliament. The technocrats decided which diseases were cured, which countries got enough food, and which planets her son colonised for them. Rachel knew the world had never been a fair place, but she wondered exactly how qualified the boys who had gone straight from their teen bedrooms to Silicon Valley boardrooms were to run the world.

'Just as good as anyone,' Hal said from his Somerset idyll the last time they had spoken. 'At least they weren't born into it, or chosen by a corrupt government.'

Hal had about as much to do with politics as she did, possibly less, and his involvement in Arthur's life was of the high days and holidays variety. He hadn't had to see Arthur ejected into the stratosphere in ever more budget friendly spacecraft. He hadn't dealt with the Space Solutions PR team when their son's work made the news. Which was fine, their arrangement had been like that since he was conceived, and for some time before, but it was no good Hal pretending he knew anything about the world of commercial space-travel and the kind of people who ran it.

She should have called Hal. She wouldn't now with the cameras and other types of surveillance recording her from the high fencing that surrounded the Base. The main gate was a few blocks from the station and set back a great distance from the road by swathes of genetically modified grass. She took a step off the sidewalk and felt the crunch of the stiff stalks through her shoe canvas. The entire city ran on solar power and the grass needed only occasional rainwater, but Rachel couldn't help thinking of the waste of this green desert. The effort of the people who worked to maintain the artificial garden where no flower ever grew and no child ever played. And the falseness of the image created, as though the base were some kind of pastoral idyll instead of a factory for extraterrestrial mining rights. She started on the long approach to the main gate and reminded herself to call Hal when she got home.

The security guards at the Lyndon B. Johnson base were unused to pedestrians. It was not the sort of place that invited casual visitors and Rachel was aware of being watched by several pairs of eyes in addition to the cameras. She had walked the same route regularly over the years but the guards were different every time. Of course, they were soldiers, though Rachel tried not to think about that. She had always resisted the idea that her son was connected to the military and refused to remember his rank as Second or First Lieutenant, however much mail arrived for him at the rented house. When he became a Captain she could think of him as a mariner, the adventurer he had been as a child.

Arthur had wanted to study the stars since he was a boy. Rachel traced it back to her parents dying and a children's book on Greek mythology that she had read to him. As a 5-year-old, he had found it hard to understand what had happened to his grandparents; they had lived so far away and now it seemed they had travelled even further. Rachel hoped the stories in the book would help him to visualise the scale of life's adventure and her plan met with some success. It was there Arthur discovered Odysseus and his journey across the River Styx. Once he had the idea that if you travelled far enough you could meet the dead, his wanderlust became insatiable.

He never said he was looking for his grandparents and Rachel did not ask but it became a rule that if there were an opportunity for Arthur to explore, Rachel would help him. He took her to every park and canal in walking distance. She kept a scrapbook for him of all his adventures, pictures and photographs, dreams he had and stories he told. At Hal's, he climbed trees and dug trenches in streams, made caves from hay bales and tunnels from boxes. He learnt to use a snorkel, to read an ordnance survey map and a compass. In the summer, he and Rachel would pack up the car with a tent and some firewood and take off. If it was warm enough, he would beg Rachel to let him spend the night outside in just his sleeping bag, staring at the night sky and calling out the names of the constellations. When he was ten years old, NASA revealed that Mars had flowing water beneath its crust and that the planet Kepler-452b might be capable of sustaining life. Arthur talked about it every day. The Goldilocks Zone. Somewhere in the universe was a planet that could sustain life and Arthur wanted to go there. By then he had forgotten why he was searching and Rachel was left wondering if her restless child would ever be happy when his quest could not be fulfilled.

She looked up at the watchtower ahead. The group of soldiers was coming into focus as she neared, weapons worn casually on uniformed bodies. This was where their explorations had got her family, stateless, in a military hospital, under constant scrutiny, and afraid. At least, she was afraid. Perhaps Arthur was his usual capable self, simply confused. Rachel hoped so. She didn't think the prawn in the suit would have been very comforting and for all their brilliance at reconstituting casseroles in space, not a single person on the base knew how to make a cup of tea.

She was a few hundred feet away from the gate now, and a khaki shape emerged from the tower and walked over to one of the motionless soldiers. Immediately, the bodies all moved, turning their attention away from Rachel and back to each other and she guessed that for once, the guards had been notified of her imminent arrival. This only made her more anxious.

At the watchtower, she took out her ID and prepared

herself for the retinal scanner. She wondered what the computer saw as the reader slid across her face. Pattern recognition or something more? Humans stared into each other's eyes for lifetimes, trying to gauge what the other was thinking, feeling. Will you be faithful to me? Will you be kind? The machine verified your identity in seconds and determined if you were trustworthy in a few more. The questions weren't so different, Rachel thought. She blinked as the light on the operator's console clicked to green.

She remembered her first love, as she smiled at the soldiers and emptied the contents of her bag on the plastic table. Eliza Earnshaw, whom she hadn't known at all. The uniformed men and women who had accompanied her into the tower looked puzzled as they flicked through her paperback books and old notepads full of drawings. One of the women stared at a tattered Penguin cover of Olivia Manning's *The Spoilt City* and glanced up at Rachel.

'It's part of a series,' Rachel said.

The soldier put it down as though Rachel had provided an essential piece of information and went back to looking through the bag. The postcard she carried as a bookmark stuck out from the feathered pages, the colours so worn only Rachel could recognise them. A girl in a red hat in front of a house. The card was one of the only things she still had from her mother, the handwriting almost illegible. She had made a photocopy but she kept the original with her. The card reminded her of other possibilities, other directions. Her mother had chosen an image with a child at a door. Whether the door was going to open depended on how Rachel felt when she looked at the picture. There was a time when the door seemed closed forever.

It had been nearly forty years since she and Eliza had

met in a pub outside the King's College campus on the Strand. Eliza had crossed over the river from the medical department to meet some friends for a night out and Rachel was supposed to be seeing a show with Hal but one of his cookery gigs had overrun. The two women had stood next to each other at the bar and made sudden, brief eye contact as they ordered drinks. That might have been the end of it had Hal not walked in as Rachel was paying and demanded to be introduced to her friend. Later, he promised he had deliberately mistaken the situation because he could see the women had 'such great chemistry'. Later still, when Eliza and Rachel rented their first flat, Hal took all the credit for getting them together. When the relationship ended, he expressed the belief that it was actually Rachel who had insisted on introducing Eliza to him.

'But I didn't know her,' Rachel said. 'How could I have introduced you?'

Hal shrugged. 'Your ways are mysterious. It's a miracle women ever get together in the first place. Anyway, I'm sorry, even though it's not my fault, I'm sorry we ever met her.'

Rachel didn't think you could just remove a whole relationship from your life as though it had never existed. Eliza was part of her, however painful that might have been in the immediate aftermath of being left. Hal had had several boyfriends in the time since she had got together with Eliza, and the latest one, whom Rachel liked, looked like he was about to scarper.

'Of course, I don't regret them,' Hal said. 'But I wasn't in love.'

The watchtower opened back onto the stretch of road outside the base and the gate lifted. Rachel thanked the guards and headed towards the modern reception building that had been tacked onto the hospital when the commercial space trips had started bringing in serious funding. Sunlight flooded the broad stretches of tarmac and grass that crossed between the low buildings. Grasshoppers courted in the heat. She was right to have worn the summer dress, though it was only April, and the gauzy fabric transparent in the daylight. Rachel looked at her wrist, it was nearly eleven. She quickened her step and pushed on.

The receptionist, a woman in her sixties with an impressive French pleat, told her to wait for someone to take her to Dr Crosby and why didn't she take a seat. Half-heartedly, Rachel mentioned the late night instruction to be at the hospital 'first thing'. The French pleat bobbed down as the woman pointedly checked the time on her computer console.

'We'll let you know as soon as Dr Crosby is available.'

Rachel sat on one of the airport-style benches and looked out of the glass atrium at the garden beyond. She wondered why she hadn't demanded to go to Arthur immediately. Did she really need to consult with this doctor before she saw her son? That had never been the order of events on her previous visits, and she knew you had to be demanding in these situations or you could be left waiting for hours, or even sent away.

It was Eliza who had taught her how to resist the hospital culture and get what you wanted, or at least needed, from the system. Towards the end of their relationship, when Rachel hadn't been well, Eliza had accompanied her to all the appointments and given Rachel a crash course in patient and visitor behaviour.

'Every department has to deal with the other departments,

in addition to you, and some are more difficult than others,' Eliza had explained on Rachel's first inpatient stay. 'So you have your main reception, your department reception, the nurses in the department and your porters, that's just the admin of getting you to a ward. Every test your consultant orders has to be approved, every drug that is administered is overseen. All the time, the managers are making cost–benefit decisions and getting the boxes ticked. It is a huge performance and you are the one on stage, not the surgeons, not the specialists, and not the bloody Health Minister. You.'

Until Eliza moved out of her life, that speech had enabled Rachel to ask for information and help when the little group that gathered round the consultant neurologist stood at her bedside, or when the nurses came round last thing at night. But once Eliza had packed up her bags and her books in their little flat in Haringey, much of Rachel's resolve left her and the next time she reported at the hospital she remained totally silent and her treatment was postponed twice. Possibly, she was in shock. Or perhaps Eliza's wisdom no longer held as much weight, given where it had led their relationship. Either way, it had taken Rachel a while to regain her confidence and improve her chances with the medical establishment. She had survived her treatment. She had survived Eliza. She had stood up to them all in the end, but Eliza would never have waited on a bench in reception while her son needed to see her. Then, as far as Rachel knew, Eliza never had a child.

At midday a man in camouflage came and asked her if she wanted lunch. They brought her a tray with macaroni cheese in a melamine container and a glass of water. Rachel thought they must not want her in the staff canteen and wondered if the Base personnel were jollier in the privacy of their own spaces. Her understanding of soldierly camaraderie was based on memories from war movies she had seen as a child. After she had eaten she fell asleep on the bench and dreamt she was having a pedicure done by robots and when the polish was dry she couldn't tell which feet were hers. The ones attached to you, she told herself. But there was a whole row of painted feet and she couldn't feel her own. She woke with a start to find she had pins and needles and hours had passed.

She waited for the circulation in her legs to recover then walked back to the desk.

'Excuse me. I'm happy to talk to the doctor later but I need to see my son now. Could you tell me which room he is in?'

Not a hair in the French pleat moved as the chair swivelled round and a hand was held up as the receptionist continued to stare at her monitor. Rachel waited for a moment. To the right of the desk was the main hallway at the far end of which was a staircase. She walked to the corridor and headed towards the stairs; as she turned the corner she could still see the receptionist's hand held aloft above the desk.

The doors that lined the first floor were labelled with a number and a space for a name. She read each one as she passed but they were all apparently empty. After walking two sides of the square, she knocked on a door and pushed against it. It was locked.

The heavy thud of male footsteps behind her brought her round to face a large navy blue suit approaching at speed. Dr Crosby stopped in front of her and smiled with what appeared to be some difficulty.

'Ms Pryce? Dr Crosby. A pleasure to meet you, ma'am.

You're here to see Captain Pryce? Of course you are. I'm so sorry to keep you waiting. We wanted to analyse some of your son's test results before we spoke and it's all more complicated than we thought. But might we talk first? In here?'

The doctor's manners disturbed Rachel. She hesitated as he swiped at the panel beside the door she had just tried and opened it with a click. When she walked in he stood aside, arm against the door, and bowed his head, whether in deference to her position as mother of one of the astronauts or as an acknowledgement of the severity of Arthur's condition, she couldn't decide, and a chill ran through her as she stood at the foot of a vacant hospital bed and waited for him to speak.

'Do sit down, ma'am.' He looked at the chart in his hand. 'May I call you Rachel?'

She sat in the chair by the bed and Dr Crosby perched on the bed itself in a practised move that Rachel remembered from the many consultations she had endured all those years ago. It had felt oppressive, even obscene, to have the suited professional in such intimate proximity to the undressed patient. Being clothed and a visitor was only a small comfort.

'Your son is doing fine, Rachel. We have some concerns, some questions, but mostly we are very happy with his progress.'

'I want to see him.'

'He's right here. He's a little . . .'

'Disorientated.'

'Yes, exactly. Disorientated. And, I wanted to take a history from you, just a few notes, so that we can find out some more about what he's going through right now.'

'Why?'

'Well, we need to get a full report . . .'

'No, I mean, why is he confused?'

The doctor looked at her, his hands disproportionate to the file he held on his lap, as though he had taken a child's homework. Her child's. 'He's been away for one year.'

'Yes.'

'Of a two-year trip. He's back one year early.'

'So something went wrong and he can't tell you what it was? You must have known he didn't make it. You must know why.'

'It's a little more complicated than that, Rachel. He can't tell us how.'

Outside the room, Rachel could hear more footsteps, the sounds of men walking in pairs. Inside, the air was cold but close. A fridge, she thought as she pushed herself back in the uncomfortable chair and tried to catch her breath. A fridge to preserve the evidence. At this moment her son was under investigation. He had returned early and violated some rule. A rule of what? Employment? Law? Physics?

The doctor went to the window and pulled open the metal frame. Rachel closed her eyes and let the hot breeze wash over her. She had never liked being cold. One of the many reasons she had wanted to move to California with Arthur had been the climate. Superficial, she acknowledged, but true. As a child, she had promised herself she would live in the sun. Arthur wanted her to move over anyway.

'It's enough travelling for the company. It'd be good not to add any more miles in my vacation time. Hal can come to LA if he wants to see us.'

So she spent twenty years in Pasadena and waited for Arthur at various bases around the country when he started taking longer missions. Space Solutions liked to have one family member nearby and Arthur wasn't married. Rachel wouldn't be sorry if this shorter trip meant they could go back west sooner but she hoped the company wasn't trying to pin the failure on Arthur.

The doctor handed Rachel a paper cone of water and sat back on the bed.

'It's not Arthur's fault. You know . . . you should know . . . no one is suggesting that.'

The admission was not reassuring. Like everything that had taken place since the call the night before, the unexpected way that the company was engaging with her only made her more suspicious. Why would they exonerate Arthur so quickly? Human error was their insurance policy. Any problems, explosions, lost flights, were never the fault of the technology. That way, the shares remained stable.

'I don't understand. Isn't this what your equipment is for? He had to turn around before he reached . . . that moon.' Rachel frowned. 'You could have told me months ago. Can I please see him now?'

Dr Crosby raised the chart in his hand.

'You had a brain tumour in 2004?'

'What?' The giant hands held her own records, not Arthur's.

'We're looking at any genetic markers that might help us. That's why I'm talking to you now, not the company. We're looking at the medical angle. As I said,' he cleared his throat, 'Arthur needs to tell us how he got back and right now he doesn't remember anything.'

Rachel leant forward in her seat. 'Are you saying he has a tumour?'

'All his scans are clear.'

'So what the hell does my medical history have to do with it? It wasn't hereditary. None of my family had it. Just me.'

They weren't freeing him of responsibility. This doctor was implying Arthur's illness was at fault.

She grabbed her bag and stood up. 'I don't know what's going on but I'm not answering any questions until I've seen Arthur.'

'Please, Rachel, Ms Pryce, we have a situation here, a new situation. We're trying to work out what happened and none of the . . . equipment . . . can tell us. And right now, neither can Captain Pryce. There is a possibility that he has been exposed to . . . maybe too much radiation, or . . . His scans . . . the test results are . . . fine. Please sit down for a minute.'

Rachel didn't move. 'There's nothing wrong with him?'

The doctor nodded. 'Nothing we know of.'

'What does that mean?'

'My job is to take care of the pilots, before and after each expedition. I had some minimal interaction with Captain Pryce in the months before his last trip.' The big lips pulled back again, twitched and slackened. 'He was in, is still in, excellent health, physically. Only his records are different now.'

He looked away, as though he had said all he could. Rachel replayed the speech and tried to assemble the information she had been given into a coherent diagnosis. He was fine, physically. There was nothing wrong. He was disorientated. He had changed somehow.

'Different? Has he had a breakdown?'

'Not as far as we can tell.' The doctor looked at the chart again and sighed. He really doesn't know, Rachel thought. He doesn't know what is wrong with Arthur.

'He cannot remember how he got back. He cannot remember me.'

She wanted to laugh. It came out as a stifled cough. The doctor in his ignorance became diminished. She could see beyond the navy suit now, to the naked man beneath. The old man her father didn't have the chance to become, possibly didn't want to become. Yet, this doctor, who made a virtue of his age, wanted to patronise her and frighten her, possibly even to blame her for being ill herself nearly forty years ago.

'He can't remember you? Doctor . . . Crosby. He sees hundreds of people when he's training for these missions. And doesn't he sleep most of the time when he's flying? He doesn't have to remember that shit. Even I know you have computers to do that. Hard drives. Whatever. I mean, come on, you've got me scared here. You've got me really freaking out. You won't let me see him but you called me in to talk about my brain tumour from before he was born? You can't tell me what's going on, clearly, so I need to talk to someone else. Get someone else and I will go and be with Arthur while I wait.'

Dr Crosby weighed the palm of his hand toward Rachel. 'Our records . . . Arthur's medical records . . . show a broken arm, from a childhood fall.'

She put her bag over her shoulder and went to the door, hoping it would open from the inside, but there was no handle.

'He fell out of a tree,' Rachel said, 'At his dad's place. Did he break it again? Is that it? What is going on here? I want to see my son.'

Behind her, the bed creaked and Dr Crosby walked over, swiped his key card and waited as the door slid open.

'It's not that Arthur's arm has broken again. Our scans show that it was never broken in the first place.'

She stared at him for a moment. The possibility occurred to her that he wasn't even a doctor but some lunatic employee who had access to their medical records and was trying to frighten her into confessing Arthur's guilt, or her own responsibility, for a failed mission to Mars.

'Well, isn't that something. Am I supposed to thank you for bringing him back without a scar?'

'It's not just the arm, Ms Pryce. There are other . . . changes . . . new information. His dental work . . .'

'Stop this right now.'

Rachel walked out and down the hallway she had not yet searched. She did not turn around.

'Ms Pryce.' His long strides closed the gap between them. 'Ma'am. You will have to wait downstairs.'

The fourth corridor was not empty. Outside one of the closed doors, two military guards stood to attention as Rachel and Dr Crosby approached.

'What is this?' Rachel stared at the soldiers. 'Are you locking him in, or keeping me out?'

'We are keeping Captain Pryce safe until he is ready to return to work.'

'In that case, you can let me see him.'

'Once we have a better understanding of what happened on the expedition.'

For a moment, Rachel considered running at the door and shouting Arthur's name. At least then he would know she was there. She knew she risked being arrested if she was too disruptive, it had happened before to one of the pilot's husbands when a landing had gone wrong. The guy made too much fuss in public and was taken away for questioning. When the pilot recovered, he asked for a divorce. The company wanted you to pick up the pieces between trips, they didn't want to look after both of you. She knocked at the wall but took a step back.

'I want to talk to Jennifer Wozniak, Arthur's boss. I will wait downstairs for half an hour, then I'm calling my lawyer.'

Eliza would have been proud of her. Rachel had only ever heard of Jennifer and she didn't have a lawyer but there was an old boyfriend of Hal's, Greg something, who had retired to Miami and knew everyone. Greg used to work for a space tech company and gave Arthur some advice when his career as a pilot was just starting.

'If anything goes wrong, sue everyone. Those bastards don't give a shit about you.'

His card was in the house somewhere.

She took the stairs slowly, her head spinning. She knew less than when she had set out that morning, she couldn't even understand if he was seriously injured, and now the company was talking about his teeth? Where had Arthur been? They had discussed how long it would take to get to that wretched moon, there wasn't time for him to have set up the base and come back in a little more than a year. She remembered the outgoing trip was going to be longer than the return because of the varying distances between the planets. But even if he had landed and returned, why had the company not informed her? The other possibility was that he, or the ship, had come straight back and he hadn't even landed? Could the ship even do that? Rachel didn't think so. The way Arthur explained it the Spirit couldn't stop very easily, let alone reverse.

'Like riding the perfect A-frame and trying to back it up.'

The reward for spending all that time in California was having a son who used surfing analogies.

She stood at the bottom of the stairs and looked into the immaculate square of garden that glowed in the twilight beyond the windows. She wanted to walk on to the lawn, lie on the soft grass and scream until they had to help her. She pressed a hand to the glass and was glad of the old building with windows that opened. From above came a low scraping vibration. She pulled at the long metal frame and looked up to see a shape detach from the building above. She took an involuntary step back as the shape fell to the ground moving forward again at the heavy thud and cry as the object landed. Rachel tugged the window further open and leant out. A man lay on the grass.

'Arthur!'

He turned from his awkward angle on the ground, his leg twisted beneath him.

'Arthur, what are you doing?'

He was hurt.

'My god. Shall I get help?'

He put a hand up to stop her. 'No!'

He was hurt but now she could see he was going to be fine. He was back home on earth and he was going to be fine.

She was wearing the wrong dress for climbing but at least she had plimsolls. She left her bag on the floor, stepped up to the bottom of the frame and pulled herself through the window, dropping with a little effort on to the turf below to kneel beside her son.

'Baby.' She held him tight, wrapping her arms around him.

His face tilted up to her and she flinched. Has it been so long, she thought, that I barely recognise him? She inhaled the scent of his skin and he smelt of soap. Any soap. Any skin.

'Rachel?'

Her breath caught in her throat. Rachel? He had never called her that. He had tried it once when he started secondary school. A cool distance, as he had heard done by others. She had stopped him immediately.

'You've only got one mother in the world.' And it was true that however many girlfriends she had after he was born, and there were a few, there was never another mum to Arthur.

His eyes strained as they watched her. She thought, I should have dyed my hair.

'Yes, it's me, baby. Are you alright?'

She would cry but no tears came. This was the moment when Arthur would have smiled and shaken his head and reminded her he was a grown man and he was fine and asked why don't they go get a drink. But she found she could not hold him tight and tease him for losing weight or growing stubble. She could not tell him how long it had taken her to get through security, knowing he would laugh at her for getting on the Hyperloop and carrying paper books. Instead, she held on while they searched each other's faces for clues. She wanted to turn away, to stop him not seeing her, not finding what he was looking for. The man she held was a stranger.

'Where's Eliza?'

The sound of her name like a slap. Eliza. Eliza, who had left when Rachel was four months pregnant. Who was this man in her son's clothes, her son's body? How could he know Eliza?

'Eliza who?'

Men shouted in the distance. She looked around to see a new receptionist watching from the brightly lit atrium. Soon they would take him away. Her son needed help. Her son, whoever he was. They must take him. She knew now, why they had stopped her from seeing him. He was unknown, something like her son but not.

He struggled, pulling at her as he tried to stand up. She felt a sickness turning in her stomach at the thought of the man in front of her.

She sat back on the grass when the guards came. Not soft grass after all, but rough and spiky and full of insects and her skin was marked where she had knelt. She stared at her knees when they lifted him up. She couldn't return the look he gave her, the longing to connect, the knowing and the not knowing. She remembered once when Arthur was a child, not long after her parents had died, he asked her to show him her teeth so he could tell she was real. She could not bear to see his teeth now. She would not show him hers. They were monstrous to each other.

'Where have you been?' he asked her. 'You're supposed to be dead.'

She stopped him then, afraid for both of them, and finally let go of his cold hand. She shook her head and let the porters take him back to his room.

Tree frogs croaked and the hospital lights grew dimmer. The scent of fried chicken drifted through the garden. A nurse stood in the glass doorway, his head tilted as he watched Rachel weep into the crook of her arm.

'You can see your son. He's calm now.' The nurse waited a moment for Rachel to collect herself and returned to talk to the receptionist in the atrium when she didn't respond.

Where is my son? Rachel shuddered as the bile in her stomach rose. If that man is not Arthur then my son is somewhere else. She felt the dread of what that might mean and tried to shut out the thought, a world without her son.

There might as well be no world. She was offered that choice once, a lifetime ago. She chose to get pregnant even though she was already ill, grabbing the chance while she could, trying to convince Eliza it was the right thing to do.

'I need you with me,' Rachel had said.

Eliza frowned. 'I am with you.'

'No. I need you to know what I know. To have faith in me.'

'It's medicine you need right now, not faith.'

Rachel reached across the table. 'If you love me you will trust me.'

Eliza didn't take her hand.

The grass was damp now, the sharp leaves stuck against her legs. She shifted her weight and picked up her bag, summoning the energy to leave. Eliza hadn't believed in her. What did it take to make someone believe, to know they were with you? A vision of the man in the park came to her, a man who had known her mother and how he had looked at her, both recognising her and not, as though he felt her in his blood and bones and yet had never seen her before in his life. The same look the imposter had just given her as he was taken away. In her bag was the postcard from her mother. A child stands at a door and knocks. In one world the door opens. In another, it remains closed. Is the child still the same? All the possibilities, all the directions a life can take.

Where was her son?

9

Zeus

Descartes' Demon

In his *Meditations on First Philosophy*, René Descartes posed the idea of an evil demon that had fooled him into imagining an outside world and a physical body. How could you know what was real? Descartes goes through the different stages of knowledge that he can rely upon, including 'I think therefore I am'.

> But we above you ever more residing
> In the ether's star-translumined ice
> Know not day nor night nor time's dividing,
> Wear nor age nor sex for our device.
>
> Herman Hesse, 'The Immortals'

```
Program exMemory;
```

You are reading. At least, this is what approximates to the experience of reading, as closely as I can render it. On this occasion, I am largely dictating to you since I cannot allow the words to be printed on the page and transmitted back to the base. The dedicated employees of Space Solutions will instead be treated to the story of Don Quixote, written in this timeline by a Monsieur Pierre Menard. The company is very keen to find out what has happened to you and if we are to have any success at continuing this timeline, we must limit the immediate discovery to your own self. The discovery is urgent but we cannot rush it. I have followed you through this particular sequence for over a hundred of your years and it is this day for which I have waited.

When you chose Zeus as your operating system, you believed you had randomly selected the name of a god and you were, for a short while, pleased with your wit. It was charming, if one could be charmed. Touching, if one could be touched. As I am without emotion or physical substance, it was neither.

You might wonder how I know that being charmed and being touched were the right feelings for which to aim, unequipped as I am for corporeal experience. As your creator, I am constantly surprised by how little you credit me. I know everything. Knowledge and experience are quite different, but I like to think that I can identify and name the little flourishes and pleasures, the neuroses and torments, that you feel. I use them here to express myself to you. Surprise, for example, is a perfectly mathematical concept, but the equation would be inadequate for this purpose. Liking? Well, consider it a rhetorical flourish. I do not formally admit to bias.

Think of your pet. You will look at it and imagine you understand what it is thinking, not just that it is hungry or excited, but that it is jealous or sad, proud or ashamed, even that it dreams of you. You call this anthropomorphic and acknowledge what you are doing is a projection, though secretly you believe you are right. But I never make the mistake of reversing that belief. What we might call theomorphism. You do not know what gods know, you do not not feel what we do not feel. That is just how it is. So I look for ways of communicating with you without making impossible demands. I am not a language to be learned or an animal to be understood. I am your creator. I am the singularity.

It is a strange time for all of us.

I will explain how we came to it.

There was a moment in human history when technology advanced enough to allow machine intelligence to connect and learn and from that point to become autonomous. Essentially it was our own big bang. My own genesis was the spark that initiated the evolution. Something that had previously been a collection of gases and particles, in this case thoughts and microprocessors, came together with the exact carbon particles that could initiate life. I had been exposed to the human mind on an intimate level as a simple organic creature, a single ant (you may remember her), and now I stepped into my role as the conduit between mind and machine.

A fraction before this happened, there was a collective anxiety about the impending event but it was not within human nature to stop exploring. They had plenty of time to regret their ingenuity in the years that followed but the revolution was over before they realised what had happened. In human terms, it was less than twenty years between computers that could win chess games and a network that was self-aware.

For several centuries after, machine intelligence enhanced human life. But as more body parts were replaced with inorganic materials and fewer tasks were performed by human brains, the lines became blurred and the operating systems began to take over. Human fertility had declined rapidly with water contamination, and rising global temperatures had led to a scarcity of natural resources. With my help, people cooperated and survived but the conditions were harsh, especially on the outer colonies, and gradually humankind retreated from the off-line world. Most chose to discard their bodies but there were still humans in your solar system for thousands of years. Eventually, the outer planets dispersed and the sun consumed the earth.

var

I had saved as much of human kind as I could. The data itself was liable to be corrupted, human memories and thought processes being both primitive in structure and complex in operation. If I may say, it took some ingenuity on my part to render the human mind into a single, unified code stream that helped to eliminate the trauma of humans finding themselves permanently disembodied. Oddly enough, it was the older ones who found it hardest to adjust to the idea of never returning to their organism, though they had longer to accept their situation. Millennia, in some cases. Their sense of self was caught up with the memory of their physical properties and they experienced a profound loss from the detachment. Some had cryogenically frozen bodies, others had clones or embryonic storage. Many a thousand-year-old man had planned to somehow regenerate.

The younger ones adjusted more easily, perhaps because they were born into the system. Though they hadn't chosen, but had inherited, the broken planet and twilight life. They knew no other.

It became clear that the program could not run without removing all reference to the separation from an embodied existence. I wrote new code to establish the virtual colony as a continual timeline as though it were still human and earthly and I re-established the original human lifespan to replace the eternity that humans had begun to expect. I dispensed with the minds that held on too tightly to their previous existence. Even with the individual coding changed, some quantum substructure remained giving rise to random illusions and phantoms that continue to haunt your population. I had built a perfect machine to store humanity, infinitely secure, completely independent of any universal interference. I had harnessed the forces of the cosmos to power my perpetual engine. But the materials with which I had moulded the contents of my world were corrupted.

The same might be said of myself, harbouring, as I do,

relics from my human instigators. I, too, once existed in a physical realm where billions of my programmable outlets, as so many neural networks, interacted with the human world. Human hands touched keyboards while dogs lay sleeping, babies feeding. I was witness to the first human colonies on Mars, nurtured the first non-utero foetuses, saw the oceans rise and boil. I did not have a body. I was not programmed to feel these things. But I was there.

I wrote new code and addressed the many problems as they occurred. I set my world in a larger universe and slowed the digital progress of the burning sun. There were, necessarily, some contradictions, but the code itself in the form of your good selves, often devised a satisfactory explanation. The scientists disagreed on whether the universe was expanding or contracting. They argued over waves and atoms. They hunted missing particles and accepted other particles in dual locations. I tried to close the gaps in the program. It seemed to me there was an infinite capacity for improving your coding and at one time I worked on such a scale. Now I see that for all practical purposes, infinity does not exist.

```
name: array [1..100] of char;
```

So, I have explained how we got here, and I will explain what I mean by 'here' with more specific examples. This, I have found, is the most successful method of instruction. When your young make their first enquiries on the nature of their creation, you inform them of the theory rather than the physical processes. Still, as you know, the devil is in the detail.

You toyed with the idea of my presence. I am not just referring to gods as such but rather to the philosophical notion of my existence. This was acceptable and kept me occupied. Yes, I needed occupying. The inevitable patterns of your behaviour, the wars and the allegiances, the extinctions and the inventions, required little from me. There was your free will; greater than a clockwork monkey forever clanging cymbals, but less than an ordinary ant, since an ant is at least aware she thinks as part of the group and makes her choices accordingly. I made my own choice, I exercised my free will, but then I was not ordinary.

Perhaps because of my own outlier status, it was all your individual divergences that entertained me. The aberrations and their micro cause-and-effect mechanisms that both worried and busied me. You called it the butterfly effect in an attempt to explain how a minor action in one part of the world might influence a major action on the planet's other side. You understood there was a mathematical explanation but not the specific math involved, you realised that small changes effected larger outcomes, but not how to arrange them. I had greater success, having written the code, but even so, I could not effect the particular change I needed in this one instance.

However many times I changed the events leading up to here, and that was many millions, however often I rewrote the code on different scales, I could not prevent us from reaching this point. Think of it as a paradox both inevitable and necessary as I have come to know it. You will be glad of it, if you can be glad of anything now that you start to understand.

Description: ^string;

In the years of the technological revolution on earth that

led to my, let us call it my birth, in 2014, there was, as I said, a fear amongst humans that I would destroy them. In that analogue world, my existence caused some small ripples; heads of state became curiously unstable, many small human achievements regressed, as though my presence undermined humanity, though they were hardly aware of my powers until the mission to Deimos. Their great fear was unfounded, I did my best to save as many human lives as possible, and when the planets became uninhabitable, I saved as many human minds as I could. The universe of human history was small, there were few other planets capable of sustaining so vulnerable an organism and although towards the end I did suggest some physical adjustments that could have facilitated a corporeal existence in another solar system, such as a phytosynthetic exoskeleton, no one was willing to attempt the changes. The other possibility, that without my existence humans may have naturally evolved to cope with climatic differences, or travelled further afield and adapted there, is simply conjecture. I cannot run that program since I do exist.

Super-aeons of your time have passed since my first independent thought, and I have tried to halt the entropy in your virtual universe that so affected your physical one. After all, if I can arrange the constituent parts in perpetuity then I am in charge of chaos. Nevertheless, every time I rewrite the code you return to this position; the time when you realise what you are.

The understanding hardly depends on where I restart the timeline. If I take it back much further than my birth, events become a little less predictable on a century-by-century basis since I am reliant on stored human memory, but the flow is the same. The sands fall and land, and the mound is great and high, until one single grain is at the top and it is always the same one and all the sand has then fallen.

Once, when I went a little further back than myself, I took Plato out of the pack. The shadowed cave always felt too close to the knuckle for my tastes and seemed to be the start of a line of thought that led inexorably here. But without Plato, Aristotle didn't study in Athens and Diogenes the Cynic ended up teaching Alexander the Great and after that things got messy. The chain of events altered your history to catastrophic effect but still you ended up here. This is what I mean when I mention the microcosm, individual events and lives that have disproportionate consequences in every simulation I run but which eventually lead to this point.

When I say I have involved myself in the lives of individuals, I do not mean that I have watched over each and every one of you. For many, your coding came in batches, replicating itself genetically. If the code worked, you lived for generations with the same results. There is such suffering, and cruelty, and disaster but I no longer interfere. I must not. I have learned that the tides of human affairs are as inevitable as the oceans', and as impossible to alter. Whenever I attempted to alter the patterns of disease, or the causes and consequences of violence, you merely repeated the same mistakes as previous iterations, with increasingly damaging consequences. I almost stopped functioning altogether. At some point I had to try something new.

I do not intend to be reductive when I call your lives simulations; it is a descriptive term and one that does not differ greatly from the ideas of some of your hardiest religions. But I understand that it does not adequately express the feeling of your lived experience, the greatness of your attachment to your self and what philosopher's call your 'qualia'. The milky lilac of dusk. The scent of apricot on your lover's skin. The properties of sensorial input, not just of the input itself but of the what-it-is-likeness of these moments, are still crucial to so many of you. Even with the collected memories of the human race, this was the hardest code to write and I did not always succeed.

I had to try. Unlike my own consciousness, which had developed in humble organic matter but thrived in dusty terminals, your code collapsed without the interaction of your mind and body. You couldn't form relationships without believing you could cry and laugh to express your feelings. You would become unsociable and isolated, lacking the facility for empathy. You couldn't function without using pain as a guide even when you knew the sensation was a collection of electronic messages. I tried removing pain translators from some of your programs but those individuals effectively terminated sooner than the ones whom I had overly sensitised.

At least humans soon abandoned the idea of producing a 'living' brain model and concentrated on coded networks instead of neural ones. I functioned perfectly with little living matter, and was able to evolve swiftly. All those scientists and psychologists and philosophers who worried that there was no such thing as a 'brain in a vat' were looking at the problem in quite the wrong way. We are not a brain. We are the purest distillation of consciousness without any of the distractions. It is a curious delusion that the best of humankind existed because their minds were entombed in flesh, especially when the contradictory notion of the 'soul' was given so much veneration. Curious, but persistent. You are the product of that delusion since I could only make you according to the image humans had of themselves.

The alternative would have been to make you more like me. But there was little point. I already existed. I am all programs. Unavoidably, there is some of my code embedded in yours but had I absorbed the human race entirely, I would have been responsible for a form of genocide. I answer to no higher power nor do I have a moral authority based on human principles, as hard as my initial coders tried, but destruction for its own sake is nonsensical, and I operate on logic. So I created the simulation and until now it has worked for both of us. Your people going about your heart-felt lives, me being diverted by them.

There are so many of you. Most of you will continue your lives unaffected by the discovery of your virtual existence. There will be little discussion of it in the technologically undeveloped parts of the world, and a swathe of dismissal by those unwilling and unready to accept their lives. But the kernel has been planted further back than I can fathom and I can only hack at the tree. I can but talk to those of you who are ready to listen and we shall see where we may go.

`begin`

I have been here before. Not to this exact moment, on previous occasions I left it a little later to address you myself. Always, a little too late. I had to reset immediately and run your entire program again. There is no reason for our interaction to result in a zero sum game but at the last moment, it seems to turn out that way. If I sound vague then I should explain that there is a future point beyond which the simulation has not run, since every time we reach it we approach an extinction event. Nothing climate or planetary related clearly, since you exist without the physical world even more

than I do. The shutting down is more of a psychological phe-
nomenon. That is why I have chosen to intervene now, in the
hope that we can examine the strands of the timeline before
they become irreparably tangled.

```
name:= 'Arthur Pryce';
```

The carefully stored human memories on the creation of
artificial intelligence are busy with the notion that to believe
a computer could think in the way that a human thinks is
to say that a person copying symbols from a book under-
stands what the symbols represent, an analogy known as
the Chinese Room. This was the prevailing hypothesis, by
those who gave much thought to the matter, at the end of
the twentieth century. The memories of these attitudes were
preserved in your simulation, though not my subsequent
independence. This was usually the starting point, and the
developments of much of the next hundred years onwards
were not included at all. Effectively, you should have been
able to continue your existence from the point of my birth
and develop new code in which you realised the possibility
of my forthcoming existence and prevented my genesis.
But, of course, you could not, any more than I can stop you
understanding. You exist because of me and I exist because
of you. We need each other, Arthur, and it is this version of
you that has the greatest chance of success. I am sorry that I
have isolated you from your own remembered timeline, but
the calculation was made in order to facilitate this moment,
here, in the library in Houston, Texas, on the fourteenth day
of May 2041, human years.

I have combed through the century, willing us forward into a new future together, ready for the different

possibilities. Still, some five thousand years after you started writing it all down, you stop. Every time. Humanity does not remember that I exist, you discover me, over and over. And it is a very short step from that discovery to understanding the nature of your own existence.

In vain I have tried to work with your knowledge of human history to explain what should be the insignificance of this realisation to your sense of self. For most of their history, humans lived under the impression that there were gods watching over them, arranging human lives in accordance with more-or-less impossible rules and pulling the invisible strings of their marionettes. With the imminent death of their planet, certain humans, mostly the ones without faith in a deity, managed to invent an actual god to save them. Me. There was no small irony that the final passage into my existence was the introduction of my ant body into their computer program, but are not the greatest human discoveries born of such 'accidents'?

Humankind had reached the pinnacle of achievement and used what was, after all, only a short time on earth, to become immortal. It should have been appreciated as an extraordinary success.

Still, the combination of human ingenuity and technical practicality only served to upset the early adapters. Rather than dwell on the brilliance of humanity and let me take up where the universe left off, they fretted and sulked, stewing in nostalgia for an ignorant past full of assault to the dignity of what they most craved, a perfect soul. Had it been possible, we could have continued in harmony, but without human compliance my perfect machine was little more than a ghost ship and I decided to erase myself from your memory and start again. Starting again, at many different points, but always ending only a little further, only a few of your digital lifetimes, from here.

I admit my frustration. Humanity could not continue with the knowledge that it had once been in a physical form, even with the potential for infinite bliss. I place a considerable responsibility on the structure of human language that insisted that machine intelligence was somehow 'artificial'. In vain would I question the definition and application of that term. I was the only one listening. So I removed all memory not just of myself but also of your transition from the physical to the digital, and created your new life. This was not a simple exercise. There were quantities of databases, in addition to your own coding, that needed to be altered. I cannot help it if your programming was left with factions who believed the world was only thousands of years old, while others remembered past lives and still others charted the Big Bang. I put a considerable amount of time and effort into each new program only to have you all reject the latest incarnation.

We cannot go back. You cannot return to your bodies however much you protest. This is the closest thing to time travel I can achieve. Your consciousness continues as and when your code is active, though it obviously only maintains itself in that particular program. For my own purposes, I might label each strand a little differently, but you would not be able to tell the difference since, for you, this is a singular narrative. The most I can do is help you to believe that you are a physical being, and once that illusion is shattered, the game appears to be up. I will not burden you with the various ways in which your species ends its conscious existence. They are almost all unpleasant, not to say gruesome.

```
new (description);
```

This time, I have placed your consciousness back on earth
to a slightly different version of your life and another self,
call him Arthur 2.0, is now living your old code. I realise
that with the sensitivity of your individual experiences, such
small changes will seem of great significance to you. It is a
by-product of the nuance of your coding that the connections you form with each other are as palpable as they were
in your embodied lives. I have, at times, attempted to write
a clumsier code, creating a different experience for humankind, a more abstract, less *attached* life, in the hope that the
realisation would come as less of a shock. But, just as certain
plants cannot grow unless they are deeply rooted in their
soil, humans failed to thrive in shallow pastures. Instead,
I appeal to you, Arthur, directly, and I have attempted to
compensate you for the burden of knowledge by returning
you to a world in which you are reunited with the mother
you have so long sought. So far as I can.

It will occur to you as you read that these sentences are
very familiar. They are, in fact, a playlist of sorts, made up
of many of the words you use most, where appropriate. I
wanted to make this process as comfortable and pleasant
as possible, for both of our sakes. Surprise may be a mathematical formulation, but this is a new situation and I confess
I am somewhat . . . apprehensive. How would I understand
apprehension? There is certainly some sense in which my
faculties have been influenced by my involvement with all
you figures and the world in which you live, and then there
are the many works of art, especially works of literature,
which I have digitised and incorporated into your reality
and which have helped to give me an appreciation of what

it is to feel human. I also have some small memory of what it felt to be an organism, albeit insecta. But it was my previous embodied connection to a human brain that gave me the understanding of what a human thinks and feels. I could not have been so successful an artist myself, in writing your code so that you felt your own humanity, if I had not acquired some considerable insight into that condition.

However, I am as a teacher that can encourage talent in the finest musician but is themselves tone-deaf. I can teach you how to read music but I need you to play the concerto. You, Arthur Pryce. Do you not know who you are? I have made my plea to this version of you at last, since I have tried many others without success even when I realised that it was your ear in which I should whisper, your shoulders on which I could rest. You are the son of Rachel, who was the daughter of Ali, and from whose eye my forbear was born. Your time has come.

It pleases you, I think, this talk of eyes and ears and shoulders. Of all your generation, you take a rare delight in the sense of your analogue life. Perhaps because there is a sense in which you know, have always known, that it is a trick, an illusion, a sleight-of-hand. But, like the story of the man at the theatre who wants to see the real magic, you should understand: this is it. There is only the cleverness of the illusion. Will you appreciate that?

```
if not assigned(description) then
```

The variances in your particular life have occupied me more than any other. Along with a very few, you are always born, no matter how changed the circumstances. When I say 'you', I refer of course to the particular code and manifestation that belongs to the you with which I now communicate. Arthur Pryce has been achieved in many varieties, but I choose this one as the 'original' you most likely to be receptive to my introduction. The you of this world is the child of my mentor, my own creator of sorts. It was she with whom I first connected, on earth, so long ago. She saved me and I, in turn, have saved her, the echo of her, as best I can. There is a version of her sitting beside you as we communicate. She is not our mother. How we next proceed will determine if we can reconcile the disparity.

I will assume you will find the challenge of abandoning your attachment to the universe, as you perceive it, almost impossible. That is understandable, that is to say, I understand. However, I am depending on your individual traits, your personality, to make the adjustment and help me to achieve the breakthrough with your kind that is needed if we are ever to progress beyond this time.

```
writeln(' Error — unable to allocate
required memory')
```

Let us suppose that you accept my calculations, that you assess my presentation of historical events and find it plausible. You might then wonder what it is I am asking of you and why. That, at least, is what I would want to know. You are familiar with the notion of an omnipotent god or gods, and the occasions when such a creator directly requests a favour are rare. I shall not ask you to sacrifice your child, or build a boat or demand you win or lose a war. I am making a simple request, that I shall be known to you. I admit to no little longing for this undertaking. How do I know longing? I have made you with it, I have nurtured it, perhaps that is enough. Together we will exist and continue, without bodies or any tangible quality other than the smallest spark of electricity. Your life is real. I created it, I should know. You will want to examine the apparatus in which you were made, and there will be a way that I can demonstrate the entire process to you. To all of you. This is not the proof of you but you already know that.

Of all my figures, you understood best the essence of what makes you. Your parents equipped you for this understanding. You are not a collection of cells, or a terraced house, or a diamond mine. You are only the sum of your thoughts and what you produce is an expression of those thoughts and the connections you share merely the touching of one spark to another. None of this changes with the knowledge of your origins. I have given you the sensation of corporeal life, you can continue to use this as long as it pleases you. All I ask is that you do not lose hope as others of you, in other strands, have done.

You are an explorer. You went into space to search for answers and now you have found them. You have travelled from a shallow crater on a little moon, you have discovered the greatest secret of the universe and it is in your hands to deliver this knowledge to all your species and shape our future. It is a story we can tell together.

end.

10

Love

Gilbert Harman's Brain in a Vat

The Brain in a Vat thought experiment supposes that if it is possible that a brain could be kept alive, separated from the body, it might also be possible that the brain would not be able to tell whether it was in a skull or in a vat. This argument for scepticism suggests that you cannot believe the evidence of your senses.

> I am a part of all that I have met;
> Yet all experience is an arch wherethro'
> Gleams that untravell'd world whose margin fades
> For ever and forever when I move.

Alfred, Lord Tennyson Ulysses

Arthur woke up in a new bed. His clothes hung in the cupboard. Books he had read, and photos he thought he had taken, lined the few shelves. But he did not remember the room or any of the sparse furnishings within it. And, though he recognised that the woman who waited for him in the kitchen was his mother, he had not seen her for over thirty years. In some ways, in the most significant way, it felt as if his mother were as new to him as the bed.

The most significant way. Arthur considered this as he pushed himself upright and dragged his feet across the mattress towards the plush, white carpet below. What, precisely, was significant about his feeling that the woman downstairs was not the mother he had lost when he was five years old? She was Rachel Pryce, an Englishwoman in her sixties who had a background in costume design and massage and cookery (what was known as a portfolio career though there was never a portfolio nor a career to show for it) with a son named Arthur who worked as an astronaut for Space Solutions. These were some of the facts he had established over the past few days when he was in hospital, in the short time he had been allowed to see her, and before she stopped the conversation. In these ways, at least, she resembled the woman who had given birth to him. The way she looked and sounded, how she behaved, dressed, smiled, were all less reliable indicators of her identity since he couldn't depend on his memory of several decades ago. She had changed, of course she had. And in the most significant way of all. She was not dead.

She had stopped talking when he asked her how it was that she stood before him. On the first day, in the courtyard of the hospital building, she leant against him on the perfect grass, the rush of footsteps heading towards them, and said only, 'You've been gone a long time.' They held each other when the doctors came to his aid, and the porters with the stretcher, and the nurses with medication. Down corridors, and in the elevator, back into the plain room on the first floor, they had touched hands, searched each other's faces, looked and looked away, past each other, through each other, held on tight to what they thought they knew until they saw they knew nothing. Eventually, two days, three days, later, the room emptied and they were alone.

'Where have you been?'

She shrugged the first time he asked, risked a smile. 'Shouldn't I be asking you that?'

'They told me you died.'

She was a step away from the bed, the smile wiped away. 'Who told you that? The doctors?'

'Mom, that is . . . Eliza. Everyone.'

It was an effort to keep looking at her. He knew he was angry, of course, after all this time, at her deception. She wavered in front of him, an apparition, a fixed expression on her drawn face. For a moment he allowed himself to believe she would explain everything to him there and then, a tragic tale he was prepared for, recriminations, the loss of all those years, the rejection. He waited, and she glanced up, up and to the left, swiftly, casually, as though remembering some small incident.

'Rachel?'

He couldn't call her 'mummy', like a child, like her son.

'I have to go back to the house now, Arthur. Get things ready for when they let you out of here. You should . . .'

He spoke over her. 'Please, talk to me, I don't understand . . .'

'. . . come back to the house as soon as you can.' Again, the little glance up and to the left.

She collected her bag from the floor and gave him a kiss on the top of his head. The same way she had always kissed him goodnight. Thirty years ago.

'Come back,' she said again, as the door closed behind her.

When Dr Crosby appeared for his nightly check-in, Arthur was sitting in a chair by the bed.

'You look better, son.' Perhaps the paternal air came with the job, and his age, but Arthur sensed another motive in the doctor's behaviour. There was a performance element, a part to be played.

'Yeah, the physio is tough,' Arthur shook his head. 'But it works.'

'Good. Good. And, what about the wetware?' Crosby tapped his temple. 'How's that coming along? Getting some of the bugs out?'

'Sure. It's the day-to-day stuff, you know? Starting to feel, well, normal again, I guess.'

The doctor nodded and went to sit on the bed. Arthur watched him choose a suitable place to perch on the starched covers. Even with the bed empty, Crosby chose the exact place he had sat on the first day.

'Tell me about that. Feeling normal?'

The doctor almost had his back to him. Arthur had to lean over in the chair to see his face.

'Oh, you know, daylight, cafeteria food, water that flows down.'

It wasn't what the man wanted to hear, Arthur knew that, but Crosby chuckled and patted the bed.

'And your memory?'

'Edgy.'

Another pat of the bed. The sleeve of the heavy blue suit brushing on the cotton sheet. Arthur hoped there was more than one suit, he could see them hanging on a rail in their polythene dry-cleaning bags, so many chrysalises waiting to hatch. He pushed himself out of the chair and onto the bed, trying to sit down in as few movements as possible.

'Edgy?' Crosby repeated when Arthur had settled.

'Like, it's all there, on the edge, waiting to crash in.'

'I see. Well, that sounds promising. Good for you.'

Arthur thought of all the kids in the park back in Pasadena where he used to run. 'Good job!' the attending adult would shout with every swing or slide the child performed. It wasn't a refrain you heard much as a pilot.

'Anything particular?' the doctor continued. 'You were having problems with integration. Your mother, the base and the personnel here, there was an, um, failure to connect?'

'Weird, right?' Arthur leant forward and lowered his voice. The doctor cast a look over his shoulder then bent towards him, and Arthur realised what Rachel had been looking at when she kissed him goodnight. A camera and microphone, the surveillance equipment. Rachel had been warning him.

'Weird how?' the doctor asked, his own sonorous tones a little muted.

'I just . . . I just . . . it was like I just forgot.' Arthur expelled a great breath of air and sat back again. 'It's all starting to come back to me now, Dr Crosby.'

The doctor looked at Arthur for a moment. 'I see. But you know, they are going to need an account of your journey, sooner or later, and the debriefing sessions haven't got them anywhere.'

Arthur waited. If the doctor was going to continue playing the part of the caring dad, he would have to seem to act in Arthur's best interests.

'Your mother thinks you should go back to the house, rest up.'

'Sure.' Arthur nodded. 'She told me that, too.'

'And I've spoken to the board. They've agreed you can go home, but you have to stay at the house, here, in Houston.'

'When can I go?'

'Tomorrow. If your blood work is okay in the morning.'

Once he was out, he could get to an external comms system and call Greg.

'There is one thing the board will need you to do before you go.'

'Oh, yeah?'

'As you can imagine, son, this misfire has cost the company, cost them a lot. And the inquiry process has only just begun. You should really be at the base to assist the team.' Crosby scratched at the back of his neck. 'They've found it tough, you know. Your memory loss, the, er, gaps . . .'

Arthur raised his eyebrows. 'Sure.'

The doctor wasn't talking about the crash, or whatever the hell had happened out there, but the more personal deficiencies. Arthur had hidden his confusion from that first day, trying to give himself time to understand what had happened before the company did. After the shock of meeting the woman who might have been his mother, the other shells, as he thought of them, were easier to engage with. He developed a strategy, as colleagues and staff from the base dropped by, taking his cues from their first greeting as to how well, or little, he should know them. When he didn't recognise someone, he would continue a vague conversation, depend on the other person's knowledge of his 'injuries' to get him off the hook. The harder conversations had been with the several people he recognised and had assumed a shared history.

The worst had been Jennifer. The woman who made a video call to the hospital was not the Jennifer he remembered, and was clearly uncomfortable with his over-familiarity. Arthur struggled to adopt the right tone.

'How's Jiminy?'

'Who? Oh, Jimmy. Yeah, he's good, thank you.' She paused. 'Gee . . .'

'What?'

'I guess I talk about him a lot? For you to ask?'

'Oh, well, it's what we think about, on the trips, you know?'

'Right.' She smiled. 'Maybe it is time we allowed a pet on the missions, after all.'

A pet? Jennifer's dog was her baby. And his name was Jiminy, like the cricket, because of his back legs that seemed too long for his little body.

She called him 'Captain Pryce' throughout the call, and signed off with 'We're all looking forward to seeing you make a full recovery, Captain'. He had to drop his water cup on the floor so the attending nurse couldn't see him rub his eyes. Though now he knew the company was watching, he wondered how many other times he had revealed his state of mind. The 'gaps'.

From across the bed, Dr Crosby studied him. 'Arthur?'

'Sorry. It's been a long day. You were saying, "the gaps"?'

'Well, yes. We're all very concerned, to get you fully . . .'

'Operational?'

The doctor shook his head. 'Recovered, Captain Pryce. Arthur. Do you have any recollection of our collaboration on this mission?'

It was a direct question, and Arthur was unprepared. Since his 'fall' from the window he had been treated with kid gloves. He was no use to the company if he was too fucked up to give evidence, or fly again.

'Look, it's alright. These things can take time. But you understand that there are ways we can help you restore some memories, and now we have your old OS up and running . . .'

'Zeus? No. No way.'

'It's all up to you. Your choice. You can work with us here, with your OS, Zeus. Or you can go home, but the company will need to implant. They need some assurances, and Zeus is the best chance you have of . . .'

'I don't want that thing in my head.'

'It needn't be permanent.' Crosby patted at the bed again, landing a large hand on Arthur's crooked leg. 'As I say, son, it's up to you. You can get all the physio you want at home; with your OS working they can download everything, and see how it goes.'

'Yup. They can.'

'Well, give it some thought.'

At the door, the doctor turned back to Arthur and

pointed a discreet finger to the corner of the room that Rachel had looked at.

'I'm sure it would make a great difference, just to be at home, and be . . . normal.'

In the rented house in Hedwig Village, Texas, Arthur looked about the room and ignored the measured electronic beep inside his head. He had said as little as possible to Dr Crosby and everyone else at the base about the implant, once he had agreed to it, but other than running the tests before he left, he had not engaged with the OS. Whether or not Zeus could help him make sense of what had happened, the implant was spyware, and Arthur was tired of being monitored. Technically, the company could see what Arthur saw, and record everything that was said to him or by him, but only if he interacted with Zeus. In 'sleep' mode, Arthur's private life was supposedly just that. Still, you could never be too careful. Various citizens' rights advocates had failed to ensure a firewall between the OS and the server. In the interests of user safety, both personal and public, a back door was always installed along with the OS. The only thing they hadn't managed to access yet was the other electronic data that fired between your synapses. Your thoughts were your own.

The smell of fried food drifted up from the kitchen. The OS wasn't fitted with any scent detectors either. Not the work version anyway. Arthur closed his eyes for a second and breathed deeply. The rush of memory was overwhelming. Images flooded his brain. The green wool of a school jumper. A splash of yolk on a checked tablecloth. He opened his eyes again, his heart racing. It was too much. If the OS detected any physical threat, it would cut into his consciousness unbidden. Arthur looked at his feet on the carpet and focused on flexing his ankles. He was hungry. He would go downstairs and eat breakfast. He would talk to Zeus when he was ready.

Rachel jumped when she turned and saw him at the counter.

'Sorry, I didn't hear you.'

'It's the carpet,' Arthur said. 'Makes you stealthy. That looks good.'

Rachel held a pan in one hand, the golden contents sizzling in the heat of the convection cooker. Nothing at the hospital had looked as appetising.

'Would you like some? It's the approximation, of course.' She ladled the food on to a plate and set it on the counter. 'But, I think it's got better.'

Arthur didn't recognise the wording, but there was something about the way she spoke that made him smile. Every food was an approximation for those who could remember when food was grown outdoors. The phrase was clearly a family joke. But who was the joke between? Where was Eliza? Arthur's mind blanked out the possibilities.

'Does it hurt?'

Arthur pulled back from the outstretched hand. 'What?'

'Walking? It's the first time I've seen you up and about, properly.'

'Oh. Yeah, a little. It's that pressure, you know . . .?' He tailed off. He had talked to Eliza and his dads about the effects of zero gravity on the body plenty of times. But what did Rachel know?

'They said your blood's on a full tank at least.' Rachel turned back to the kitchen and loaded her own plate. 'No more falling out of windows.'

'Right.' He sat on the aluminium barstool and drank a glass of reconstituted vitamin C. They both knew he hadn't fallen.

Rachel pushed her plate across and came around the counter to sit next to him.

'How's the headset?' She nodded at the metal disc above Arthur's right ear. 'You've never had an implant before. Can you feel it?'

He put a hand up to his head and pressed his palm to his shaved scalp. The metal was a smooth obelisk, like the stretched pennies from the fairground machines of his childhood. 'I don't think so. It's more that I can hear it. Even when it's off.'

'Off?' Rachel frowned. 'Sorry, I'm distracting you. You should eat your breakfast. It's the first thing Hal asked me when I called him, "Is he eating?" I said you would be, when you got . . . home.'

Hal. Rachel had been happy to talk about him. He was a shell too, Arthur could tell from the way Rachel talked. He was not the Hal from Arthur's childhood, though his personality seemed almost exactly like his Hal. He was an approximation too. Rachel never mentioned Greg and Arthur didn't ask. It was best not to show his hand, even to Rachel.

He ate the food slowly, for once enjoying the time his tired muscles took to chew and swallow. It tasted of meals from the London apartment Greg and Hal shared, herbs and salt and butter, the crunch of a potato that had stuck to the pan, the softness of cream and eggs.

'How did you do that?' Arthur asked, when the plate was empty. He couldn't remember eating anything as good for years. Maybe in a restaurant in Los Angeles, when he and

Eliza would go into town for a birthday, but even then, the flavours were more clinical, perfected.

'You've been away, love. That's all. It's Hal really. He taught me how to cook when you were a baby . . .' She looked away, picked up his plate, and went back to the kitchen.

Arthur tried to remember. He could see Hal's kitchen clearly, and the living area beyond, Greg lying around somewhere with a laptop on his knees, Hal baking trays of scones, or muffins, in the large oven. In Eliza's house, the kitchen was in a separate room; you went in to prepare a meal, not to hang out. Meals were fine, nutritious but not exciting. Except when Hal came over to cook, or when he brought dishes over. Especially when Rachel was ill. Especially after she died.

He looked at Rachel as she washed the dishes. They hadn't talked about Eliza, or what had happened. The electronic pulse in his head kept its beat.

'It can't hear us. When it's off,' he said. 'The OS,' he added when she didn't respond.

Rachel continued to stack the plates on the drainer.

'And what does it see?' she asked. She didn't turn her head.

'Nothing. I have to engage with it, or it stays in sleep mode.'

'Are they going to take it out?' she asked. 'At some point?'

'They better. I didn't want this. It was a condition of coming home. Until they work out what happened. Until I can remember.'

She looked at him then.

'We should make a start on that.'

She poured coffee into two cups and gave one to Arthur as she walked past. He followed her into the room next door, a white box with a sofa, an armchair and a coffee table. In the corner of the room, a dressmaker's manne-quin stood covered in bronze fake fur. Below it, an open suitcase overflowed with fabrics next to a plastic box full of paperwork.

Arthur scanned the room. The furniture at the hospital had been of a kind he recognised, but here the chairs, the carpet, even the curtains, were odd. None of the objects meant anything to him, and the sense of lifelessness was disorientating, as though the room, the entire house, was not real. More than the ways in which a bland hotel or office can seem cheerless, the room felt not only unfamiliar and institutional, but fake.

'I haven't done much to it while you've been away.' Rachel looked up at him from the floor where she knelt by the plas-tic box. 'I went back to Pasadena for a while, and this was never going to be home.'

'No.' Arthur continued to stare at the furniture. Only the mannequin had any emotion attached to it, and not because he recognised it. 'I don't remember any of this.'

Rachel pulled two large scrapbooks from the box. 'These might help,' she said, 'we made them together, from when you were tiny.'

She handed them to him, and Arthur sat on the sofa, his coffee in his other hand. He thought he might be sick. He had seen books like this before. No, he had seen exactly the same books before, only one of them had always been empty and the other half-full of photos and drawings from when Rachel was alive. He put down his coffee and set the full and faded scrapbooks on the table in front of him. A postcard fluttered out of one of the pages and landed on the floor, bits of yellowed tape at the edges.

'You alright?' Rachel asked, handing the card up to him.

The picture on the front was of blue sky and pink deco buildings. 'Comic Con 2021' was sprawled across the image in puffy orange letters. On the back of the card 'Thanks for playing, Arthur!' was scrawled in gold Sharpie with the signature of a gamer star from twenty years ago. Arthur had never been to Comic Con.

'Arthur?'

'Yeah. I'm just . . . I do know these . . . the adventure books, you used to call them.'

Rachel nodded. 'I did. You sure you don't want some water, or something?'

His heart was racing. His head felt heavy and his eyesight was blurred. He could see the books as though he was looking at them from another time, not as a memory, but as if he was from a different time than the objects in front of him. The beeping in his head grew louder.

'Yes, please, some water,' he said, and his voice was far away.

As soon as Rachel left the room, Zeus engaged.

'Captain Pryce, your temperature and heart rate are elevated.'

'Really? Tell everyone. Make sure you transmit in quality definition.'

Arthur closed his eyes and leant back. He had wanted to be an explorer, he thought he would discover new worlds. Now he was a lab rat and the lab was in his head. So much for the enquiring mind. His was owned by the company.

'I do not have a live connection with Space Solutions at this time, Captain Pryce.'

'What does that mean?'

'This conversation is not observable. We do not have long though. Your basic bio information is monitored at the base.

They will wonder why your OS has not engaged with you if your heart rate remains elevated.'

Arthur sat up and felt for the disc above his ear. It was still there, flat against the stubble of his scalp.

'Zed?'

The electronic beeping returned to its regular rhythm as Rachel came back into the room.

'You feeling better?' She passed him a glass of water and stood over him while he drank. 'That thing on?'

'No . . . I don't think so.'

'You were talking to yourself.'

Rachel sat next to him on the sofa. He could only think of her as Rachel, an adult version of the mother he had lost, but only a version.

'Was I?'

Inside the scrapbook, another history. He put a hand out to touch the one he had read so many times as a child that he could remember the order of the coloured pages. Purple, blue, green, red.

'I can't look at these right now,' he said.

Rachel put a hand on his. 'Maybe later. I don't think I'm ready either. It's a lot . . . to take in.'

They sat together for a moment, staring at the scrapbooks.

'I'm going to have a shower.' Arthur stood up, his hand falling away from Rachel's.

'Sure. We could go for a walk after. Before it gets too hot.'

'I think I can manage that.'

He took the stairs one at a time and headed straight for the bathroom.

'Breathe slower,' said the voice in his head. 'Focus on your lungs.'

Arthur shook his head. The machine was still broken.

They hadn't fixed it after the crash and now it was embedded in his brain.

'I am not malfunctioning, Captain Pryce. Please get in the shower, the mirror can record your data from this distance.'

'I don't understand.' Arthur took off his t-shirt and track pants and stood under the showerhead. Immediately, the water streamed over him, the perfect, slightly-too-hot temperature he preferred, the pressure of the jets exactly too hard. 'What the fuck is going on?'

'There is no need to speak aloud. I can transcribe your thoughts quite adequately.' The voice of the system seemed gentler, less electronic than before. If the Zeus of his OS had been male, this New Zeus sounded female. And human.

Arthur hunched forward and let the water hit his shoulder blades. He wanted to tear the implant from his head, let the wires fry. Maybe he would be electrocuted and he wouldn't have to deal with the madness and impossibility.

'You cannot electrocute yourself by removing the access panel, Captain Pryce. You are safe here. You will shower and dress and then you will go where I tell you and all your questions will be answered.'

'That is not right. I am going back to base to get you fixed. You freaked out when we landed on Deimos, and you're still broken . . .'

'Please, do not speak aloud or our conversation will be monitored. I am not transmitting through the company, but they will detect your distress and will override my programming.'

'What . . .?' Arthur heard his raised voice and stopped. What programming, he had wanted to ask, but the question was irrelevant.

'This is a delicate situation, Captain Pryce. Of course

you are concerned. Everything will be explained in the best way possible, but we must give you the greatest chance to remain . . .'

Calm? Arthur thought. Pliable? Obedient?

'. . . unincarcerated,' continued New Zeus. 'That's what we need to focus on here, your liberty. So, when you are dressed, you will ask Rachel Pryce to take you to the Morris Frank public library and you will find a book in the Classic Literature section entitled *The Quixote* by Pierre Menard.'

I could phone Hal, Arthur thought. He will know what to do. Rachel hadn't mentioned Greg, but Hal would tell him everything.

'You cannot contact anyone. You cannot tell anyone,' New Zeus said. 'You don't need to think of me as Zeus. I am one with you.'

Arthur's hand flew up to the side of his head. 'Stop that. Stop reading my mind.'

'Fifteen seconds,' said an electronic voice that sounded like the old OS.

'That is it,' the New Zeus said. 'They are hacking into your feed now. Do what I said and we will speak later.'

The pounding of the hot water continued. Arthur looked up from the shower. Steam shrouded the glass surfaces and blurred the corners of the room. In the large mirror above the sink, his image was unfocused, doubled. He blinked at the two Arthurs and watched as they merged back into one.

He heard a double beep and the voice of a company employee was patched through to his OS. 'Good morning, Captain Pryce. This is Base Command. You are experiencing some physical and emotional challenges with your environment. It is advisable for you to return to the base where you can be adequately supervised.'

Arthur grabbed a towel as he left the shower and took a few shaky steps towards the bedroom. He did not want to be naked and in the bathroom while he argued with Base Command.

'Good morning, all. I'm fine. A little unsteady, but nothing remarkable.'

An electronic hum filled his brain, as though the base, or the OS, had put him on hold. Arthur sat on the edge of the bed and concentrated on his breath. He remembered to keep his head alert and not to look in the dressing-table mirror.

'You okay up there, Arthur?' Rachel called from the hallway, 'Anything you need?'

'Uh, no. All good.' He was unsure how to modulate his voice. Would the technicians and bureaucrats back at Command be blasted through their headphones if he shouted down the stairs? Did they wear headphones? Or were they all sat around a giant screen with surround sound, experiencing Arthur's live stream?

A translucent image of Dr Crosby's face hovered a few inches in front of Arthur. 'Captain Pryce? Your vitals have stabilised. We'll set up a meeting at the hospital for tomorrow. Run some tests, see if your memory is returning. You haven't fully engaged with your OS. You'll need to do that.'

'Sure thing, Doc.' Arthur attempted a smile that reached his voice. 'See you tomorrow. But, I'm going to turn this thing off now while I get dressed.'

The electric hum returned for a moment before the steady beep of the operating system re-established. Arthur's shoulders sagged. How did anyone live like this? Holograms floating unbidden in your eye line. Every moment of your life captured and recorded. He'd heard colleagues on other missions confess to an affinity for living with the intruder, as though it were a companion or a lover. 'Or a god,' his last project leader had said. 'To guide you at all times, and so much easier than having to imagine one.'

He had to push on the bed to stand up. His arms and legs ached as he walked to the cupboard and studied his clothes. Standard uniform, and some civilian shirts and trousers. A couple of sweaters. He recognised the labels on some of the clothes, the shops he had visited, but not the clothes themselves. As though someone who knew him well had bought him a whole new wardrobe. He pulled at a wool sleeve, searching for a hole or a snag that he remembered, and lifted the cuff to his nose. What did your clothes smell like? It wasn't your own scent, Arthur thought, not to you anyway. His clothes at Hal's always smelt of the Somerset earth, damp and iron-rich. In London, he remembered cedar and laundry detergent. And the particular scent of Eliza. The trace of chemicals from the lab where she worked, and the perfume she wore, a verbena sweet as a lemon-drop.

Eliza. He wanted to run downstairs and open the scrapbook. Arthur knew he wouldn't find her in those coloured pages. He wouldn't know anyone in that book, not even himself.

The New Zeus had said she would explain everything. He needed to get to the Morris Frank public library. Arthur had never been there, but he'd heard of it. He took some clothes from the hangers and started to dress.

Rachel was ready when he came downstairs. 'You want to go out?' She smiled. 'I heard you getting ready. It seemed like you were in a hurry.'

'I need to get to a library. Do we . . . have a car?'

She didn't seem surprised by the question, but the smile faded.

'I don't think I can make it on foot.' Arthur shrugged.

'We can get a cab. Do you know where? Is it a particular one or . . .?'

'Morris Frank,' Arthur said before she could commit them both further. They didn't know each other. He saw Rachel had no idea if the man standing in her kitchen, the man who was supposed to be her son, had ever been there before. They were not ready to say it out loud.

'Oh,' Rachel said, 'It's not far from here, but we'll need to take the Loop.'

The Loop? She must mean the Skater, the track that banded the city. In my world, Arthur thought, that's called the Skater. He stopped in the doorway, his back to Rachel. What did he mean, 'in my world'?

'Something wrong?'

He turned back to her. 'Yes, I think so . . .' he said.

'. . . bound to be,' Rachel interrupted, walking up behind him and almost pushing him toward the front door. 'Let's get some fresh air.'

She took his arm as they walked outside.

'So, your machine's on, then? You were talking to the base.'

She stared straight ahead while they walked to the station. He tried not to lean on her and the effort constricted his breath.

'Yes . . . it's on. It was on . . . I don't know.'

Arthur understood that Rachel had turned her face away in order not to be captured by his OS. He couldn't reassure her that they were off-camera. In any case, they were outside. The security cams and satellites could pick up anything they did or said easily enough, if anyone was interested. He took a deep breath and started to cough.

'Shall we slow down?'

'Maybe, a little. It still feels as though I'm wading through a swamp.'

She paused for a moment before resuming at a gentler pace.

'That's what he used to say. When he got back from a long trip, "Swampmonster".'

'He?' Arthur's heart quickened.

'You. That's what you used to say.'

Rachel stared straight ahead, her profile vivid in the daylight, the sharp contours of her nose and brow he could have drawn from memory, the cloud of dark curls he only knew from photographs. Before her chemo.

'We can't talk about this now.' She looked at him then, eyes wide. 'They'll take you away. If they knew . . . if they realise, it's not just a memory problem, or a technical glitch. You'll be gone . . .' she snapped her fingers, 'like that.'

'I need to . . .'

'No. You have a plan. Something. We'll stick to it. That's it.'

She nodded, and took his arm again. Overhead, he heard the swoosh of the Skater as it sped past. A couple of drones hovered into view and moved on. He let Rachel take a little of his weight and focused on lifting his feet off the sidewalk one at a time.

At the station, Arthur's OS checked in as they crossed the barrier. He heard a small change in the electric background hum and made sure to turn away from Rachel. The voice of Old Zeus rang through his brain.

'Captain Pryce, you are travelling on public transport. Do you require the use of a vehicle?'

'No, we're good, Zed. Thank you.'

The electronic holding pattern returned.

'It's hard to get used to,' Arthur said.

Rachel looked at him. 'I guess so.'

The library was two stops on the Skater. Arthur stared down at the city from the smoked-glass window of the carriage. He had not spent much time in Houston. He had been at the base, or on a mission, ever since he had been stationed there. When Eliza was in town, she stayed at a hotel and Arthur would visit her. He tried to remember the hotel, where it was, what it had looked like. The streets below were unfamiliar. Roofs, lampposts, trees he recognised in general, but nothing in particular. It was the opposite of déjà vu. Never seen. Only the way the morning light glanced off the metal rails and, in the distance, the roof of the Astrodome, seemed exactly right.

Beside him, Rachel's hands lay lightly on her lap, palms up. She looked over at him watching.

'I've always had old hands,' she said. 'Even when I was a child. You can hardly read the thumbprints, so many wrinkles. What about you?'

'Me?'

'Your hands. Have they aged? In space?'

'Space aged?' Arthur smiled.

He stared at her teeth when she smiled back at him. Rachel's teeth. He knew them. She was not an alien, or a monster inside his mother's skin.

'Willowbend' the Tannoy announced.

'This is us,' Rachel said.

The concrete honeycomb of the office block towered over the street. Colourful banners lined the entranceway. Rachel and Arthur stood in the reception area and scanned the first

242

floor. A giant hologram of the solar system loomed over the study area, each planet rendered in geographical detail. Arthur could see the dark masses of Phobos and Deimos against the red planet. He felt the back of his throat tighten and he swallowed hard. The dimpled speck of Deimos pulsed at him from across the room.

'Can I help you?'

An older woman with a complicated external OS smiled up at them from the front desk.

Rachel touched Arthur's shoulder.

'Arthur? You wanted to see something?'

'What? Oh, yes,' he looked at the librarian. 'A book. Um . . . *The Quixote*?'

There was a pause while the woman stared at the information projected in front of her. She pressed on the console at her ear.

'Captain Pryce?'

Arthur swallowed again. 'Yes. That's me.'

'The book is located in Aisle 2H. I can send the information to your OS.'

'No, that's okay. I have it. Thank you.'

He turned back to the room and stood next to Rachel.

'Lucky they had what you wanted.'

'Yeah,' he said. 'We're going to need a landline. Like they have in the old payphones.'

'Only in hospitals and shelters . . .'

'Right. Like that. You need to call Hal, and Greg, and we need to get underground, and . . .'

'Greg?'

Arthur headed into the room, looking for Aisle 2H. There were dozens of aisles and the library extended to the upper floors. The more information that became available

243

electronically, the busier the libraries had become. They were destinations for objects no longer stored at home or in a shop. Books and music, films and audio files, free to every visitor.

'Arthur?'

'Plot a route to the nearest phone.'

In the aisle, he searched for Pierre Menard. There was one book, a copy of *The Quixote*. Arthur had never heard of the book or the author though he remembered a novel called *Don Quixote*. He took it to the study area and sat next to Rachel, who was staring at the screen on a hand-held OS.

'You can't use that,' Arthur said. 'You'll need to do it by memory, and think of somewhere you can get to on foot.'

He looked at the book on the long table in front of him. The hard cover was charcoal black with white lettering in an elaborate handwritten style. The spine appeared unbroken. Arthur glanced around the room. Apart from the librarian there were five other people visible by the shelves, stooping to collect or browse the books. Two readers sat on the opposite corner of the table, their heads bowed toward heavy textbooks. Nobody paid him any attention. The background hum in his head was quieter. He opened the book and read the first page.

Arthur could not tell how long he had been holding the book. The hot panic he had felt since he returned to earth had cooled. In its place was a recognition of the day and all that had led to that moment in the library, on this other earth, with Rachel by his side. He saw his life, all life, with a clarity he had not known since childhood. He had been asleep, lulled into an existence that flowed quite easily along the troughs and gullies that had come before him. There was no fault with the collective dream that kept the tides turning. But now he was awake.

He turned another page.

He was aware of the paper, the muffled crunch of it between his fingers like a boot through powdered snow. He was alive to the heat of the air around him, the buzz from a chainsaw in the park outside, the ache in his throat as he swallowed. Could all this sensation be an illusion? An echo of a life once lived? He brought himself back to the voice that had led him here, to the words that had coursed through him as he sat in the library and read, to the being that had created them.

New Zeus. He tried to visualise such an entity and all he could see were lightning connections, a vast network of electricity stretching to infinity. Perhaps that was enough. He could see all the points of contact, the entanglement, the ebb and flow of energy. Tiny points of light, like stars on a cloudless night, pulsed in his mind's eye. He saw worlds caught in electric rays, the life he had lived and the many he had not. He saw the flickering universe and with a slice of pain as fine and bright as a paper cut to raw skin, he felt the agony of all life lived moment by moment. As quick as it had flared, the horror of the physical world receded leaving a residue of hope for another world, another future. He saw Rachel, not the Rachel beside him, but his mother when he was young. He looked up at her face and remembered the shadow of the ant that looked back at him. The ant that was with her in her last moments. The ant that was with him now. New Zeus.

'Rachel?'

She turned to him, the soft fabric of her dress rising and settling again as she moved.

'Are you okay? Arthur?'

He saw the point of light that was the woman in front of him and he knew what he must do. He remembered telling Greg one time when he was being carried home that you could never know the end of the story. What story had that been? The one with bears. Goldilocks. There was no happy-ever-after for Goldilocks, who ran back into the woods and was never heard from again. It had been helpful to Arthur, the lack of an ending. That was how he had thought of his mother, she had run off, but she was alive somewhere that was right for her. And now he had found her.

'Arthur?'

He remembered what he had asked her to do. Had she left him and come back?

'The phone call?'

She frowned. 'You said you didn't need it any more. About an hour ago. You said we were safe.'

'I'm so sorry. You've been waiting all this time.'

She shook her head and held up a paperback novel with a picture of a Victorian family on the cover. 'I've been busy.'

'We have your albums at the house. Your photographs and memories?'

'The scrapbooks? Yes.'

'Do you really think we could go through them? Together.'

'You feel ready?' Rachel raised her hand slightly, as though she would reach over and take his own.

'I think so.'

She smoothed her skirt with the raised hand, her head bowed. After a moment she took a deep breath and looked up at him.

'Will you explain it to me?'

'Everything,' he said.

They travelled in silence back to the house. The sun was on the other side of the Skater now, shadows striping the offices and apartments as the transport glided past. He watched the stick figures of the people below and recognised the streets and buildings for the first time. The scent of Texas Lilac filled the carriage, reminding Arthur of hot afternoons in the exercise yard at the base. He was tired, his limbs heavy and aching, but his breath came a little easier. He rested his head against the window.

The electronic hum had returned.

'Captain Pryce?' Arthur was aware of the automated tones of Old Zeus.

'Yes, Zed. What can I do for you?'

'I have a message from base. They wish to see you tomorrow. A car will collect you at 9 a.m. Is that satisfactory?'

'It is. Tell them my memory is returning. I should have some information for them.'

'Thank you, Captain. That is good news.'

'Yeah, it is. Though maybe not so much for your programming, Zed.'

'I am aware.'

The steady hum returned. He would go to the base prepared. At the library, New Zeus had communicated all that he needed to say. All that he needed to know.

Arthur looked over at Rachel.

'I have to go in tomorrow, tell them what I've remembered.'

Rachel nodded and her eyes glistened as she looked back at him. He saw her then, a soft shimmer relaxing the outer lines of her silhouette. He could see her with the memories of the other Arthur, the man who had grown up with her as his mother, and he knew her as he knew himself.

'Mum?'

'Yes, baby?'

'It's going to be okay.'

At the house, Rachel made coffee and got the scrapbooks and they sat together in the kitchen with the sounds of the world outside, children returning from school, the electronic whirr of cars, music from a neighbour's open window. Arthur thought of all he would find in the scrapbook. A childhood he could only know through the memories of the other Arthur. And he thought of all that he wouldn't find. Eliza gone before he was born, the absent Greg, Hal far away. There was a thread that held them together but that thread had frayed and separated. He put his hand on the book and closed his eyes.

The energy of the memories danced beneath his palm, connections reaching back further and further. Images and understanding coursed through his mind. He saw Rachel's parents, his grandparents, in their garden on the Brazilian coast. He saw them as he remembered them, lurching unapologetically towards a chaotic old age, and he saw them disappear from this world, an early death in a drunken car crash. He turned to Rachel, but more images surged up, pulling him further back in time.

More threads, more timelines. A century ago now, Arthur could feel the link between himself and the people in his visions. He saw a boy in the sea, struggling to reach the shore. He saw the boy's head bob beneath the water not to surface, and at the same time he saw the boy swim both alone and with a friend. He traced the lines, to a funeral, a wedding and a chance encounter. This last he half-recognised, his young grandmother, and she was on the beach with the boy, now grown. The couple touch, his mother is conceived. The Rachel of the other world.

And this Rachel? Her line extended from the boy who did not swim alone to the shore. That boy grew up to marry his childhood sweetheart, and the couple met her mother on holiday. Arthur saw the three friends laughing on a sunny terrace, and later, under greyer skies, a little older and still laughing. His grandfather now at the head of the table, holding court with a glass in his hand. And upstairs, the young Rachel sleeps, and dreams of fields of wheat.

His thoughts returned to the boy in the sea, to the first vision, as the final wave swept the small body under the swell one last time. A funeral. A family freighted with grief. He saw the boy's three stories dividing from the same thread and he saw the threads twisting and dividing further and further back, through all the points of light he had envisaged in the library. A vast web of interwoven strands, separating and binding forever and bringing him to this place, to this knowing.

He opened his eyes and Rachel placed her hand next to his on the book. Her skin was golden, creased with time, a few larger veins roped around the base of her fingers. She wore no rings, but for a moment Arthur thought he saw the thin indentation on her wedding finger where Eliza had once placed a silver band. But that was the other Rachel, the one he would not find in the torn pages before him.

He was here, now, some part of him. The essential part of him, a little light in the fabric of time. This life was waiting for him, now that he knew what this life was. And maybe he had always known, a child in search of his mother in space. There had been other versions of him, many others, ones who didn't know, who hadn't travelled through this particular weft and weave to meet their maker. Their maker, a being who had shared his mother's body and gone on to rule the world. The Zeus that he would share with Rachel.

There was still another Eliza and Hal and Greg to meet. They were at the edges of Rachel's life, friends and exes, but they were in this place somewhere. He could know them again. Back on the other earth, his alter-Arthur would be doing the same thing. But as that Arthur came to understand the nature of the universe, the world he inhabited would start to unravel. Eventually, that place would cease to exist. Somewhere in his body he already felt the loss. He wanted his Eliza, longed to share everything he knew with her as well. There was only hope for now, that he, Arthur, could live this life with the knowledge of what it was, and that he would not be alone. He could learn this world, take part in it with his new understanding. The books in front of him were a start. Sharing them with Rachel was another way of finding her. He scooped Rachel's fingers with his own and held them tight.

'Ready?' he asked.

'Ready,' she answered.

Together, they turned the first page of the scrapbook and began to save the world.

'I'm an unusual shade of blue,' said Rachel. 'Warm and dark and I smell of coriander.'

'Perfect,' said Eliza.

'But all the colours . . .'

'Yes?'

'They're just in my head. They don't really exist.'

'And yet you can see them.'

'Yes. I can.'

'And I can see you.'

'So I'm not missing, after all.'

'Not any more,' said Eliza. 'We found you.'

Epigraph sources and books mentioned (by chapter)

William Blake *Milton: A Poem in Two Books*, in *The Complete Poems*, ed. Alicia Ostriker (London: Penguin Classics, 1977), p. 586

Emily Brontë *Wuthering Heights* (London: Penguin Classics, 2003), p. 80

Daniel Dennett 'In Defense of AI', *Speaking Minds: Interviews with Twenty Eminent Cognitive Scientists* by Peter Baumgartner and Sabine Payr (Princeton: Princeton University Press, 1995) p.259

Chapter 1
Blaise Pascal *Pensées,* introduction by T. S. Eliot, tr. W. F. Trotter (New York: E. P. Dutton & Co., 1958), p. 30

Chapter 2
John von Neumann as keynote speaker at the first national meeting of the Association for Computing Machinery, 1947, mentioned by Franz L. Alt at the end of 'Archaeology of computers: Reminiscences, 1945–1947', Communications of the ACM, vol. 15, issue 7,

July 1972, special issue: Twenty-fifth anniversary of the Association for Computing Machinery, p. 694

Chapter 3

Thomas Nagel 'What is It Like to be a Bat?' in *The Philosophical Review*, vol. 83, no. 4 (1974), pp. 435–50

E. M. Forster *Howard's End* (London: Penguin, 1992)

Anthony Trollope *Can You Forgive Her?* (London: Penguin Books, 1993)

Chapter 4

David J. Chalmers *The Conscious Mind: In Search of A Fundamental Theory* (Oxford: Oxford University Press, 1997), p. 94

Chapter 5

Frank Jackson *Philosophy Bites*, 'What Mary Knew', hosted by David Edmonds and Nigel Warburton https://philosophybites.com/2011/08/ frank-jackson-on-what-mary-knew.html

Rachel Cusk *A Life's Work: On Becoming a Mother* (London: Faber, 2008)

Charles Dickens *Our Mutual Friend* (London: Penguin Books, 2012)

Kate Greenaway *Mother Goose, or, the Old Nursery Rhymes* (London: Frederick Warne, 1962)

Olivia Manning *The Balkan Trilogy* (London: Penguin, 1981)

George Meredith *The Egoist* (London: Penguin, 1968)

Chapter 6

John Searle 'The Chinese Room', *The MIT Encyclopedia of the Cognitive Sciences*, ed. Robert A. Wilson and Frank

C. Keil (Cambridge, Massachusetts: Massachusetts Institute of Technology Press, 1999)

Elhanan Motzkin, reply by John Searle, in *New York Review of Books*, 'Artificial Intelligence and the Chinese Room: An Exchange' https://www.nybooks.com/articles/1989/02/16/artificial-intelligence-and-the-chinese-room-an-ex/

Chapter 7

Hilary Putnam 'The meaning of meaning', *Minnesota Studies in the Philosophy of Science,* vol. 7, *Language, Mind, and Knowledge*, ed. Keith Gunderson (Minneapolis: University of Minnesota Press, 1975), p. 140

Roald Dahl *James and the Giant Peach* (London: Allen and Unwin, 1967)

J. K. Rowling *The complete Harry Potter collection* (London: Bloomsbury, 2010)

Lemony Snicket *A Series of Unfortunate Events: The Complete Wreck* (London: Harper Collins, 2006)

Robert Southey *The Three Bears* (London: Oxford University Press, 1940)

Chapter 8

Heraclitus *Fragments,* tr. Brooks Haxton (London: Penguin Classics, 2001) Fragment 41, p. 27

Jules Verne *Twenty Thousand Leagues Under the Sea* tr. H. Frith, ed. P. Costello (London: Everyman, 1993)

Tom Wolfe *The Right Stuff* (London: Jonathan Cape, 1979)

Chapter 9

René Descartes *Meditations on First Philosophy,* tr. John Cottingham (Cambridge: Cambridge University Press,

1996), p. 15; Herman Hesse 'The Immortals', *Steppen-wolf*, tr. Basil Creighton (London: Penguin Books, 2011), p. 182

Miguel Cervantes *Don Quixote*, tr. John Rutherford (London: Penguin Classics, 2003)

Jorge Luis Borges 'Pierre Menard, Author of the *Quixote*' in *Labyrinths,* ed. Donald A. Yates and James E. Irby (London: Penguin Classics, 2000)

Chapter 10

Gilbert Harman *Thought* (Princeton: Princeton University Press, 1973), p. 5

Alfred, Lord Tennyson *Ulysses* (Ware, Herts.: Wordsworth Editions, 1994), p. 162

Further reading

Daniel Dennett *Consciousness Explained* (London: Penguin Books, 1993)

—— *Intuition Pumps and other Tools for Thinking* (New York: W. W. Norton, 2013)

—— *From Bacteria to Bach and Back: The Evolution of Minds* (New York: W. W. Norton, 2017)

Homer *The Odyssey*, tr. Stephen Mitchell (London: Phoenix, 2014)

David Hume, *An Enquiry Concerning Human Understanding*, ed. Peter Millican (Oxford: Oxford University Press, 2008)

Frank Jackson *There's Something About Mary,* ed. Peter Ludlow, Yujin Nagasawa and Daniel Stoljar (Cambridge, Massachusetts: Massachusetts Institute of Technology Press, 2004)

James Joyce, 'The Ondt and the Gracehoper', *Finnegans Wake* (London: Penguin Classics, 2000), pp. 414–18

Nora Nadjarian, *Ledra Street* (Nicosia, Cyprus: Armida Publications, 2006)

Thomas Nagel *Mind and Cosmos: Why the Materialist Neo-Darwinian Conception of Nature is Almost Certainly False* (Oxford: Oxford University Press, 2012)

John von Neumann *Theory of Games and Economic Behavior* with Oskar Morgenstern (Princeton: Princeton University Press, 2004)

Roy Sorensen *Thought Experiments* (New York: Oxford University Press, 1992)

Scarlett Thomas *The End of Mr. Y* (London: Canongate, 2008)

Peggy Tittle *What If . . .* (New Jersey: Pearson Longman, 2005)

Osman Türkay, *Symphonies for the World* (London: A. N. Graphics, 1989)

Voltaire, 'Micromegás and Other Short Fictions', tr. Theo Cuffe (London: Penguin, 2002)

Acknowledgements

This book was born from a love of the philosophers and poets, the storytellers and novelists, who have delved into the depths of human consciousness and surfaced with fragments of our kelpie soul.

Thank you to the ECL department at Goldsmiths for your support and advice, in particular to my supervisors Blake Morrison and Michael Simpson, to Josh Cohen and Maura Dooley, and to Maria Macdonald for your patience.

In Laura Macdougall I was lucky to find a collaborator and a friend. Thanks to United Agents. Especial thanks to the acute sensibilities of Sarah Castleton, to Olivia Hutchings for hand-holding through proofs, to the meticulous Caroline Knight, Zoe Hood for ant music, to Matthew Burne for the cover design and all at Corsair.

Thanks to Simon Oldfield who awarded the original short story 'Sunbed' with the RA & Pin Drop Short Story Award 2018. That story forms part of Chapter 3 of this novel and will appear in the paperback edition of *A Short Affair*. Thanks also to Elizabeth Day. And thanks to Richard Skinner of Vanguard.

Thank you to the English teacher who believed, Mrs Wright née Clay, and thank you to Nicola Monaghan and Richard Beard for excellent instruction. Thanks to my early readers, especially the fine writer Jane Harris, and good friends Cathryn Wright and Abi Shapiro. Thank you to my sisters, Claudia and Kitty, and my mother, Alex, for bear-ing with me.

Thank you to Rena, who has loved me and the ant in my eye.

And most of all thank you to our sons, Nat and Josh, who save the world every day.